Jane Augusta Terry Gunn

Memorial Sketches of Doctor Moses Gunn

Jane Augusta Terry Gunn

Memorial Sketches of Doctor Moses Gunn

ISBN/EAN: 9783337044015

Printed in Europe, USA, Canada, Australia, Japan

Cover: Foto ©Raphael Reischuk / pixelio.de

More available books at **www.hansebooks.com**

MEMORIAL SKETCHES

OF

DOCTOR MOSES GUNN.

BY HIS WIFE.

WITH EXTRACTS FROM HIS LETTERS

AND

EULOGISTIC TRIBUTES

FROM HIS

COLLEAGUES AND FRIENDS.

CHICAGO:
W. T. KEENER, 96 WASHINGTON ST.
1889.

$$\mathfrak{D}\text{edicated}$$

TO

MY HUSBAND,

THE CENTER ROUND WHICH ALL MY MEMORIES REVOLVE

PREFACE.

I have sought in these sketches to present a portrait of my husband limned from different points of view.

Letters, like autobiography, bring us nearer to the personality of the writer, especially when these are unpremeditated. This is the quality of Doctor Gunn's correspondence—a family correspondence—which was never intended for publication, but which now largely makes up these pages.

In the language of his letters is seen a shadow of his living self; those from the army describe his experience as a surgeon in a military camp.

His protestations in behalf of General McClellan, while they may be of no value to his memory, are strong expressions of his individual belief in the man.

His hurried letters written during a rapid tour through Europe, are inserted simply to show his temperament and his keen sense of enjoyment.

To those who have set forth their conceptions of his character and attainments, which are herein embodied, and to others who have in any way aided me, I feel most grateful.

J. A. G.

2101 Calumet Avenue, Chicago.

CONTENTS.

CHAPTER V.

PAGE.

CHAPTER VI.

CHAPTER VII.

CHAPTER VIII.

CHAPTER IX.

CHAPTER X.

CHAPTER XI.

CHAPTER XII.

CHAPTER XIII.

CHAPTER XIV.

CHAPTER XV.

CHAPTER XVI.

CHAPTER XVII.

CHAPTER XVIII.

CHAPTER XIX.

CHAPTER XX.

CHAPTER XXI.

CHAPTER XXVII.

CHAPTER XXVIII.

CHAPTER XXIX.

CHAPTER XXX.

CHAPTER XXXI.

CHAPTER XXXII.

CHAPTER XXXIII.

CHAPTER XXXIV.

ILLUSTRATIONS.

AUT PAX AUT BELLUM

INTRODUCTION.

There is no better way in which to introduce these sketches than by some quotations from Professor James Nevins Hyde's Report on Necrology, so graphically written, and published in the Transactions of the Illinois State Medical Society for 1888.

.   .   .   .   "Professor Gunn's reputation as one of the leading surgeons of the country was, however, largely attained after the establishment of his connection with Rush Medical College, Chicago, Illinois.   .   .   Here he remained actively engaged in his practice as a surgeon, and in his duties as a teacher of medicine, up to the time of his death, which occurred, after an illness of several weeks, on the fourth of November, 1887.   .   .   .   .
Professor Gunn was granted the degree of Doctor of Laws, by the University of Chicago, in the year 1877.

"At the date of his death, he was a member of the American Surgical Association, an original member of the American Association of Genito-Urinary Surgeons, and in each capacity a member of the Congress of

American Physicians and Surgeons, a member of the Illinois State Medical Society, of the American Medical Association, and of the Chicago Medical Society.

"Besides the work required in his college professorship he served as a surgeon on the active and consulting staff of a number of the public charities of this city, including the Cook County Hospital, St. Joseph's Hospital, St. Luke's Hospital, and more particularly the Presbyterian Hospital, where in later years some of his most brilliant surgical operations were performed.

"Like most of the truly great surgeons of the civilized world, Professor Gunn won his exalted place in the ranks of his profession by his success, first, as a judicious, yet brilliant, always neat, and wonderfully successful operator; second, by his fame as an oral teacher of his art. He was indeed a scholarly and accurate writer, and had composed a systematic treatise on Surgery which was destroyed in the Great Chicago Fire.

"But his fame, like that of Velpeau, Nélaton, Hunter, Parker and Mott, will always rest rather on what he did with his knife than with his pen. All of his accomplishments, and they were not a few, were subordinated to his surgical skill, on which his reputation was firmly based. He was, for a physician, an unusually accurate accountant, a good churchman, an excellent horseman, a lover of the best general literature, a skillful architect, an amateur astronomer, and a man of refined tastes in all matters pertaining to art. But upon none of these subjects did he set his heart to any extent comparable with the untiring zeal and zest displayed in the discharge of his professional duties.

"With the enormous demands upon his time, he never, when in health, was known to fail to enter his lecture room at the stroke of the bell, or to be punctual at the appointed hour for a consultation. The clinical work he did in public was the chief delight of his life. There he was truly royal in word and act. His superb figure and commanding presence in the amphitheatre are the imperishable souvenirs of thousands of young medical men, who have learned from his life their first lesson in practical surgery, and have followed with their eyes the wonderful play of the instruments in his hand, guided by an anatomical knowledge that few, as fully as he, possessed.

"Professor Gunn came thus to be known to the world at large, as one of the most eminent surgeons of his day—a man of remarkable presence, of high moral character, and of the best social position. But to those who were admitted to share the intimacy of his friendship, he exhibited qualities which others often scarcely suspected. He was in all these non-professional relations, found to be singularly modest, gentle as a woman, light-hearted as a boy, faithful in his friendships, fixed in an honest hatred of all shams and pretenders, and exhibiting in every judgment of his mind a strong common sense that illumined every dark corner into which he looked.

"Professor Moses Gunn was one of those men who would have been great in any sphere of life. He was, viewed from every side, one of the greatest of the great men whose names the medical profession will always treasure with gratitude and respect. His memory is enshrined to-day in that pantheon of honor, where the most learned of jurists, the ablest ecclesiastics, the most successful military heroes, and the immortal poets and artists of America are numbered with its famous physicians and surgeons."

MEMORIAL SKETCHES

OF

DOCTOR MOSES GUNN.

CHAPTER FIRST.

THESE desultory memoirs were begun in those first days of enthusiasm, when as the pages grew under my hand, I found they were shaping themselves into something like a domestic romance. And though this tendency may still in a measure cling to them, I have as far as possible divested them of their original character. Knowing that husks only, with a few approved kernels can be used, and realizing that there is nothing heroic to relate, according to the world's idea of heroism (physicians' battles with disease are seldom recounted), and that my husband's colleagues and friends have kindly chronicled his professional accomplishments and many of his manly qualities, I yet desire to add a few incidents in his life. If in delineating these my personality has been intruded where it might have been avoided, I hope for a lenient judgment.

Friday, November 4th, 1887, dates the close of a useful life; the life of a man whose devotion to his family and to his profession, services to the world, aid to suffering humanity, and earnest counsel to those whom his enthusiasm aroused to nobler effort, must make his removal keenly felt by all.

To me his loss is irreparable. All I have left is the rich legacy of his love, my choicest heritage; in that I live, and if from the garnered recollections of the past, I can frame a tribute to my husband, it is the only task that can bring relief or make less insupportable each day of my life. I think of him in every sleepless hour; and in my waking, endless dreams—I dream of him.

If, among the thousands with whom he was connected, there are any who find interest in these pages, it will repay my days of labor and my nights of tears. The labor has been no hardship, only an unremitting struggle lest I should too frequently reveal the undercurrent of deeper feeling, or portray too often the reverse of the picture, showing the trivialities in our lives.

Moses Gunn was a man who made the world better for having lived in it. Not that he was more charitable or more amiable than his peers. On the contrary, he had a high-spirited nature, impatient sometimes; but underlying this, he had great geniality, the highest sense of honor, the keenest sensibilities, and the liveliest sympathies.

He was born in East Bloomfield, New York, April 20th, 1822—the youngest of four children. His father, Linus Gunn, was of Scotch descent; tall and powerfully built, he was the embodiment of vigor. Many stories are told of his prowess and endurance; and the ancient tradition of the universal hospitality of the Scots seems to have been transmitted to him. His liberality, his honesty of purpose, and his Christianity, which consisted not alone of being a zealous member and supporter of the Church, bore fruit in acts of benevolence that made him respected and beloved.

His wife, Esther Bronson, was a comely, clever, thrifty woman, who served as a balance-wheel to keep in bounds her husband's sometimes ill-advised generosity. She was kind and affectionate, a loving wife and loving mother; to her he was indebted for the many comforts of his home and for much of his success.

Their pioneer days were over, their early home exchanged for one in East Bloomfield. Here they had settled, and though not exempt from the necessities of economy, were, in farmer phrase, "fore-handed," or well-to-do.

Bloomfield suggests its counterpart in the large cultivated farms, the rich fruitful orchards, broad meadows and fields of feathery, waving grain, the comfortable farm-houses—all indicating prosperity.

In the distance were the blue Bristol Hills; those nearer were covered, in summer, with velvet verdure, in winter with glistening drifts of snow. The grand old elms that cast their cool and grateful shadows across the highway, the school-house, and the mill with its murmuring, unceasing accompaniment of dam and stream, completed the summer scene of rural loveliness.

Their house on the main stage-route from Rochester to Canandaigua, was known for miles as a convenient resting-place; even stragglers along the road soon learned where to ask for food and rest, until the demand became so great, that a wayfarer's bed was suggested and finally located in a remote corner of the house and ever after called "The Beggar's Bed."

Not alone to these mere tramps did their hospitality extend. It was a delightful place for visiting. Clergymen were welcomed and here made a pleasant sojourn, friends were cordially received and entertained, and poor relations here found a haven for their woes.

Thanksgiving was the day for family reunion; from the aged grandmother, almost ninety, to the prattling child, all were often seated round the same board, where delicious viands were served to tempt their appetites.

On one of these occasions a little fellow of four or five, a frequent and favored guest, was overlooked when some delicacy was "*handed round.*" Reproachfully turning to his aunt, he said, "Whatever that *was*, you did not pass it to me." Instantly it was placed before him. But with quaint humor, he said, "O! never mind, I do not *want it!* only I like to have folks *pass me things* when I'm around."

The following incident, though trivial in itself, illustrates one phase of my husband's boyish character: His sister (fourteen years older than himself) he almost idolized, and his youthful fancy endowed her with marvelous beauty. When any allusion was made to her approaching marriage, though she was to live only across the way, his grief was so intense that he would wander off alone, lest he should hear their discussion, and would ponder over, by himself, what appeared to him the direst of calamities.

When the eventful, but to him distasteful, day arrived, the wedding breakfast over (it was not called a breakfast then), and the guests departed, the bridal pair began preparations for their short trip. With jealous eyes he watched them reach their dwelling, then his plan was made.

Early the next morning he gathered together his few belongings. Some of these possessions he crammed into a small hair trunk that he had made for himself; with this upon his shoulder, two hats upon his head, and an extra pair of shoes dangling by his side, he marched across the road, and announced to his astonished sister that "he had come to *live with her!*"

His comical appearance and still more comical "announcement" was so convulsing, that it almost prevented her, at first, from saying—"That will be very nice. I have a little room upstairs that will exactly suit you." The families winked at this droll proceeding and allowed him to remain. One day, however, hearing his mother's voice, he thrust his head inside the door, and called out—"Hello! mother, is that you?"

"Yes, my son; and how do you think I feel to be left alone? Is it not bad enough to lose my only daughter without having my boy go off and leave me too?"

The pathos of her words and voice brought him to her side; still with hesitation and some slight patronage, he said, "It is pretty bad, and I will go home with you to live; but, mother—I want it *distinctly under-stood*, that I shall come here *once a day to eat!*"

This was too much for their equanimity, but the compromise was made and the boyish threat carried out almost literally for years.

His brothers delighted in exciting his childish ire, sometimes to test his youthful logic. He was tinkering at some vehicle (he manufactured all his own), when one of his brothers came along and carelessly asked, "Why don't you hitch up old Buff and make him pull?"

"You know the reason, Lou, as well as I do; he is *too old*."

The superannuated subject of their debate was dozing in the sun. Making a stride towards the unconscious animal, Lou called out, "I am going to kill this dog! for he is old, and useless, and takes up too much room."

Instantly the boy was on his feet. With flashing eyes and quivering voice he cried, "If you are going to kill everything that's *old*, you had better go in and kill your *grandmother!*"

His father seldom chastised his sons, but when he did, invariably prayed with them afterwards. The doctor always said it was hard to tell which he dreaded most, "the thrashing or the prayer."

He once said of himself that his youth was remarkable for nothing but a love of fun and mechanics.

His sister mentions an act of their father's discipline:—"My brother, when a lad of ten or twelve, was in the habit of interchanging visits with his cousins, 'The Gunn boys.' They all anticipated the greatest pleasure in these visits. One evening when the boys were going home, Moses gained permission to walk part of the way back with them, the distance not being specified. When sufficient time had elapsed, and he did not return, my mother was fearful lest something had befallen her boy. You know he was her Benjamin.

"At last her anxiety became so great, that my father decided to go in search of him. When he arrived at his brother's, he found the 'young rascal,' as he called him, in bed with his cousins! He said nothing, but returned. In the morning, when the small culprit appeared, he was told that for this misdemeanor he could not go to his uncle's for *one year!* At times this seemed a greater punishment than he could bear."

Fifteen years after this memorable little episode, the doctor and his wife were taking tea with these cousins and their sisters, when she fully realized what a cruel deprivation his boyish palate must have undergone during that long year!

The doctor's mother was a remarkable woman, and needs more than a passing notice. She lived to the age of ninety-three, with all her faculties unimpaired. She survived her husband many years, he (dying at the age of sixty-seven) leaving her his small estate, which by her providence she increased, though her gifts were many and munificent. When her children were young, after attending to her household duties through the day, she would sit up far into the night, and while the others slept, accomplish the greater part of her sewing, which was of no ordinary kind. Two weeks before her death (it must be remembered she was then ninety-three), she had been engaged on some fine needle-work.

After giving up her home she resided with her daughter living directly opposite. There she found a melancholy satisfaction in looking over at the house where, through the lights and shadows, the hospitalities of other days had transpired. One night she saw this old home burn to the ground.

She spent a part of each alternate year with the doctor's family, and as a labor of love (after she was eighty) hemmed and "whipped" many of the fine linen cambric ruffles he then wore. He told her of an excitable French patient who said to him one day—

"Docteur! I shall tear off ze frille, some time, it make me so exasperate! I nevare get zings don up like zat!"

She was fond of making written extracts from her Bible. Up to the time of her death, her letters were written in a clear, neat hand.

Her face, slightly severe, was intelligent, and often and easily lighted up with a peculiarly humorous smile. She was of medium height, her form plump and erect, and her step vigorous. Her clothes fitted her perfectly, and were of handsome material. She was particular in her personal appearance and always made a point of *dressing* for dinner. Among other graces she was wise, never allowing her son to imagine she saw any shortcomings in her daughter-in-law. She was amiable —in fact she was exceptional.

This little tribute is due from one who, under all circumstances, received her warmest affection.

The doctor, averse to his name when a boy, once asked his mother why she called him "Moses."

"Because, my son," she answered, "it was the name of your grandfather,—a courteous, amiable old gentleman, whom we hoped to have you emulate."

"That is a good reason, but I could just as well have emulated him—without his name."

He never quite forgave her this infliction, and never, until maturer years, signed his name in full.

When writing to his wife, he indulged in a *nom de plume*.

The rudiments of Doctor Gunn's education were begun very early, so early that he was allowed a pillow in school. He was twelve years old, when a young theological student became a member of his father's family, and was his tutor for three years. Then he entered the East Bloomfield Academy, where he pursued his studies until they were interrupted by a serious illness followed by prolonged invalidism. During a part of this time he rode on horseback to the academy, though a painful side often prevented his riding faster than a walk. A constant inclination to bend over either when walking or riding, he fought against, and a supreme effort of his will alone enabled him to sit upright in his saddle. His mother watched him with extreme solicitude for two years; finally a change of climate and a sea voyage aided in his recovery.

When on his way to New York, he was informed by a sympathetic passenger on board the "Packet Boat" (which was then the popular mode of travel in that section) that he would die of consumption, in less than a year.

His sister says:—"After the first winter of my brother's illness he was always busy binding books or engaged in some mechanical employment. It was during this time he traced the ancestral line in both his grandfathers' families."

A few months after his return from the South, he entered Dr. Carr's office in Canandaigua, as a student of medicine. He soon became a favorite with Dr. Carr; close attention to his duties won the doctor's regard, and he often drove with him on his professional rounds. His preceptor wore a large, blue camlet cloak, then much in vogue. One morning as they were starting out on their expedition a corner of the cloak blew over the young student's arm. Turning to Dr. Carr, he said:—" How proud I should be if your mantle could fall upon my shoulder." Looking at him earnestly, his preceptor replied, "My boy, you will wear a *greater mantle than mine.*"

CHAPTER SECOND.

A N old-time friend, J. S. R——, writing about his early acquaintance with my husband, refers to his student-life at that period:—

"I often met Moses Gunn when he was studying medicine, and a member of Dr. Carr's family. I invariably noticed him intent upon his work; this made a deep impression upon me. After he had been studying a year, Dr. Carr would frequently take him when he had a difficult case, and always when he had an operation. Few physicians outside the cities had a reputation equal to his, for skillful and successful operations. He did nearly all the surgery within a radius of many miles; it was beneficial for your husband to be associated with such a man. Yet I recall a time when, speaking of a certain operation at which he assisted, he said 'If I ever have a case like that I shall manage it differently.' The treatment which he had in mind was radically different from that of his preceptor. Thus, while he studied, he thought for himself. Years after, when recalling old times, it occurred to me to ask him if he had ever had such a case. I remember the satisfaction with which he replied 'Yes, several, and was successful according to those early convictions.'

"It is not necessary for me to speak of the doctor's splendid achievements; those you already know. My only object in writing this brief retrospect, is to make you better acquainted with the kind of man he was, before you knew him."

These are the recollections and impressions of one who knew Doctor Gunn in boyhood, as well as in later years:—

"When I first entered the family, the doctor was a boy of eleven. From that time forth, he had the same lovable nature which characterized his life; ever ready to contribute to the pleasure of others, or to the relief of their pain.

"Especially was he endeared to me during the last illness and at the bedside of my dying husband. .   . A student of medicine, he left his books, to devote himself night and day to the almost entire care of him.

"I can never forget the stay and comfort he was to me while passing through this, my first great affliction. No matter how often I disturbed his snatches of sleep by day or night, he awoke to my relief with unabated tenderness.   .   .   .   .   .

"His purity of character and unselfishness were so transparent, that I watched his development with interest and affection, and I believe there are few whose lives, from childhood onward, are kept so free from stain or blemish.

"I am very glad I was permitted to meet the doctor so recently, by which the sacred memories of the long ago were revived."   .   .   .

Professor C. L. Ford writes of his early and later associations with Doctor Gunn:—

"I was a student of Dr. Edson Carr, of Canandaigua, N. Y., and after being graduated at Geneva College, was appointed Demonstrator of Anatomy, which office I held for several years.

"On my way to and from Geneva, I occasionally spent a few hours in Canandaigua, and there I first met your husband, who was then a student of Dr. Carr, as I had been before. By these occasional interviews, I became aware of his earnestness in whatever he undertook, and especially of his enthusiastic devotion to the study of anatomy.

"In October, 1844, he became a member of the medical class, and was at once recognized as a man of more than ordinary promise. The session passed as do most college sessions, without any specially exciting or noteworthy incidents, and he was again energetically at work as before in Dr. Carr's office. At the opening of the session of 1845–6, Dr. Gunn returned and resumed work as usual. During this session my health was by no means good, as I had not fully recovered from a severe pneumonia, and my friend had already obtained such a knowledge of anatomy and had shown so much skill in dissecting, and imparting knowledge, that he became to me a valuable assistant and I often assigned to him duties that belonged to me. In all these, he evinced so much aptness and skill in instructing others, that it foreshadowed his appropriate field of labor as a future instructor as well as operator.

"During the college session, while mutually engaged in instructing others, we sometimes, as was very natural, talked of the future, and built air-castles, as young men occasionally will do, and even went so far as to hope that in the not distant future we might be associated in some medical college, where he should be professor of surgery, and I should teach anatomy.

"At the close of the session, the College received from a prison of the State an unclaimed body, which was to be devoted to scientific uses; and as we had no means of preserving it, and no occasion to use it after the college was closed. Dr. Gunn was allowed to employ it for purposes of instruction.

"As an illustration of his enterprise, he received his diploma on Tuesday, left his home on the Monday following the day of his graduation, and started for Michigan; and in two weeks from the day he left, he had made arrangements, and commenced a course of lectures on anatomy in Ann Arbor, for which his previous earnest devotion to dissection had made admirable preparation; and the thorough study he had given the subject ever after inspired the confidence and self-reliance, based on accurate knowledge, with which he undertook formidable operations.

"Here he began his professional life and surgical career. His facility in lecturing, and his manifest acquaintance with the subject he had undertaken to teach, attracted attention and marked him as no ordinary man; and on succeeding seasons he repeated lectures on anatomy, accompanied by dissections and demonstrations,—the first ever given in Ann Arbor, if not in Michigan.

"In the fall of 1850 Dr. Gunn was duly appointed Professor of Anatomy and Surgery in the Medical College. In 1854 it was deemed desirable that he should no longer be required to teach anatomy in connection with surgery, and in June of that year I was appointed

Professor of Anatomy, and our youthful aspiration was realized, wherein one taught anatomy and the other surgery, from that time till he resigned and went to Chicago; making us co-laborers for thirteen years of harmonious co-operation and friendly rivalry, as teachers of our respective branches of medical education.

"The doctor and I roomed together in Geneva, where began a friendship of forty years. He was always most earnest in whatever he undertook; no half-way work ever satisfied him. He acted upon the principle of doing well whatever was worth commencing, and he evinced the same energy and enthusiasm as a student, that characterized all his subsequent career in active professional life. He was always remarkably self-reliant and self-respecting, never doing anything unworthy the man or the occasion, always commanding the confidence of the public and of professional associates. . . . .

"For four years he taught anatomy and surgery with a success that placed him at once in the front rank of teachers. I may say of him he had a 'teaching diathesis'. He grasped truth clearly, believed it firmly, and stated it impressively; so that, as has been said, 'with him truth had horns, to lay hold of and to hold on to. One is sure that he knows it, and is convinced that he believes it.'

"Doctor Gunn removed to Detroit that he might have a larger field for surgical practice, and thus do greater service to the institution and give to students the benefits of a wider experience.

"Of those who have aided to make the College what it has been and what it still remains, who have finished their course, Moses Gunn I may almost call the pioneer in all this enterprise.

"His honorable and useful life-work was finished at the age of sixty-five, after almost forty-two years of service in his profession." . . . .

CHAPTER THIRD.

SOON after entering upon his medical studies in Canandaigua, Moses Gunn met a young girl whose home was in that Western town where subsequently he commenced his professional and matrimonial careers. She was at Mrs. R——'s school in her native state and was spending her first vacation with relatives. She says in reference to this time:—

"Though these memories are unimportant, they have a bearing on this little history, and bring to mind the old residence, the trees, the well into whose glistening depths we peered and tried to penetrate; the bee-hives we shunned for the garden and orchard less dangerous; the in-door and out-door pastimes; the drives about the country, and horseback-riding, which filled up the measure of our joys.

"It was a pleasant, hospitable country home; the house was large; some rooms had corner cupboards filled with quaint old china and queer souvenirs bequeathed by an 'Ancient Mariner,' a relative on the father's side. A venerable clock ticked slowly in the hall; a corner fire-place disclosed curious andirons supporting grotesque heads that in the flickering flames appeared to nod, and smile, and silently gossip with each other. These unique andirons and some other odd old articles would delight a modern antiquarian.

"Invitations for a party had been sent for twenty miles around. East Bloomfield was within the limits. Moses Gunn and a favorite cousin of his own age had just received and were opening their invitations, when C—— exclaimed, 'What luck! I have been on the *qui vive* for weeks to see that cousin of the T——s, and now it is impossible to go. But, Moses, you can find out if she amounts to anything.'

"A drive of eighteen miles brought 'Moses' to the spot where he expected to encounter a full-fledged young woman, instead of which he found a diminutive specimen of girlhood in short dresses! Astonished, but determined to fulfil his mission, he approached and with mock gallantry, offering his arm, said, 'Let us go out on the porch.' The night was glorious! the moon was full, and the maiden not too young to take note of his personality. He had brown, waving hair, a blonde goatee; was pale, near-sighted, and wore eye-glasses. His tall, slim figure was rather noticeable, and he talked well. Some guests from a distance remained all night, he among them. In the morning he said 'good bye,' and his youthful listener of the previous evening thought of him no more.

"The Sunday following he spent at home. C—— came over and began his catechism. M—— replied, 'Our friends romanced about their cousin simply to arouse your curiosity. She is only a school-girl, and a small one at that, but I carried out your enterprise, and afterward she sang a song; then before the evening was half over, *she went to bed!* I thought of her once or twice (after the song), but in the morning she reminded me of the L——s we neither of us lost our heads about.'

"The critical young man little dreamed that the small individual he then discussed would six years later *become his wife!*"

CHAPTER FOURTH.

FIVE years!   What sorrow can be crowded into five
years; and sometimes, what joys! It was five years
since the student had looked down upon his small companion and criticised her. Since then he had been
graduated with honor and some distinction, and had
(with those memorable trunks, which are hereafter
mentioned) emigrated westward.

In the following personal reminiscences written by
Doctor Gunn forty years later for "The Chronicle," in
1886 (the year before he died), he alludes to this
journey and describes the university town as it then
appeared:—

"It was on one of the bright and beautiful days
with which we were favored in the early part of February, that the writer, in sentimental indulgence, found
himself once more in the beautiful arbor-city of Washtenaw. What memories are awakened by those two
names—Ann Arbor and Washtenaw! Just forty years
before, I had looked for the first time upon the fair

scene which once again greeted my vision. How changed! and yet the same! Boyhood and ripening years show the same changes and resemblances. At that time many of the primitive trees of the aboriginal oak-openings which captivated the first settlers and induced them to locate on this spot their romantic town, still remained to justify the strikingly original name which they bestowed upon it. A pretty bit of history is that which originated the town name, and which is all familiar to Ann Arborans.

"A bleak, uncomfortable and fatiguing winter journey through Canada by stage-coach—there being no railroad communication between Buffalo and Detroit—a three hours' trip in a very primitive car by rail, or, rather, pieces of old strap-rail, from Detroit, landed me in Ann Arbor on a day, the mildness and sunny-smokiness of which suggested Indian summer rather than February. From Ypsilanti, where the railroad strikes the valley of the Huron, we had crept along under the bluffs, following closely the windings of the river, the engineers of the road having avoided the building of bridges, by increasing the distance to be traveled over, on rails that would have been dangerous had the speed been greater. 'Ann Ar-r-bor!' called the conductor as faithfully and impressively as duty required; though the indefinite rests which were indulged in at stations

would enable a reporter of the present day to gather or
invent facts enough for a gazetteer item.   My objective
point was reached; and seated in an open 'bus' the hotel
was sought.   At the top of the hill which we rise from
the station my attention was arrested by a huge boulder
that reposed just at the fork of the road, and which now
ornaments the college campus and perpetuates the
enterprise of one of the university classes.   This
thought-suggestive boulder, which has thus become a
part of the *res gestæ* of the campus and student life,
has other associations in the memory of the writer,
which ante-date by many years the commencement of
its classic association, but which are too personal to be
more than alluded to in this connection.

"The hotel which opened to me its hospitable doors
was the 'Ann Arbor Exchange,' situated on the south-
west corner of Main and Ann streets, an institution of
very indifferent merits, but with a rather showy bar in
the general office or reception room, at which within a
day or two of my arrival, I saw a gentleman of the bar
legal from Jackson indulging with some of his *confrères*
in an extremely social glass of something that passed
current for French brandy.   Now, this circumstance is
worthy of note only from the fact that the last time I
had seen our hero, he was delivering a most eloquent
temperance lecture down in the Empire State, from

which he had emigrated, bringing up in the Wolverine State, and now, to my surprised vision, before another bar than that for which he had been educated. It was one of many observations which served to put me appreciatively abreast the novel phases of Western life; for Michigan was then a Western State, and her university town was not an intensely temperance one.

"The city—for I believe it had a city organization—consisted, then as now, of the upper and lower town. The business portion of the upper town lay principally on the south and west sides of the Court House Square, while the residences were scattered somewhat promiscuously on the northwestern slope of the eminence which is crowned by the University. Between the university grounds and the first of the residences quite an unoccupied space intervened, while to the north, east and south of the campus the eye rested only on fields or common.

"On the forty acres of the university campus which, at present, emulates the old town in arborescence, there was scarcely a tree. The north wing of the present western façade was built, and was devoted to recitation rooms, dormitories, and a single room each to library and museum, while in the attic were stored numerous boxes of cured skins which have since been mounted and which, probably, are now to be found in the museum. The four residences for the use of the Professors' families were also built, and were occupied respectively by Professors Williams, Ten Brook, Wheedon, and Agnew. These four university magnates, equal in authority, constituted the executive head of the university. In teaching they were assisted by Tutor Smith and Dr. Douglas; the latter acting as instructor in chemistry, Dr. Houghton, late professor of that branch of science, having lost his life the previous autumn while prosecuting geological and mineralogical surveys at Lake Superior. There is now in the museum, probably, a specimen of native copper bearing the marks of his chisel which Professor Houghton laboriously cut from the, at that time celebrated, copper mass which was removed, by the United States authorities, to Washington in 1844 or 1845. This valuable specimen cost the efforts of four successive seasons to secure, the professor having used up his available chisels for three seasons without success. Dr. Sager, then a resident of Jackson, was Professor of Zoology, but was not on duty. Death had already invaded the professorial ranks, and a broken shaft near the present location of the Chemical Laboratory commemorated the virtues of Professor Whiting.

"I have alluded to Dr. Douglas as instructor in chemistry. After he became Professor Douglas he began to develop his department and finally organized and for many years administered the affairs of a model practical chemical laboratory. In fact, he was a pioneer in this kind of work. I therefore hesitate not to speak of his day of small things. Shortly after my arrival in Ann Arbor he invited me to be present at one of his lectures before the senior class. A room not exceeding sixteen by twenty feet served him for both laboratory and auditorium. His illustrative appliances were remarkable for what they lacked—nothing more. In no department is the contrast between 1846 and 1886 more marked than in that of chemistry.

"The Regents of the University were, at that time, appointed by the Governor with the confirmative action of the Senate. In their selection, party affiliations were wisely ignored. The Governor, Lieutenant-Governor, the Chancellor and the Justices of the Supreme Court were *ex-officio* members of the Board of Regents, the Governor being the presiding officer. Already had Governors Mason, Woodbridge, Gordon, Barry, and Felch, the last of whom is yet a venerated resident of Ann Arbor, filled the chair, while the names and wisdom of Farnsworth and Manning had ornamented and benefited the Regent list. Surely the university had been fortunate in the character of its early conservators.

"But neither the wisdom of the Regents, the zeal and fidelity of the Faculty, nor the sacredness of the cause, had saved the infant university from malicious enmity. Emanating from this source were estimates showing how much it had cost to educate each of the ten graduates. The first class of ten had been graduated the autumn previously (1845), and afforded a basis for calculation sufficiently plausible for the use of jealousy and blind opposition. Such opposition was, of course, unreasoning and unreasonable, and although the authors have ceased to be remembered, their efforts were not without influence at the time.

"The aspect of the town, as contemplated from the present time and status, seems a little grotesque. The infant university, which now in its vigorous adolescence almost constitutes and sustains the city, was, even then, a prominent feature in the equally infantile town, and gave to it the appearance, so to speak, of a college town in short dresses. The students were, many of them, poor, but nearly all strove to don the Oxford cap and sustain college characteristics and dignity before the village maidens. Thus early the 'college widow' was recognized; one class had flourished and vanished from town. As spring ripened into summer the young collegian would sally forth from his dormitory in the college building and wend his way to his morning repast under the ægis of the square cap; and, occasionally, for comfort or economy's sake, or for both considerations, he would appear clad in a calico morning gown, in which bright colors and conspicuous figures reigned predominant. Still the girls admired and courted the widow's weeds.

"*Apropos* is an anecdote, *une vraie*, in which figure the collegian, the possible college-widow, and her young brother. The student was a member of the first class, who subsequently attained high official dignity in a territory which has since become an important state. He was of eminent social position, bright in intellect, pleasing in manners, but diminutive in stature. Starting out, on one occasion, to make some formal social calls he donned a dress hat. Approaching the portals of a certain residence, he was discovered by *l'enfant terrible*, who, standing at the open window, called back to his sister: 'O, sister —— ! here comes Tom C—— with a *man's* hat on!' Imagination can picture the vigorous hustling off of young America and the reception of her visitor by the blushing maiden.

"Junior exhibition was the chief spring event: the junior hop was not then an institution, though hopping was a familiar and popular step with the collegian.

"The second annual 'commencement,' occurring in August, 1846, took place in, or rather under, a huge tent, which was pitched on the campus just west of the present central or chapel building. The exercises were of the stereotype pattern, and for the town, made it a gala day. The burlesque programme failed not in its appearance, nor in its cheapness of strained wit and pun; nor did professorial dignity fail in its perceptible annoyance thereat.

"At the annual meeting of the Board of Regents which occurred at this time Dr. Douglas was made Professor of Chemistry. It was at this meeting, also, that the first steps were taken calling into existence the medical department. A memorial asking for its establishment was presented and referred to a special committee which reported in favor of the project a year or eighteen months subsequently—I think in January, 1848. The report was adopted, and the two medical men, Drs. Sager and Douglas, who already held professorships in the university, were made professors in the new department; and a committee was appointed to select additional professors.

"The Board had been contemplating for some time the erection of a chemical laboratory, and now determined to enlarge the contemplated building in order to accommodate the medical school. The outcome of this determination is to be still seen in the Grecian-temple portion of the present medical building. Professor

Douglas was the architect and superintendent of construction; and whatever may be thought of its architecture, or of the general architecture of the University, it is quite certain that it made a convenient home for the new school for a number of years.

"In July, 1849, the committee to nominate additional professors, named, and the Board appointed the writer of this paper Professor of Anatomy. Six months later, viz: in January, 1850, Professor J. Adams Allen, M.D., who had for two years held a chair in the La Porte Medical College, and who is now President of Rush Medical College, Chicago, and Samuel Denton, M.D., a former Regent and State Senator, were made professors, respectively, of Materia Medica and Physiology, and of Theory and Practice of Medicine. At the same time the subject of Surgery was added to the chair held by the writer. The medical faculty was thus organized with five professors.

"The primary announcement of a course of instruction in the new school was issued in May, fixing the time for the opening of the course on the first of October, 1850. Thus was inaugurated a new medical college, with new and comparatively unknown men for a faculty, three of whom were yet, in medical parlance, boys, and none of whom could show a gray hair. To supply this deficient sign of erudition Zina Pitcher,

M.D., of Detroit, a Regent of the University and an ex-officer of the U. S. A., was made an Emeritus Professor.

"The first medical class numbered ninety-two students,—a number, I think, quite unprecedented, at that time, for the first class, in the history of medical colleges. The size of this class exerted an amusing influence, for one year at least, on the practice of hazing. A mild form of hazing had been in vogue which consisted of the initiation of the freshmen by the sophomores into the 'Bumptonian Society.' The department of Arts and Science had opened early in September. The sophomore class had lost in numbers while the freshmen were unusually numerous. Under such circumstances, the Sophs. hesitated in opening the campaign. Finally, deeming 'discretion the better part of valor,' they effected a compromise, whereby the Fresh. were to enjoy immunity on condition that they would join the Sophs. in the initiation of the expected Medics. Exultingly the confederated Lits. awaited the advent of the poor Medics. But when on their arrival it was discovered that they outnumbered all four classes on the other side of the campus, and that among their number were many stalwart and matured men, more remarkable for physical development than for refinement of face and manners, consternation seized the confederates, and there ensued a status, described in later times as 'all quiet on the Potomac.' All was quiet on the campus. The 'Bumptonian Society' ceased to exist and was heard of no more.

"The medical readers of 'The Chronicle' will, I feel sure, be interested in, and others will pardon a few additional observations upon this department. Its opening session had closed upon a remarkable success; the faculty were egotistic enough to regard it as even brilliant, and from that egotism sprang an ambition to gain for the college a position in the foremost rank. The eminent men who were subsequently added to the faculty brought to their work the same ambition and energy backed by recognized ability. The writer looks back with the greatest pride and pleasure upon the seventeen years during which he labored in the University, and experiences the satisfaction of knowing that the ambition of the faculty had been realized before he severed his connection with his colleagues and the University. The last course of lectures which he gave in Ann Arbor was to the largest class assembled, that year, in the United States, viz: five hundred and twenty-five students.

"Though nineteen years have passed since the ties were severed which bound him to the university of Michigan, his affection for the institution and his old colleagues remains ever green. Even to the body of professors and instructors who have, since that time, become attached to the university, he feels in a measure related."

CHAPTER FIFTH.

DOCTOR GUNN, learning that a university was established at Ann Arbor, knew that ultimately the departments of Medicine and Law would be inaugurated. He came, as he and others have mentioned, and was instrumental in organizing that department where, later, as Dr. Ford says, "Their youthful aspirations were realized, wherein one taught anatomy and the other surgery."

Almost immediately upon the doctor's advent to this "infantile town" he met the girl who had been the subject of his five-years-before adverse criticism. A month later he gave her a problem which required *more than a year* for her to solve. During this time of probation his practice increased, his knowledge of the German language brought him a German patronage, his manhood's struggle had commenced, and some of his ambitions were beginning to be realized.

The young physician named his first horse "Satan," for iniquities that came to light after he had bought him.   He needed a strong horse; this one looked not only strong, but reliable, and his purchaser made no inquiry into his character.   The beast's trangressions were chiefly committed in the stable, except on rare occasions when he would go through his programme in the harness.

I had just returned from an absence of five months, when on a cold, crisp, sunny day, the young doctor asked me to drive with him.   He wore a light drab overcoat, becoming because it made him look stouter. I never afterwards refused to go *anywhere* with him when he wore *that coat!*   "Satan," with the subtlety of his namesake, divined this to be a "rare occasion." With a vicious shake of his head he started on a keen jump, and never stopped till he reached the brow of a high hill, some two miles distant from the town.   Here he paused—just long enough to tower on his hind legs (I thought he would sit upon us); but gathering himself, he plunged down what seemed to me a precipice, and when fairly at the bottom, with dextrous agility shivered the dash-board into a hundred splinters!   At this climax the young Esculapius looked for me—*I had slipped out behind!*   Shortly after this exciting drive, "Satan" was presented to some one who could better appreciate *all* his unusual eccentricities.

"Bishop," "Satan's" successor, was a reliable, handsome chestnut who was never known to commit the slighest indiscretion.   He was speedy and untiring in his long drives into the country, several of which were famous.

O'Brien, a bright young Irish student or physician I don't remember which, often drove with Doctor Gunn on his rounds.   One morning, by appointment, O'Brien was to call for him at the church.   It was just before Christmas, when the young people were especially devoted to St. Andrew's.   Evergreens with their spicy fragrance filled the aisles.   All the girls were there with one or two exceptions, wearing old party gloves to protect their fingers while they religiously fashioned their emblems and at the same time carried on their small but interesting flirtations.   He came—his eye scanned each separate group even to a remote corner of the church, where two more zealous at their task were seated beneath a pine that seemed to be growing for their benefit.   Not finding the one he sought, but who lived near, he turned his steps toward her home.   An hour later he saw Bishop passing, and stepping out hailed O'Brien, who, taking in the situation, accosted him: "Ah, Doctor, I see ye are at yer devotions!"   After returning from the country, when nearing the

office, O'Brien asked, quizzically, "Now, Doctor, shall
I *take ye back* to yer devotions? for sure—

> " 'Love is like a dizziness:
>   It winna let a body
>   Gang aboot his bizziness.' "

CHAPTER SIXTH

DOCTOR GUNN was twenty-five! we had been married three weeks! when one night he was called up in haste. I had never taken kindly to the profession, but my antagonism was then in its infancy. There was some small excuse for timidity, ours being the only sleeping-room on the first floor. Making his preparations to go out, I dolefully inquired, "Doctor, are you really going?" "Going?" he reiterated, and looked as any impecunious young doctor might look at the wife whom, wisely or unwisely, he had taken to support. With a few reassuring words, and saying that he would be back soon in all probability, I relented, but called out after him: "Remember, I shall not sleep *one wink* until you return."

He said:—"This was my first experience, and on the whole my best. I hurried to my patient, was not detained, prescribed, and was back in less than an hour. With winged feet I flew to my sleepless wife, with eager hand unlocked the door, crossed the hall, and approached our room. I had endowed her with every feminine attribute; but, ye gods! what sound was that? Oblivious to me, to her bugbear, and to her fears, snored my unconscious wife. Yes, actually *snored!* in the face of her last promise. Ignored, so soon! I began to think I was not of much account after all. Then I reasoned: It is better thus, she has learned her first lesson (I hope the others will come as easy); but O! false delusion, this was the first nap and the last she ever indulged in when I was out at night on professional business."

Doctor Gunn concluded, before entering upon his service in the University, to spend the winter of 1849–50 in New York, Philadelphia and Boston, visiting the hospitals and schools. We were then at the "Franklin," which had gone through many metamorphoses, but the rooms en suite were desirable and were furnished according to the plethoric or attenuated purses of their occupants; giving to them an individuality and a home-like appearance.

My husband's practice, though not large, was very laborious; the long drives over execrable country roads made it fatiguing. He had some prominent patrons among the town's people, and others that were not so prominent, but his most lucrative practice was among the Germans. His tastes were extravagant, but he abhorred debt, and rather than incur one, would undergo privation. As an illustration: When first we went to housekeeping, he sold his watch, bought another less expensive, and with the surplus purchased a desired piece of furniture. He was not, however, an adept in commercial enterprises. If he wanted an article he was ready to pay its full value, or, his friends said, usually "a little more."

Doctor Gunn's mother once asked a nephew how her son was doing. "O! he is doing well; don't trouble about him. You know, Aunt G———, the doctor never pays a dollar for anything *if he can get it for a dollar and a half!*"

The doctor told with amusement an incident of a rich old Irish farmer who never paid a doctor's bill if he could help it. He held the Irishman's note, but said there was little prospect of ever holding his money. After a year or more he turned the note over to a sharp business firm. When their collector presented the note, O'Connor said: "Sure, an I'll not pay that!" Being informed that the note was held by the M———s, he shouted: "Is thim the divils? Troth, thin, I may as well be afther payin yez."

———

Leaving for the East a few weeks in advance of my husband, his letters will give a glimpse of his daily proceedings for the next few months.

"ANN ARBOR, *September 26th, 1849.*

"I have just returned from the country, driven to the postoffice, found your letter, read it twice, and am seated to respond to its contents. The day after you left I went to Lima, from there to Portage Lake, into Livingston county, and home by the way of Hamburg. I arrived at six, but avoided my rooms on account of the loneliness. . . . . . .

"On Tuesday C. L—— returned and remained until Thursday, when F—— came, and they both went home together. Fenton has been nominated for lieutenant-governor. While they were waiting for their carriage to come round, I said, 'Come, let us go up to my room.' F—— replied, 'Is not your wife gone?' Upon being answered in the affirmative, 'Well, then, what is there to go up for?' . . . . .

"*Afternoon, Five O'clock.*—I had written thus far when called away, and have been driving all the afternoon. . . . I am tired and chilled but must say a few words and mail this letter to-night. I am sitting at the dressing-table, shorn now of everything except 'Jules Haules,' the only object between me and the glass from which is reflected your lone lord, red whiskers and all. The rooms look so desolate that I don't know how I shall manage for the next six weeks." . . . . .

"ANN ARBOR, *September 30th, 1849.*

"I have abstracted this sheet from your portfolio; therefore the blot with which it is embellished is probably your own—so much by way of apology for its presence. It is Sunday evening, and a cold, wet, melancholy day it has been. Mr. Taylor is ill, and instead of his ministering to me and others of his church, I have ministered to him.

"*Thursday Morning, Eleven O'clock.*—Yesterday I came from the country at eleven o'clock, found your letter, read it and was prepared to answer it when a man made his appearance for me to go into the country to one of those ——— cases, which if I could I would forever foreswear. I went, and returned at half-past two this morning—fourteen hours!! Owing to this, I was unable to send you a letter by return mail, but I could not avoid it. If there is anything I hate, it is one of these cases.

"I shall be very busy until the first of November; shall not get away, perhaps, before the tenth. . . Knowing your fondness for details, I shall commence a history of my daily thoughts and doings, that on the arrival of your letter, I can send you a long one in return." . . .

"Ann Arbor, *October 5th, 1849.*

"Agreeable to my promise yesterday, I begin my journal.

"Last evening was spent in Mrs. D——'s room playing euchre with Mrs. D——, Mrs. P—— and Mr. A——. You know I am not fond of playing, but euchre is my fate, or to be left to my own forlorn society.

"The other evening in W——'s store, talking with a circle of men, the conversation turned upon a certain charity. B——, with plenty of means, is not much of a favorite; he proposed giving *two* barrels of flour! I offered my services. B——, evidently considering this a small contribution, inquired, 'About how much, doctor, do you consider your services worth?' 'O, not much; possibly about as much as *your flour!*'

"Do you recollect the darkey who did some work for us and took such a fancy to you? (all the darkies do). Well, while I was in W——'s store this evening he came in. I noticed that one of his hands was deformed. I asked him to let me look at it. As he showed it to me, he said, 'Doctor, you have seen it a hundred times befo'! Why, I knowed you, and you' father, and all the folks in Bloomfield. I was mos' suah it was you the fus' time I heerd you' name' He was raised in Canandaigua, knew every one there, was very talkative, and wanted to know *all about* 'How de young missus was.'

"*Sunday Morning.*—It is cold, and continues to rain, and with the wind in the north-west is drear and horrible as you can imagine. The quicker I get out of these rooms and let Mrs. D—— have them the better. M—— about once a week sweeps and dusts, then arranges the chairs, *all in a row*, round the room. I come in and scatter them about in double-quick time, but they never look right. I am growing unfriendly to the surroundings and shall vacate the rooms without much regret, leaving Mrs. D—— to get all the pleasure out of them she can.   .   .   .   .   .

"To-day has been miserably wet and unpleasant. I have been ten miles into the country this afternoon. During these drives I ponder a good deal over the future.   .   .   .   I have an invitation to Mrs. M——'s to night, but do not intend to go. The H——s expect me to dine there every Sunday, which I cannot. I forgot to mention dining there the first Sunday after you left.

"*Saturday Evening.*—Again I am seated in my dismal room, while you are wondering why you received no letter from me to-day.   .   .   :   This moment that I have begun writing, I am summoned away.   .   .

"*Sunday Evening.*—I promised to call at J. P——'s to-night. It is now ten o'clock, and another evening has been whiled away. When leaving, H—— handed me this parody to send to you. I affix it to the sheet; the last stanza strikes me as particularly *apropos*."   .

"*Monday Noon.*—Your two sorrowful letters have come, and I stop in the midst of moving to close this and dispatch it to your comfort. Only one night more in the dreary old rooms! Everything is out of the parlor, and nearly everything out of the sleeping room. .   .   .   I shall start just as soon as I can deposit my vote in the ballot-box, which will be four weeks from Tuesday."

"Ann Arbor, *October 9th, 1849.*

"It is just after dinner, Tuesday. I have everything arranged, and stored away. Mrs. D—— is now moving down. She occupies C——s parlor for a day or two, and has ordered a fire made and has just told me to go in and make myself comfortable. I have done so, and finding pens and paper on the table, have appropriated a sheet, on which I begin a letter to you.

"'Time seems to creep as decrepit with age,' when I think of the time set for my departure. .   .   .

" *Wednesday.*—I am only half recovered from a cold, taken while engaged in that laudable enterprise of moving, which needs your commendation.   .   .

"To-day is the beginning of the fair; the town is full of the queerest specimens of humanity that ever took premiums at any fair! I have been out on business, in the mud and wet, through it all, when I ought to have been at home.

"*Thursday Evening.*—By another miserable mistake of the Detroit postmaster, our mail was sent on to Battle Creek, while we received theirs. I am a little better of the cold, but have a voice like a young bull. I should like to establish a momentary telegraph between us. Friday and Saturday's mails bring no letter from you. What can it mean? To-day is the eleventh; only twenty days more, before I hope to join you. Business is about over, and nothing but collections shall detain me. Mrs. D—— has just told me she wished I had my old rooms back again, for she might as well try to sleep in bedlam as in rooms so near the dining-room."   .   .   .   .   .

"ANN ARBOR, *October 14th, 1849.*

"It is Sunday morning, I have no country patients, and my village business is finished for the day, unless something new comes up. It is a beautiful morning, and so unlike any we have had for the last two or three weeks, that it is indeed a novelty. Next Thursday evening is disposed of. I am going to the R——s to dinner. . . . .

"*Sunday, Nine P. M., October 21st, 1849.*—I have just finished a very interesting picture founded on the history of Chillon and the long captivity of the unfortunate Bonnivard in its dungeons. Thus I manage to while away the time. During the week, I am able to get along quite comfortably till evening; then I find it impossible to keep myself from sinking into a melancholy musing, and dwell on thoughts sometimes, I could hardly write to you. .

"My patrons seem to take an interest in my plans for the coming winter and exert themselves to help me off. My good German friends come up to the mark and pay the money on bills of from fifteen to twenty-five dollars less than two months old. I am often surprised at the cheerfulness with which they acknowledge and liquidate their indebtedness. Governor Fenton sent a man from Flint to consult me in a case of surgery which will lead to an operation. . . .

4

"*Friday Evening.*—Nothing can exceed the dullness which surrounds me.   I meditate on my approaching escape, and count the days before leaving.   .   .   To-morrow, I have to go to Hamburg, a consultation case.   In eight days I start for New York.

"*Saturday Evening, October 27th.*—I leave next Thursday, and this will hardly reach you in time to announce my coming.   I am very tired to-night, having ridden from here to Hamburg and back over the worst kind of roads."   .   .   .   .   .

Doctor Gunn arrived in Bloomfield, according to his date, remained a few days, and then went on to New York, where he writes from the Irving House, on November 28th:

"The loneliness I felt at our dear old Ann Arbor, after you left, was nothing compared to this I now feel in this bedlam city.   .   .   .   To begin back. I had a cold, unpleasant ride to Vienna.   When I arrived at Geneva, amused myself by going up to the College and calling upon Dr. Hoadley.   The evening dragged until nine o'clock, when I sought refuge in my almost never-failing friend Morpheus.   I was called in the morning, to take the boat at six.   The trip up the lake compensated in a measure for the wretched staging from the head of the lake to Elmira. We were till half past four, making the distance from Elmira, twenty-two miles. The wild scenery of the Delaware, through which the Erie railroad passes, is not unlike the Mohawk at Little Falls. We arrived this evening, and New York is noisier and more like Babel than ever. The whole day I have run and run, until my feet ache with pressing the pavement, the hardness of which is only exceeded by the flint-like expression of the countenances of the Gothamites.

"It is six o'clock, the house is full, but I feel entirely alone.   .   .   I will find your friends the D——s to-morrow."   .   .   .   .   .

"IRVING HOUSE, NEW YORK,
"November 29th, 1849.

"I wrote you last night out of the fullness of my heart, and to-night, my heart feels about as full as it did last night.   .   .   .   One little bright spot is the recollection of my call at D——s.   .   .

"There are many pleasures and conveniences in this city, and there are also many drawbacks. With my present feeling, any desirable inland town suits my ideas of comfort better than New York ever could. For two or three days past, Broadway, from its beginning to its end, has been one puddle of mud! Thirty thousand people who are constantly threading this great thoroughfare keep the pavements covered with mud an inch deep, about the consistency of thick cream, and on the cross walks, about as thick again. When crowded with carts, omnibuses and carriages, if you wish to cross from one side of the street to the other, you must run the gauntlet of the numerous vehicles, with other pedestrians like yourself. If you escape without being knocked down, you are fortunate. This is no exaggeration, if one wishes to cross Broadway at any time, or at any point between the park and Wall street.

"This is the unpleasant side of the picture. But now take the glowing evening view of Broadway on a fine dry night when the magnificent and varied display in the shop windows bursts upon the sight almost like the magical changes of stage scenery. The prodigal expenditure of money to unfold nearly everything of which the brain can conceive, is used to engage the attention of the passer-by. You meet the same vast multitude, ever busy, ever changing, and over the whole are thrown the brilliant gas-jets of the streets and stores; you move along in the throng with the thundering of omnibuses on the one side and the brightly lighted shops upon the other. The large glass fronts expose to view the illuminated interior, the marble floor, the carved and gilt tables; while above and upon the sides are tastefully arranged the costly wares. Here is a gentleman's furnishing establishment with ten thousand fancy articles; next comes a dry goods house of bewildering attractions in silks, laces, velvets, and gorgeous imported costumes to rivet the attention. A glance shows how one would like to linger and partake. Contiguous to this is a jewelry house where beautiful designs and novelties gleam entrancingly on the view. Then the druggist's display of fancy jars and glass, in variegated array. But I will go no further in the category.

"Now let us revert to the darker side of the picture. The evening is bitterly cold. You are passing the 'Astor,' with its shops as alluringly bright as those already described above; the windows of splendidly furnished apartments are sending forth rays of dazzling light, exposing borders of rich drapery, while in others through a filmy web of lace the soft light gleams. All is gay and bright within. We turn a corner just outside of all this luxury. Sitting upon an old stool, beside an old table, beneath the glimmering street-lamp, is the venerable vender of her daily and nightly wares. She, poorly clad, shivering with cold, waits for some one to buy,—it may be to feed some starving ones at home. Here a little fellow, young in years, but old in sin, with scarcely clothes to hide his nakedness, shakes a paper in your face, crying lustily, 'Evening Express! third edition! great mob in Boston!' when it contains no such announcement. There sits a miserable mendicant holding out his hand for a penny. Farther on you are met by an apology of womankind with a little *abortion*, almost, in her arms, who, while she begs, if you would stop to listen, tells a story of distress that would sicken you to the heart. You can't imagine the tenth part of the misery in this city; much is real, and some, of course, is feigned.

"*Sunday Afternoon.*—I have not seen a pleasant Sunday since I came to New York. If you arrive in Bloomfield by the 25th, I will direct my next to Centerfield."   .   .   .

This was the nearest point for receiving and posting our letters. An old red brick house which had once flourished as a country inn, bore over its door the magic word, Post Office. Always, when driving through Centerfield, to and from Canandaigua, I felt impelled to stop and inquire for some *impossible letter*.

"IRVING HOUSE, NEW YORK,
"*December 8th, 1849.*

"You were right in saying my first day in New York would be my loneliest. My time is more occcupied, yet it sometimes drags heavily. I contemplate an alteration in my projects which may enable me to finish in Canandaigua, what I have begun here.   .   .

"I found my old friend Thomas Rochester. He lives on Houston street. Yesterday, going up Broadway, I met T——; he is at the Theological Seminary. There is now in New York a member of every class that has been graduated at the University. This morning on the Ferry I met J. W——: was introduced, and then gave him your Uncle Van D——'s letter of introduction. He is a very elegant man. I frequently pass your Uncle A. L. J——'s office, but shall not present my letter to your *eminent relative* until I return from Philadelphia.   .   .   .   .   .

"I have just learned that my brother, who has been a year in Buenos Ayres, had a very tedious time in getting to California. They were blown three thousand miles off their course, off the Horn, and during the gale the first mate was blown overboard and lost! For two days the ship lay on her beam-ends, and no one thought she would right up again; but finally she did, and then had six feet of water in her hold!"

> "IRVING HOUSE, NEW YORK,
> "*December 22nd, 1849.*

"It is too rainy to be out as much as my business demands. I have just come in, and after reading some of the Detroit papers in the reading-room, have seated myself at the public writing-table to begin a letter to you. Yesterday was bright, clear, and not cold. I went to Greenwood; saw many fine things, and as many that were ridiculous—every variety of taste, and every way of its exhibition. . . . . .

"There is a new comic pantomime, by the Ravels, just out at Niblo's—the scenery new, made expressly for them, and said to be gorgeous. I have not yet been to the theatre, but shall go next week. . . .

"I attended Grace church this morning; sat with J. W——. He is a very polished man, and very polite to me, and I like him. I had a letter from Dr. Carr yesterday, in which he expresses great satisfaction at the prospect of my coming there to make the preparations. He is a trump, and the ace at that. I have made some very pleasant acquaintances in the profession, here in New York, some capital fellows. Will tell you more when I see you." .

"New York, *January 6th, 1850.*

"Yesterday I spent at Blackwell's Island at the penitentiary hospital; dined with Dr. Kelly, the physician to the Island. The hospital is filled, principally, with those abandoned creatures who are victims of their own folly, and if the poor outcasts on the brink of destruction could see half of what is to be seen there in that hospital they would stay their downward career and *starve* rather than anticipate such an end; and if men who forget the laws of nature and of God, and trample them under foot, could see such convincing proof as is to be seen in the male wards of that hospital, that 'the way of the transgressor is hard,' self-preservation, if nothing else, would make them alter their course. . . . .

"I shall go to Philadelphia on Tuesday. Direct your next to the 'Columbia Hotel,' Chestnut street. There is a mighty sight of humbug going on here. The power of humbugging is as good as a fortune here in New York. I shall stop at the 'Astor' on my return, before going to Boston; direct your other letters there.

"I called, last week, upon my old friend Dr. Rochester and found him with the badges of mourning for his brother, who had just died in California. It was the brother who was graduated with him at Geneva College, the commencement you were there; you must remember them both. How much sad news of this kind comes with every steamer, and yet the half is not told!

"Write by return mail, and send H—— to Centerfield with your letter. I have a pocketful of letters to Philadelphia men which I think I shall use."

"PHILADELPHIA, *January 10th, 1850.*

"Here I am in Philadelphia, in a medical point of view, the Paris of this country. There is a medical atmosphere here that is really refreshing. If you were here you would enjoy it as much as I do. . . . There are now in this city some twelve hundred medical students in attendance upon the different medical colleges. One thousand of them are members of two of the schools, so that the professors of each of these two schools lecture to classes of five hundred.

"The politeness of the faculty here is unsurpassed. To give you an example. I arrived Tuesday evening at nine o'clock. I had some half-dozen letters to the most eminent men in the profession. Yesterday (Wednesday) morning, I called at one of the colleges and found that there was no lecture until twelve o'clock. Then I went to Dr. Meigs' residence and handed him my letter. He was just going out on his morning expedition and could devote but a few minutes to me then, but said: 'To-day my children come home to a family dinner. You must come and dine with me.' I went, had a fine dinner, met a son and his wife, and a daughter and her husband, a Mr. Biddle, a cousin of Major Biddle of Detroit.

"Before going there I visited the hospital, and at one o'clock went to hear Professor Pancoast. I had a letter to him. On presenting it, he was very cordial and asked immediately if I had a wife with me; said Mrs. Pancoast had some friends engaged for the evening and I must certainly join them.   .   .   .
On my return I found a note from Dr. Neill inviting me to a medical club at his house to-night.

"This morning presented my letter to Dr. Muter, Professor of Surgery, and from him received another invitation to a party at his house to-night, also a medical party. I am going to both. Professor Horner of the other school said he considered me engaged to him for Saturday night to attend a Wister party. These had their origin in, and were named for Dr. Wister, Professor of Anatomy in the University of Pennsylvania. You see the M.Ds. of this City of Brotherly Love have a kind of hospitality peculiarly their own. Dr. Pancoast came to me last evening and regretted that Mrs. Gunn was not present.

"The New Yorkers have a good deal of suavity, but

the politeness of the Philadelphia doctors is extended
in the way of generous hospitality, and almost every
member of the profession that I have met seems to be
imbued with the same disposition. As I said before,
Philadelphia contains a medical atmosphere that is most
refreshing, and if you could see the way the doctors do
it up here, you would admire the profession more than
you now do."   .   .   -   .   .   .   .

                    "ASTOR HOUSE, NEW YORK,
                        "*January 15th, 1850.*

"I came here from Philadelphia this morning and
found your two letters which arrived last evening. I
find this a more central point for doing business in the
shortest possible time, and as I have only a few days
more, am hurrying with all possible expedition. I shall
leave for Boston on Thursday and hope to receive a
letter from you there. Direct to the 'Tremont.' Do
not disappoint me; you will have no more letters to
write after that.   .   .   You may look for
me by the 26th."   .

CHAPTER SEVENTH.

IT was perhaps a year after the doctor's return from the East, that he purchased a roomy house nearly completed. It was on a corner, as were those he subsequently owned. The long pillars in front suggested a style of Grecian architecture now almost obsolete. There remained one thing for the doctor to plan: an outlook from the roof, enclosed by a railing; which if it did not beautify the house, afforded a view of the country, the Lower Town, and the valley where the Huron flowed.

All our energies and aspirations were centered in this new home. A house is a woman's universe; a small world of glories, struggles, and semi-tragic comedies which the graphic pen of Jane Carlyle so delightfully reveals. It was more than forty years ago the doctor squandered some of his mechanical ingenuity on household adornment. There were two chairs that derived their prestige from his cleverness in upholstering; none since have ever seemed half so beautiful.

He would say, "My wife is in her element if she can inveigle me into attempting some almost utter impossibility about the house. She has great faith in my creative powers, and watches with interest (she says) 'the deftness of my execution'. She is remarkably amiable at such times, waits on me, brings me all the tools, and while I tug, and hammer and pull things into place, she complacently sits by and *holds the tacks!*

"On one of these occasions while working on a bracket my eye-glasses caught and were demolished! 'There is economy for you!' I exclaimed. 'I could buy *six such traps* for what one pair of glasses cost'. Wheedlingly, she replied, 'But, doctor, you know there is twice as much sentiment when *you drive in the nails.*' "

Time for hanging pictures came, and with them came the tug of war; the doctor was tall and I was short; what looked well to him never looked right to me. At last, losing his amiability, he declared, "These pictures will be the death of me. You must get A—— to help you; perhaps you can make him do the impossible which you require of me."

Years after this, at Christmas, I began giving him presents for the house; an economical practice sometimes indulged in by those who are not impecunious.

He forestalled further repetitions by relating an anecdote (he usually had one ready) of a woman who "adored" her husband, but at Christmas gave him *bric-a-brac* or other things she desired for herself. For years Mr. T—— had been the unappreciative recipient of these favors; at last he determined to turn the tables.

On this occasion his wife had presented him with a rocking-chair,—not a large one in which he could recline, but a small sewing-chair! If he had ever felt a twinge of compunction, he did not now. Taking from a closet near. a long, narrow case, that baffled recognition, he crossed the room and with great *empressement* handed it to her. With delight she cried, "What is this costly, curious thing?" with eager hands unlocked the case, and—gasped—"*A shot gun!* "

This sagacious hint from the doctor secured to him ever after (from his wife) personal and expensive presents—which *he* paid for.

The doctor's voice in earnest conversation often became very emphatic. A maid who for some unexplainable reason was quite attached to me, hearing one day his "earnest tones" as he himself called them, turned to my mother with an anxious whisper, "Listen, ma'am; can it be that the doctor is *scolding Mrs.*

Gunn?"   But even this speculative joke failed to keep his voice toned down.

He disliked an argument, especially with me, and had little patience with people who could not "grasp an idea."   With a softening preface would say: "*My dear, you should never try to argue, for you have no logic in your composition; naturally you are bright but mentally you are indolent; you never like to dig down to the root of things; if knowledge could be painlessly injected (hypodermically), no doubt you would absorb a good deal! but as it is you only know what sticks to you in spite of yourself.   The variety of your schools—first it was a convent——"

"Please don't recapitulate my schools!   I am in one now where I expect to *learn* more than I was ever *taught* in all the others!"

With an arch look, he said, "I hope so."   Then with a half-amused smile, "There is, however, one rare accomplishment in which you already excel.   You would make a capital cross-questioning lawyer."   I was accustomed to his raillery and deserved nearly all his good-natured irony, but at this, I gave him a Roland for his Oliver.

He enjoyed this sharp artillery tongue-practice and was never happier than when calling out a quick repartee.

In 1853 we were living in Detroit, not far from the beautiful river in whose depths, fourteen years later, a tragedy was enacted that cast a shadow on our lives.

Besides a general practice, the doctor was obliged to go twice a week to Ann Arbor to lecture on surgery, making these days full of arduous labor which required physical endurance. In his last lecture, just before dissolving his connection with the university, he told the students that in order to *talk* to them he had traveled fifty-six thousand miles. equal to twice around the globe and three-quarters of the way through it.

In all these years I had not learned to be a philosopher. I had allowed my antagonism to increase and magnify the small vexations of my husband's profession until one day I proposed the visionary scheme that he should study law. "*Study law!*" he echoed; "what would become of our children while I studied law? before I could *practice* law, we should *starve!*" To this I had no ready answer.. He continued, "How practical it would be for a man who had lived more than half his days to commence *reading law!*" Still facetiously: "I have a Blackstone! I might begin with that, peruse Chitty for recreation, and so on through the whole catalogue of *light reading.*"

Checking his satirical badinage, and regarding me

with earnestness, he said, " My ——, be sensible. Do not for a mere whim urge me to renounce an honorable profession in which I have some knowledge and some reputation (though God knows I have enough yet to learn). My study of medicine and surgery has almost just begun; there are mines of knowledge to be explored in science and in medicine that will never be exhausted until time is no more. Do not deter me; I must continue in the profession which I have chosen. Be patient. If I am prospered, in a few years I will practice *surgery alone*."

I have heard women say (the men were probably angels) "My husband never spoke a cross word to me in his life." My husband's impatient words were few, but had there been thousands, they would stand as nought against his acts of nobility.

I have often wondered whether only undisciplined women are aggrieved when, on the threshold of some anticipated enjoyment, they are intercepted by a message that " Mrs. So-and-So wants the doctor."

It is not much, only a few words, besides it is your husband's business; but how it does upset one's equanimity, and if perchance it is a " chronic case " that one has heard of all one's days, the very name has power to exasperate. These trifling disappointments, and some sleepless nights are the exposition of our discomforts.

But what are our benefits? It is so agreeable and convenient to have a *doctor* of one's own, to rely upon and to interrogate at will. Surely this is the law of compensation, but how little do we prize it—how careless are we of the hand that shields and brings us all we have! In one brief hour, it may be gone, and we be left in isolation and in gloom.

Now, in the retrospection, how gladly would I take those grievances back again, and in the maturity of my grief, how infinitesimal they seem!

CHAPTER EIGHTH.

A FTER residing some years in Detroit, in rented houses on which the doctor had expended time and money in alterations, making them convenient for an office at his residence, a wealthy patron induced him, not greatly against his own inclination, to take a large and convenient dwelling, near his own, on Jefferson avenue.

This friend owned the residence, and made liberal terms, but these seemed formidable considered in connection with the furnishing of so large a house. However, the matter was discussed and the venture made. The house was old-fashioned, well finished, with a large hall opening on a back gallery. A handsome dining-room and remarkable cook, were inducements to give occasional dinners and other entertainments which, turned over to this rather wonderful individual, caused no further anxiety.

Here we lived in comfort and some extravagance, until the summer of 1861, when my husband purchased a handsome place more than a mile from the center of the city. The grounds were embellished with horse-chestnut trees, their foliage being so luxuriant and beautiful, that a cousin somewhat given to romance named it "Chestnut Place." Here we spent many of our happiest, as well as some of our saddest days. We were only fairly settled in this second new home when the doctor decided to go into the army. This involved change, pecuniary loss, and the breaking up of our family.

On the First of September, in the Autumn of 1861, Doctor Gunn joined the Army of the Potomac as Surgeon to the Michigan Fifth. He found the climate of Virginia delightful, and the excitement and novelty attractive. Winter quarters were less agreeable, and later, the march up the Peninsula became intolerable. His discomforts, together with the lack of means to make those under his charge less uncomfortable, annoyed and distressed him; the climate impaired his health, and in July, 1862, he resigned.

The following extracts from Doctor Gunn's letters while in the army may interest some who did not participate, and may, perhaps, be of more interest to those who, as he did, went through the Peninsular campaign with General McClellan.

"CAMP RICHARDSON, *September 20th, 1861.*

"*Friday Afternoon.*—Did I only consult personal comfort I should pronounce myself a very great fool for leaving home to become a camp pack-horse for a thousand men, for such is a surgeon to a regiment in the field.

"I have twelve in hospital and forty-six in quarters, for every one of whom I have prescribed this day. Not a few come with fancied or feigned diseases: the first low-spirited in consequence of the hardships of a soldier's life; the last, indolent and anxious to shirk duty. These two classes give great trouble.

"I am now seated in my tent divested of superfluous clothing, uncomfortably hot and thirsty; how I should like a goblet of iced Detroit river water!

"Our camp is well situated as regards ground, with the Potomac sweeping around at a distance of three miles on the north and two on the east. In sight, three-quarters of a mile south-east of us, on a high hill, is Fort Richardson, a work of great importance, now in process of construction. West of us, three miles distant, is Munson's Hill, occupied by the enemy, on which they have erected important fortifications. The Michigan Second and Third are encamped three-quarters of a mile east of us, and all around, on the north-west, north, north-east, east, and south-east are encamped an immense number of regiments.

"The forests are levelled to the ground in some instances, and even orchards, in others. A part of our camp is located upon ground where was, a month or two since, a fine young orchard; at the edge of my tent is the stump of a young apple tree, the brush of which had to be removed for its erection.

"Such, however, is war! From its horrors, let us pray for deliverance. When or where an engagement will occur it is impossible to say; many predict an early one. Both parties probably will be somewhat wary and avoid coming together unless with an advantage real or supposed. When the engagement does occur, it may be the result, to a certain extent, of accident.

"We shall change quarters to-morrow; that is, our mess will, the colonel making his head-quarters in a large, double three-story house, in a sightly place close by, vacated by the owner, gone South. The first night on this side of the Potomac, I slept in Captain Whipple's tent at the camp of the Second regiment.

"*Saturday Afternoon, Four O'Clock.*—I have had a hard day; my assistant surgeon was ill and the work nearly all devolved on me. I was constantly busy till half past twelve, and to-day pulled and hauled until your letter was received at four o'clock. I have had some half dozen interruptions since I commenced writing, but now a heavy shower has come up and is pouring down on my tent. The camp which half an hour ago was resonant with all varieties of sound, is as still as a country retreat, the rain having driven all to their tents. There is a novelty in writing under such circumstances, though I do not particularly admire the novelty. As the rain increases a few drops begin to penetrate the cloth, and fall upon me like mist. I shall realize my later experience before this letter is closed, for no mail bag will go to Washington before Monday."

"*Evening.*—It continues to rain, and blows considerably, and I am experiencing all the wet realities of camp in a rain-storm. My buffalo robe makes a capital bed, and gives an air of comfort to my tent. The rain has prevented moving into the house, and I must spend the night here. I have just been called out to the hospital to see a very sick man. My heart bleeds for the poor fellows who fall ill under such circumstances, lying on the floor with a little straw interposed between it and their blankets.

"This war is bad enough on the poor soldiers. God send us a speedy deliverance, is my earnest prayer; but here I am down in old Virginia, camped out in a deluge with an enemy determined and strong, close upon our lines. Our men, many of them, are cool and expect to meet death. One said to-day he expected to be killed! if he escaped should be glad of his good luck. I overheard others say the night we crossed Long Bridge, 'Well, boys, probably many of us are crossing this bridge both for the first and the last time.' Such are some of the reflections that present themselves to these men." .   .   .

"*Sunday Evening, September 22d.*—I have to-day moved over to our head-quarters. From the housetop, with a glass, we see the enemy upon their fortifications on Munson's Hill, three miles west of us. We saw them walking, color of their uniforms, motion of their limbs, etc. A number of mounted officers were present.

"The place we occupy is known as Hunter's Chapel or Hunter's Cross Roads, originally a fine place, but the trees are now gone, and the house greatly damaged. A company of the New York Thirty-Seventh, before we came, nearly ruined the house.

"The colonel inhabits the front sitting-room on one side of the hall, Ladue the front and I the back-parlor —folding doors between; Mr. Jacokes, the chaplain, has the chamber over the colonel's room. We dine in the regular dining-room, and 'Cam' has a stall in the stable and is becoming a great cruiser.

"There are some attractions about this kind of life which compensate for many of its privations.

"You may remember I told you of the wife of a lieutenant from S—— who was going to accompany the regiment. Well, she proves to be a second cousin of yours.   .   .   .   Her husband, Lieutenant O. D——, a brave, harum-scarum fellow, has been through the Kansas troubles, was twice shot and now carries one ball in his leg. She accompanies him through all these times and is devoted to him."

"HEAD-QUARTERS, CAMP RICHARDSON,
"HUNTER'S CHAPEL, *September 23rd, 1861.*
"*Monday Evening, Nine O'Clock.*—I have just re-turned from a review of the whole brigade by General Mc Clellan; was obliged to turn out in full uniform and take my designated place in the regiment, that place changing in the various evolutions. Naturally I felt somewhat awkward, but got through all straight. It was necessary to don a sword and twice salute the general; that too I accomplished without a blunder. General Mc Clellan is quite a young man, and looks not unlike Degarmo Whiting. He was attended by a large retinue; among them, Prince de Joinville and his suite.

"To-day I met Captain Todd, formerly of the United States Army. He told me he had just received a commission as brigadier-general, and takes command in south-western Missouri.

"This evening a bright fire burning west of us is supposed to be a large barn on Munson's Hill, close to the rebel fort, full of hay, and large stacks of grain about it. It has been used as a picket stand from which they shoot at and occasionally wound our pickets. News has now arrived to confirm our suspicions; the barn is burning and was fired by Michigan pickets shooting red-hot rods of iron into it.   .   .

"I have lost a patient to-day; a poor soldier died of brain fever brought on by lying outdoors after a hard march. The nights are damp from heavy dews that settle upon us, commencing at sundown. It is important to take the utmost care of one's health here, but the soldiers are proverbially careless on that point."

.   .   .

"*Tuesday Evening, 24th.* — Another hard day's work done. I have been over to Washington on business connected with my department. It has been warm and I have had a great deal to do, and am quite ready to retire to my, not bed—but stools! Picture me sleeping on three camp stools, drinking coffee without even milk, and calling it good!

"Our pickets are just in, reporting they have killed five of the enemy's pickets in the last twenty-four hours, the order being no firing on their pickets unless to return a first fire. They sent out a flag of truce, and the agreement was made not to fire any more, but this will not long be maintained in all probability. The loss of the barn crippled their picket service, and now they are on a par with our men; before, they had the advantage."

"*Friday Evening, 27th.*—I resume my journal this evening for your edification. To-day has been a stormy one; more or less rain all day; this afternoon and evening very high winds, two or three tents having been blown down, and an elevated temporary observatory which had been erected on top of this house, shared the same fate. One of the timbers struck the roof of the back wing, breaking a hole completely through, frightening my darkey, who jumped out of a second story window! He thought a shell had 'struck us, sure.'

"To-night is intensely dark and the wind continues to blow hard. Three musket shots have just been heard where some of our regimental pickets are stationed. What it means we do not yet know. There is an alluring excitement about this life; were it not so, it would be intolerable.

"There is (thank God!) one woman in camp whose influence is humanizing. . . . Her husband is the oddest of all mortals, has the credit of being brave, but says of himself, that he thinks it is getting dangerous, and that he shall resign. He said this afternoon that in case we were called upon to advance, he would be found in the rear. I asked him how it would be in case a retreat should be sounded. He replied that in that case he should deem it his duty to lead his forces."

"*Saturday Evening.* — I snatch a few moments before retiring. to relate the history of the past twenty-four hours. I was called up last night about midnight to dress a man's hand which had been shot by his own carelessness. amputation of part of the hand being necessary.

"This afternoon word came that the enemy were evacuating Munson's Hill. This news was followed by the order to send the right wing of our regiment up to reconnoiter. The companies composing it were soon under way, and about sundown I followed. to be of service in case there was any skirmishing. My services were not necessary, as our men took quiet possession of the place. I returned to our quarters, but the left wing, and two other regiments have moved on to hold the hill to-night.

"We may strike tents, and encamp up there to-morrow, though this is mere supposition. We would not be surprised to see hot work within the next twenty-four or forty-eight hours. I can see a bright light on the hill to-night, and one to the north-west, as of a burning building, probably at Ball's Cross Roads. Thus you see we are in a constant state of excitement."

"*Sunday Evening, September 29th.*—I must devote a few moments to you before retiring for the night. Perhaps recounting the day's transactions will interest you as much as anything I can do.

"I repaired this morning, after seeing the sick in hospital, to Munson's Hill, where I found that during the night large reinforcements had taken place. Regiment upon regiment had accumulated in the vicinity, and from the hill a wide range of view opened itself to the beholder.

"While on the hill, General McClellan, attended by his body-guard, composed of two companies of cavalry, came up. It was a fine sight. In the return I met Captain Whipple, who introduced me to Dr. Magruder, who was stationed at Fort Randall when the Redfields were there. He has a cousin, General Magruder, in the Southern army.

"After this, in company with Dr. McNutty of the

New York Thirty-Seventh, I started on an exploration of the enemy's country. We rode on a couple of miles toward Falls Church, finding our pickets had been pushed on as the enemy had withdrawn. Just before reaching the church, Dr. McNutty's horse ran with him, tearing on through the little hamlet, past our last picket. The doctor's cap flew off; picking it up, I followed on to our last picket; further I was not allowed to go. Beyond this his horse ran half a mile before he was controlled. I fully expected him to be taken prisoner, but fortunately on his return he reported that he had seen nothing. The enemy has retired, perhaps hoping we may run into another Bull Run trap. We have not yet received orders to strike tents, though an order to that effect may come at any time."

"*Tuesday Evening.*—I write from Munson's Hill, where I came at noon to-day. Four of our companies are bivouacked in an orchard close by; they sleep on straw under the apple trees. I found a German company here, raised in Saginaw, singing inspiringly. It was really beautiful.

"Munson's has been greatly devastated by the rebel army while they were here. Munson, a Union man, was returning from Alexandria, four weeks ago to-day, when the enemy took possession of this point. He was fired upon and had his horse shot under him, his horse now lying where he fell. Munson came here yesterday, for the first time since then, feeling terribly to find everything so completely destroyed. But we have nothing to boast of in the line of anti-vandalism, some of our troops acting as badly as it is possible for men to act. Unhappy Virginia has indeed suffered from this unhappy war! . . . .

"The mail is this moment brought in, and sitting round on the floor are several officers reading letters from their wives. All is noise and confusion, with some rejoicing, others disappointed." .

"*Saturday Evening.* — I write from Hunter's Chapel at the old room. I came down to look after matters here, and as the day is oppressively hot, and as my assistant surgeon has never been to Munson's Hill and wished to go, I sent him there for the night, and remain here myself.

"To-morrow we are to have service there. I shall go up, and then return for the night. This evening I made the first draft on the sperm candles you so thoughtfully furnished. Hitherto Uncle Sam has provided all that was necessary, but to-night there is a screw loose somewhere and no candles are in quarters.

.　　.　　.　　We shall probably march on Monday. I have given you our destination."　　.

"*Sunday Evening.*—I have been across the river this afternoon to visit Broadhead's Cavalry camp. They occupy a position near our first encampment. All appeared delighted to see me, as I certainly was to see them. I saw Dr. Johnson, Fred. Bachus, Colonel Broadhead and Jed. Emmons, the latter without his seeing me. Stepping up behind him, and putting my hands each side of his head, I said: 'Now, Emmons, tell me who it is?' 'By George!' said he, 'I can't, unless it is Dr. Gunn, and he is in Detroit.' We had a good laugh, he never having heard I had left Detroit.　　.　　.　　Dr. J——looks well and was writing to his wife. The major of that regiment has his wife with him.

'　"It is rumored that Mrs. General Richardson, Mrs. Colonel Poe, and Mrs. Lieutenant Whiting may join their husbands soon. Should we be ordered South, I shall telegraph you to come on to Washington.　　.　　.　　.　　.　　.

"We have two more men shot; one by his own carelessness lost a thumb, the other was shot in the shoulder while out scouting."　　.　　.　　.　　.

6

"Hunter's Chapel.

"*Monday P. M., Five O'Clock.*—I am now writing after a somewhat furious ride from Munson's Hill, in the midst of a refreshing rain attended by thunder and lightning. For several days the weather has been oppressively hot, like our July days. This rain seems doubly grateful. I mailed you a letter this morning, and this afternoon on the postman's return he brought your letter of October first mailed on the third. I need not say how thankfully, aye eagerly, I always receive them.　.　.　.　I could not accept a brigade surgeoncy if I had the opportunity, for then I could not get away for the lectures. A brigade surgeoncy is desirable as an easy post of superintendence of four regiments, but of little professional responsibility. I heard a surgeon say a day or two ago, that, as a rule, brigade surgeons were made of those unfit for the active duties of a regimental surgeon.

"Our brigade surgeon is a very gentlemanly, easy-going sort of a doctor, who will not interfere with the world very greatly. He visited our regimental hospital the other day, and said that in keeping our records we had given him some hints that he should profit by. We have not yet received orders to move. I am sorry, for this rain has caught our men at Munson's Hill without tents."　.　.　.　.　.

"*Tuesday Evening.*—There is so much to say that would amuse you, yet hardly worth writing. One speech of O'Donnel's, however, I must repeat. Speaking of some woman, he said, 'I should like to get a mould of her face to run greyhounds in!'

"Last night between eight and nine o'clock it rained furiously. I think I never knew it to rain harder. It continued through most of the night. I thought of the exposed men on Munson's Hill without tents. It became cold before morning, but the men seem well to-day. We have been under marching orders for a week, and are daily expecting to move hence. General Richardson has not thought best to move the tents to Munson's Hill. It is surprising how the men stand the cold, but most of them are in good spirits. Tents last night were almost inadequate to resist the storm.

"Mrs. O'Donnel has had her things moved to this house (Hunter's), and by the aid of two or three darkies, things have assumed quite a homelike appearance. It takes a woman's hand to' make a house look right. To-night the colonel, chaplain, two or three captains, Lieutenant O'Donnel and his wife, and myself occupy this house, and while I write all is life and animation here. I have never relinquished the back parlor; Captain Trowbridge occupies the front; O'Donnel and wife a room on the opposite side of the hall, while the colonel and chaplain are on the second floor. So, you see, poor Mrs. Hunter's house is quite lively to-night.

" I have been to Munson's Hill again to-day—have had the sick sent down to the hospital, and consequently I shall remain here." .   .   .

"*Wednesday Evening.*—Camp Richardson is about deserted, tents all gone, except the hospital tent and Dr. Everett's. We shall probably march to-morrow to our new camp below Alexandria. In that case Dr. Everett will remain here with the patients until they are fit to be moved, protected by a guard of six men. I go with the regiment."

"*Friday Evening.*—We are yet at Munson's Hill. You have noticed my allusions to Bailey's Cross-Roads in former letters. I am writing from his house. B—— is from the North, twenty years since; owns a large farm, and his house is capable of holding one hundred persons. He fills it every summer with people from Washington, being only six miles from there. He has been for weeks between the two fires, a line of our pickets across his farm directly by his barn, and a line of the enemy's twenty or thirty rods back. He and his family stuck by this property, blew hot and cold as occasion required, and thus saved it! Yes, and made money by feeding officers! His house shows bullet holes from both sides.

" Well! here I am to-night and hope to have a good sleep in a bed. I came down at eight o'clock, and it is now nine. After a delicious bowl of bread and milk, I sat out in front listening to the band of the regiment which is stationed at the corner. This, 'like most Virginia houses, is back something like a third of a mile from the road, the music at that distance sounding very finely.

"The evening is mild and with the moon shimmering through the grand old trees, all seems charming; but O! the devastations of war; you can have no conception of its influence.

"Definite orders have come to-night to march to-morrow morning at ten o'clock. We shall have a hard day's work, so I must retire in order to be ready for it. I carry my half-written letter in my pocket, that I may add to it the proceedings of the day, and reiterate the old words which are forever new."

"FORT LYON BELOW ALEXANDRIA,

"October 14th, 1861.

"I am, you see by my date, writing from our new location, below Alexandria. I am very tired to-night, having had much to do through the day; the scattered condition of the sick increases my labor and responsibility. To-morrow I return to move my hospital tent and some who are ill. I cannot write more to-night, for I am very tired.

"A band has just struck up between my tent and the colonel's. I suppose it is a serenade to Colonel Terry, but I also get the benefit; it is fine and exhilarating and almost takes the pain out of my feet. The chaplain looked in from his tent, saying, 'How can you write? I had to stop.' Perhaps my soul is not as sensitively attuned to music as his; but whether it is or not, I should have stopped writing, had it not been for its enlivening effects.   .   .   .   .   .

"There is much in camp life that is attractive as well as annoying; the music is always good, and even this cheerless tent might possibly seem tolerable to you. Loneliness is not one of its concomitants; sometimes one would be almost willing to be lonely."

.   .   .

"Tuesday Evening.—I have been over to Washington to-day, but lost the object of my journey.

Warham Brown sits by my side and hands the enclosed specimen of Secession money, saying: 'Present that to Mrs. G—— with my compliments.' Will write to-morrow night if possible."   .   .   .   .

"OLD CAMP RICHARDSON.

"*Sunday Afternoon.*—I date thus, although all that remains of that camp is the hospital and its twenty patients, nurses, and cook. A regiment of miserable, grimy cavalry now occupies our old camping ground, while the hospital and guard of six soldiers alone remain.

"Yesterday morning we marched to our new camp, two miles below Alexandria, where we arrived about noon. By four o'clock, the camp was arranged and looked like Camp Richardson duplicated. Some baggage had to wait for a second train; my tent was among the left baggage. I slept in an ambulance, with my buffalo-robe, and was snug enough though the night was cold. I was very ill through the night, taken with cholera morbus, and was obliged to take so much morphine that I felt wretchedly this morning. Mrs. O. D—— brought me some toast and coffee to the ambulance, which seems better, made by a woman's hand.

"About noon I started for this place, which is distant from our camp seven or eight miles. I found myself obliged to ride on a walk most of the way, and once here, I concluded to stay for the night, and send Everett back there. He will return here to-morrow, and I intend then to go back to camp. There is a room with a fire and I shall be quite comfortable. Don't be frightened. I shall be all right by to-morrow.　　·　　·　　·　　·　　·

"Yesterday as we passed along the Leesburg turn-pike from Bailey's Cross-Roads to Alexandria, I saw one of the most lovely building spots I ever beheld. In fact the face of the whole country is beautiful."

CHAPTER NINTH.

DOCTOR GUNN'S sympathies were easily aroused. He said, "Any one with the most attenuated milk of human kindness, must commiserate all, upon whom the calamities of war have fallen."

"CAMP BUELL, FORT LYON,

"*October 16th, 1861.*

"Although extremely tired to-night, I will write you briefly, that you may not be disappointed in your regular letter. Our marching orders were countermanded this morning at four o'clock, to the disappointment of the regiment as a body, who were desirous of having the attendant excitement. But all had to submit, and some had to go to work on fortifications.

"The whole country where we are is most charming and picturesque. From one point we can see for miles in all directions, overlooking the Potomac in the distance, Alexandria and the hills of Maryland. Alexandria is a strange old town. It not only seems finished but worn out; nearly everything having a dilapidated appearance. Yet to me it is not without interest as being a town of the old Colonial times, bearing even yet the impress of ancient monarchical Britain. The streets are named after royalistic ideas, such as King, Queen, Prince, Duke, and St. Asaph. Many of them have been paved, but the pavements are worn out, and are not repaired. The whole impress of the town is that of something belonging to the past.

"The country around is magnificent, broken and rolling, giving fine sights and extended views; but O! how unhappy in being the seat of war. You can have no realization of the curse, without seeing its immediate effects upon the face of the country. . .

"I have been very busy getting through a vast amount of work to-day. There are many ill; the assistant surgeon is yet at the old camp. This throws all the labor here on me, and it has been very tiring. . . . . . "To-morrow evening I will commence regular journalistic letters to be mailed at the usual time." . . . .

"HOSPITAL, OLD CAMP RICHARDSON, ARLINGTON, VA.
"*Friday Noon, October 18th, 1861.*

"I did not begin a letter last night as usual, for two or three reasons: First: instead of a private, three lieutenants were sent to carry and bring the mail to and from Washington. The result was that they engaged in too much private business of their own, and thereby lost the last boat. Consequently we lost our mail, or rather the reception of it last evening. Second: it rained terribly, and everything was damp and unpleasant. This, with fatigue and the non-reception of a letter from you, made me feel wretchedly unlike writing.

"This morning, after my hospital rounds, I came up here. In coming through Alexandria I met the three truant officers, with the mail. I made them stop in the streets, and on a corner one block from where Ellsworth and Jackson were shot, they opened the bag and fished out your letter. It was the last one, and whether the first was in the bag or not, I do not yet know. I waited only to get the one, and rode on, giving 'Cam' the rein, while reading your words in the public streets of Alexandria.   .   .   .   .   .   .

"In coming here to-day I took a new route, passing a fine place whose owner, a woman, continued to occupy it. The front yard contained a great variety of flowers, among them some beautiful roses. A colored girl whom I asked for some of the roses picked a bouquet of them, and I send you a specimen of each. .   .

"I hope to get the eight remaining patients here transferred to general hospital to-morrow; then my assistant will be with me and lighten my labors not a little. Neither you at Detroit, nor we here, can tell what the plan of the war will be. Your information there is almost wholly unreliable; much is absolutely manufactured and much is crude. Our means of obtaining information outside of this army on the Potomac is no better than yours. This much I think is pretty certain, that there will be no more falling into traps. Skirmishers will ever precede the advance of the army and the enemy's positions be ascertained, before any advance is made.

"My time is used up. I will take this back with me and if your other letter is received I will add to this."   .   .   .   .   .

"CAMP AT FORT LYON, *Evening.*

"The second letter I found here on my return. I have a great deal of writing to do connected with my duties, which prevent me sometimes from writing you long letters. My time is wholly occupied. I really have been too hard worked the last week. I lost another patient to-day, and you know what an effect that always has on me."   .   .   .   .   .

"FORT LYON, VIRGINIA,
"*October 19th, 1861.*

" We have had another miserably wet day, and our camp would not present many attractions were you to look in upon us to-night. The soil, of sticky clay, makes the muddy state of the camp detestable, but it is camp life, and we must expect neither pavements without nor carpets within.

"I have been to-day down to the city; and to ascertain the location of a certain office, I called at the Jackson Hotel, where Jackson shot Ellsworth! The house is used by troops and the stair rail is completely gone. . . . .

"I don't know how you will like my pencilled letters, but writing on my lap makes it the most available method. A quiet Sunday leaves me but little to communicate. I suspect, however, that we shall not remain here much longer, for our pickets are already ten or twelve miles in advance of us. Mount Vernon, some six miles in front, I have been anxious to visit, but have not yet been able to do so.

"I have just seen a large collection of flowers gathered by one of our lieutenants, some seven miles south of this, consisting of roses, verbenas, dahlias, etc. Think of roses, the last of October! I am positively in love with Virginia; yet attractive as is this country there are unpleasing offsets; insects, spiders especially, are numberless. While at Hunter's Chapel and Munson's Hill the ground at night was as starry as the heavens with the myriads of glow-worms, which are not noticed by day. Perhaps blessings and curses are about equally distributed everywhere."　　.　　.

"Fort Lyon, *October 21st, 1861.*

"Your letter arrived to-night with its accustomed punctuality, but before I could finish its perusal word came that Lieutenant V—— had just had another 'spasim,' and was very bad! I felt like sending him and his 'spasims'—well, never mind where!　　.　　.

" Previous to this interruption, the cry of fire had been raised; a tent came near burning. All rushed to see the cause of the alarm, but it was insufficient to draw me from your words, and I read on.　　.　　.

"You express anxiety about my health. I assure you it was never better than it is now. I was only ill one night. I slept in the ambulance from preference, and there was no one else to sleep in it. It is a better and warmer bed than I have in my tent. These tents are passable for summer but wretched things for win-ter. I could get a brigade appointment at once, and should take it if I could get away after assuming its duties. Now I hope to get a leave of absence; in the other case I could not."

" *Wednesday Evening.*—Yesterday was one of those unpleasant rainy days and last evening was so uncomfortable that I did not attempt to write. To-night, though windy, it is dry, and our tent is comfortable; I say 'our,' for to-day I have had the assistant surgeon's tent pitched directly in front of mine, close upon it, serving for an ante-room, making a two-roomed house or tent. Mine, the inner appartment, constitutes our sleeping-room, while the other serves as a mess room. I left the original mess some time ago, for various reasons. Since then it has broken up and I have formed one with Dr. Everett.

"I wish you could look in upon us to-night. I have built a fireplace in the first room, and here we have a fire. In the rear apartment, or bed room, the floor is thatched with evergreen boughs, forming a green carpet! On either side are arranged the couches, while between them, at the head of the room, is placed a dry-goods box with a cover on it, on which are arranged papers, writing materials, candles, etc., thus giving it quite a home-like appearance. You may wonder at the pains taken to 'fix up,' when at any time we may be ordered away, and probably soon shall be; but the true method is, to make yourself comfortable at once, if you can, even though you may encamp only for three days. . . . . .

"I got out the forks and spoons to-night for the first time. Dinner was ready about dark; after we sat down, I wanted more light. Involuntarily, I spoke out, 'Billy, light the gas!' This of course raised a shout from both Everett and myself." .

"FORT LYON, SOUTH OF ALEXANDRIA,
" *October 24th, 1861.*

"I have been to-day down to Acatink river with Major Fairbanks; the country is beautiful. The extreme point of our visit was three miles below Mt. Vernon. We dined at a house which Washington built for a relative of his family, Major Lewis. The house is known as the 'Lewis Mansion.' It is a fine, old, double brick structure, with wide hall, high ceilings, and handsome finish, located on a high bank overlooking the Potomac at one point and showing Mt. Vernon in the distance, though the house is not visible.

"The place and grounds bear evidence of former elegance, but are now much out of repair, and unfortunately in the possession of a family both pecuniarily and æsthetically unable to keep them in order. For any one who has a love of the beautiful, and would have a care for the house and grounds, this residence would be a treasure. The war over, I would be the happiest man in Virginia if I owned that place.

"A man from Maine purchased it some twelve years since for a mere song. He paid only seven thousand dollars for the mansion and four hundred acres of land! The house originally cost not less than twelve or fifteen thousand. When I thought that Washington himself had built the place, had undoubtedly feasted in these rooms, had once owned all that domain, I realized that in addition to its natural beauties, it had a charm that, once in my possession, money could not buy. I passed the site of an old mill owned by Washington at the time of his death. In fact it was the last point on his vast estate that he visited.

.   .   .   .   .

"It is cold and windy to-night, and while I am writing to you, am shivering in my half-warmed tent."

"FORT LYON, *October 26th, 1861.*

"Your extra letter in answer to my extra from Old Camp Richardson, bearing the roses, was received this evening.   .   .   .   Yesterday we had a review of the whole brigade, composed of twelve regiments; it was a good deal of a bore.

7

"This has been a leisure day. I have enjoyed it less than those more actively employed. I think much of home and the children. . . . If I come back in the spring, I trust you will come with me. . . . I cannot send this letter off till Monday. Will say good night and finish to-morrow evening."

"*Sunday Evening.*—Last night, after saying good night to you, in came Colonels Grosvenor, Hammond and Crowl, with sundry other gentlemen from adjoining regiments. The first three are on the governor's staff in Michigan, and were just from home. I was glad to see any one from Michigan, particularly so in regard to Jerome Crowl. It was pleasant and natural to hear his voice, and see his familiar form and face.

"To-day we made up a party for Mt. Vernon: Governor Blair, General Richardson, Colonels Hammond, Terry, Grosvenor, Crowl, a couple of captains on General Richardson's staff, and your humble correspondent. We were attended by an escort of some twenty cavalry. To say we had a pleasant time, is perhaps useless. But I was not satisfied. I did not stay half long enough. I was interested—wanted to see, linger, and ramble over the grounds more than I was then able to do. I want to go again, go alone, and not talk to any one, unless perhaps to you, if you could be with me; otherwise I would be alone.

"The place is very beautiful but the buildings out of repair. Some repairs have been made during the last year by the Association of Ladies. The house is large, with low ceilings, except in the state dining-room, which appears more like a drawing-room with an ante-room. Washington's family dining-room, his library, and sleeping-room interested me most. The arrangement of these was such, that by a separate entrance from the front gallery he could pass by a private staircase to his sleeping apartment, a pleasant room looking out on the Potomac; thence, to his library. In this last room he died.   .   .   .

"The tomb contains the two sarcophagi of Washington and his wife, visible through the grated door. Further on, is an entrance into an inner chamber, where are entombed other members of his family.

"Outside are seen four monuments, one erected to the memory of Mrs. Conrad, who died in Mississippi, at the age of twenty-seven. She was born at Wood-lawn, the house before described. Mrs. Lewis, her mother, was a grand-daughter of Mrs. Washington and an adopted daughter of Washington. Major Lewis, for whom he built the house, was a nephew of Washington.

"I cannot describe all I saw nor half I should have enjoyed seeing, but that Virginians are proud of their state, with all its interesting and venerable associations, is not wonderful. Well may it be called 'sacred soil,' and sorrowful indeed is the day and cause that made it the battlefield of a striving and divided brotherhood."

CHAPTER TENTH.

DOCTOR GUNN'S veneration for Washington recalls an hour twenty years afterward, when, in the Hôtel des Invalides, we contemplated another tomb, round which the interest of a world centers.

It was not the veneration nor admiration he felt for Washington that enthralled him there, but an overwhelming magnetic influence that was communicated to him, through the entire air, which seemed to be pervaded with the powerful but unseen presence of Napoleon!

He writes: "I have been again to-day to Mt. Vernon; I looked over all those interesting relics; trod the paths which he planned; drew water from his well and quaffed the pure beverage, and finally looked once more upon the marble receptacle which contains all that is left of his mortal being, and bears the simple inscription, 'WASHINGTON.'

" Among other things I saw the old modeling plans which were used in the construction of Woodlawn. I obtained a leaf from a magnolia planted by Washington himself, which I enclose and wish you would carefully preserve. I was fortunate in procuring this one, for if permission were given to pluck them, the tree would soon be dismantled."   .   .   .   .

"FORT LYON, ALEXANDRIA,
"*November 1st, 1861.*

"I should have received your letter Thursday, but there was no mail messenger sent to Washington, every man of the regiment being required to be present to be mustered for pay. I had a letter from my mother and Glynn yesterday; G——'s was remarkable for brevity. .   .   .   I received the medical journals in due course of mail. Let them accumulate in my postoffice drawer until January. After you leave, direct that letters may be sent on to me at Washington.   .   .

"I am glad my descriptive letter of our respective rooms interested you as it did. Cold weather is upon us; *i. e.*, all nights and some days are cold. The leaves are beginning to turn and the woods to assume that richness which comes to us a month earlier. This has inaugurated the necessity of inventing something to warm our tents. Consequently we commenced the fireplaces described so glowingly. The first day's trial was grand, as I told you, that day being breezy, but the next morning was still, and when the boy built the fire, it literally smoked us, not only out of our beds, but out of the tent, rubbing our eyes and weeping vigorously. Then followed a series of experiments to improve on our first. All failed! Then another attempt at a fireplace. It also was a failure. Finally, the third was a success! This consumed all the time until three days since. But although we succeeded in building a fireplace that would *not smoke*, it did not warm us, neither could we cook; another fire out of doors was required for this. To-day I have been to Alexandria and purchased a sheet-iron cook-stove; a small light affair with good oven, and sundry pieces of stove furniture; stove, pipe and all can be picked up and carried with one hand.

"This is now roaring in our first room, and I am sitting at the edge of the second, comfortably writing to you. . . I feel quite elated with it; the pipe goes through a hole in the top of the tent, wherein is sewed a tin collar. One of your darning-needles (with an expert at one end) did the sewing!

"To-day, when returning from Alexandria, I rode up on a sightly eminence, from which the view was delightful. Seven or eight miles of the Potomac can be seen; at your feet Hunting Creek, a broad bayou of the Potomac. Just beyond is Alexandria, while in the distance, six miles further up, in plain sight, lies the

City of Washington. As I drew rein there on this first day of November, 1861, I made a prayer, foolish perhaps, that I might be permitted some day to plant a home on that spot.

"*Sunday Afternoon.*—Just as I closed the above (Friday evening) it began to rain and soon increased to a terrible storm; tents blew down, exposing the inmates to a pitiless tempest. I slept delightfully through it all, though everything inside, including the covering over me, was wet the next morning. The rain poured in torrents all through the day (Saturday), obliging nearly everybody in camp to put up with cold fare, no cooking being possible outside. Then my luck was apparent in getting my stove up in the nick of time, for I had a warm breakfast, and the nicest dinner I have had since coming into camp.

" On through the day until dark, the rain continued to pour and the wind to blow. Everything was piteously distressing; the camp was a mud-hole, the tents dripping, men were wet and cold, and yet there was little discontent. Everybody laughed; now and then a noisy shout announced another tent blown down, its inmates struggling under the wet canvas, from which they crawled forth to re-erect their flimsy cloth covering, fit only for paper-rags. The storm raged, no messenger was sent to the city for the mail; consequently your extra letter was not received until to-day." .   .

"FORT LYON, *November 4th, 1861.*

" For the first time I am disappointed by a Monday's or Thursday's mail without a letter from you. It must be the fault of Uncle Sam, and not your own. You cannot imagine how great a comfort your letters are to me in camp.   .   .   .   .   .

" We were literally in a mud-hole after the storm and one day afterward. Our camp presented a dilapidated appearance; not a step could be taken unless through the mud; but these discomforts are met philosophically."   .   .   .   .

"CAMP UNION, FORT LYON, NEAR ALEXANDRIA,
"*November 13th, 1861.*

.   .   .   "Get some reliable person or family (if you can) to take charge of the house and keep 'Maud.'[1] If not, you must take her with you.   .   .

" I last wrote you from Washington. Whenever I am there through the week my time is wholly taken up with business, and I have never yet been able to see any of the interesting things there. I returned on Monday evening and found that the 'cullud pusson'

---

[1] A pet greyhound.

who does us the honor of cooking for us, had obtained a leave of absence. So, cooking my own chocolate, I went to bed too tired to write you anything last night.

"It was ten o'clock when I retired. At twelve, I was aroused by an order to be ready for marching at three! The brigade surgeon was in Washington. As the whole division was to move, I was obliged to act as brigade surgeon. I sent for the hospital cook, to make coffee for us; then I started out to see which of the medical officers of the brigade were present, and to determine who should be sent into the field, and who should remain behind with the four hospitals.

"By four o'clock we were in motion, and for the first time I was moving with a large army; the whole division moving on to our destination, which was Pohick church, twelve miles distant, as that point had been discovered to be occupied by the enemy, the day previous (Monday), the object of the expedition being to dislodge them. The division moved by two routes. A portion of our force was detached about four miles this side of the church to take a side route and attack on the flank, while we advanced in front.

"We (to make a short story of what to us was a slow and cautious movement) arrived at the church at eight o'clock and found that the enemy had 'vamosed the ranch.' Scouts were then sent out in every direction, to find any trace of them. The Fifth were ordered to advance on the road to Ocoquan, a small village where the enemy's pickets had been stationed up to about an hour before we arrived. They had been withdrawn on our approach. This advance was made by keeping our scouts ahead, and to both the right and left. My curiosity led me to go with the scouts a portion of the time. I was with the captain of a battery, a 'regular,' and we reached the deserted picket in advance of all except a party under one of our lieutenants which reached them by flank movement, just ahead of us.

" Before the regiment and battery came up Captain Thompson proposed that he and I should ride on toward the village; but seeing nothing of interest, returned, though, had we seen the enemy, we probably should have returned rather sooner. The captain proposed the trip, I think, merely to see if I would go, for regulars are inclined to test volunteers when they get a chance.

" On our return, just before coming to the place where we left the scouts and where the regiment and battery had arrived, our horses took it into their heads to have a little run; we indulged their whim, and came in at the top of a break-neck run. As we came tearing in, several soldiers sprang from the ground (where they were resting), and seized their guns, supposing we were flying from pursuers. This advance was very unmilitary, as my place is properly in the rear, but I had taken advantage of my temporary brigadier-ship to do more as I pleased. Well, after 'marching up the hill we marched down again.'

"Fording a river on our return, about a mile from the deserted picket-post, 'Cam' slipped into a deep hole, and fell flat on his side, landing me fairly in the water! Rather an inglorious ending, I thought, while wading about to regain my cap and horse. This feat accomplished, I again mounted, having fourteen miles between me and dry clothes! Arriving at Pohick church, where we found all the other skirmishing regiments, the order was issued to move the column on the return. After getting the ambulances and hospital transports in line in their proper place, I put spurs to my horse and made good time in pursuit of dry clothes. I arrived two hours before the column, and when back had been fourteen consecutive hours in the saddle, while poor 'Cam' had hardly had time to lunch on two quarts of oats.

"Now you know why I did not write last night. After a busy day, then fourteen hours in the saddle on Tuesday, I was not in a writing mood. Now, although I have spun out a long account about myself, I am going to tell you of something far more interesting to me.

"Pohick church is one of the churches in Fairfax county which Washington contributed largely to build, and of which he was a vestryman. This church is a square brick structure without spire or tower. It was finished very finely for those times—that is, the pulpit and altar. The pulpit is on the side, while the altar is in the east end. Both are richly carved and decorated. The church must have been handsome. The pulpit has a sounding-board, and under it is the little box of a desk for the clerk, just as we see it represented in pictures of old English churches. The floors are of flagstones, such as we use for sidewalks, but sadly out of repair. The pews are the ancient square, high-backed boxes of the olden time. The church has been badly mutilated by having the carving and decorations broken off. The pulpit is supported on a hexagonal column; it is of Norway pine and very quaint. I was anxious to possess myself of some relic, and must confess to a strong inclination towards vandalism.   .   .

"We all felt angry that we did not have a brush, instead of a march and counter-march. Good night!
.   .   .   .   I am at the bottom of my sheet and must close.   .   .   .   .   .

"Camp Union, Fort Lyon, Va.,
"*November 27th, 1861.*

"Last evening I wrote and directed to Cincinnati, and you will probably find the letter there on your arrival. I have always expected to return on the first of January, unless we were ordered into active field service. Now, as the prospect is that we shall not be so ordered, it will not be long before I join you in Detroit.

"So you really feel afraid I may have spoiled my coat in that unfortunate ducking? That would indeed be a pity compared to the loss of my neck! To relieve you on that point, the old grey was worn on that memorable occasion, for the double purpose of preserving the blue, and at the same time being somewhat disguised in case we had a skirmish, for the old grey would not be so attractive a mark to sharp-shooters as a bright uniform. You may have noticed that these Southern gentlemen pick off officers with most admirable discernment. The green sash, which has to be worn to distinguish one as a surgeon, suffered some from the baptism. Now are we quits?"   .   .

"Fort Lyon, Va., *December 4th, 1861.*

"If you have again postponed your journey, you will have a large batch of letters waiting your arrival.

Your information of John Bagley's testimony in my behalf gave me great pleasure. I saw very little of Mr. Bagley when he was here, and was not prepared to have him speak so warmly in my favor. I have, however, conscientiously tried to discharge my duties in the somewhat difficult part which I have had to fill, and am glad to know that my efforts have been appreciated. I have seen a 'Tribune' of the 29th ult., in which appears a letter from 'Peter Smith,' giving me the same credit that Bagley did, and I judge that Bagley must be the author.

"I will mention one fact to you by way of illustration: On Monday last, about three P. M., a messenger came over from Washington with a note from a Mr. Russell, a clerk in the 'Interior,' begging me to come and see his brother, whom he had removed from the hospital here, with my consent, to more comfortable quarters in Washington. The young man was dangerously ill, and he told the messenger not to return without me. I obeyed the call, getting leave of absence until the next evening, thinking I would visit Dr. Johnson and also the capitol (Congress being in session). Well, that night the patient died. The next morning I began thinking of matters here in camp, and instead of going on my recreation trip, I set my horse toward camp and made good time in my homeward progress. I found all going on smoothly, but my anxiety about the hospital had cheated me out of a day's enjoyment."   .   .   .   .

CAMP UNION, FORT LYON, VA.,
"December 8th, 1861.

"It is a most glorious Sunday. I am sitting in my tent without vest, in my dressing-gown, and without fire. For three days past the weather has been beautiful, and I can hardly realize that there is sleighing in Michigan. The climate at this season is delightful. We have had some cold days, but have seen snow but twice, and then in small quantity. The rain has been considerable, but to any one living in a house, that would be nothing. If you were here to-day we would have a delightful gallop across the country. I think so many times, on my trips to and from Alexandria, how much I should like this.   .   .   .   .

"An interesting piece of news is that Mrs. Fairbanks sent to her husband, the major, a full Thanksgiving dinner, everything desirable in the way of a delicious repast.   .   .   .   . The prospect now is that we shall go into winter quarters. I should not be anxious only on account of the university.   .   .

"I have a new cook; and as new brooms sweep clean, all goes off nicely. He seems neat, and can cook. Two friends are to dine with me, and I will give you our *menu!* Boiled turkey with oyster sauce; I pass over *vegetables*, to an excellent apple pie, which the pastry woman in Alexandria made for us; after dinner coffee. . . . . .

. "*Evening.*—We had at dinner, Mr. Morley and Mr. Lacey of Detroit. Mr. Lacey told me he saw you on the cars when he started from Detroit; he came as far as Toledo on the same car with you. So you see I have later news than any letter from you. This evening we have had a capital gallop over the hills and through the valleys—Colonel Poe, Captain Newell, Dr. Lyster, Lieutenant Draper, myself and others. Aside from being away from my family I have never enjoyed three months more than I have the three I have been in the army." . . . .

"CAMP MICHIGAN,

"*Sunday Evening, December 15th, 1861.*

"You speak of the weather. Here it has been perfectly delightful. Our new camp, to which I alluded in my last, is one of the finest spots you can imagine. From the front of my tent I can look out upon one of the most beautiful valleys the sun ever shone upon. Beyond is the Potomac, seen between Mt. Vernon and

8

Dogue Point, while the tent is embowered by ever-greens.

"The hospital tents are on the same prominence and are alike embowered. From just back of mine, you see a ravine, and on the opposite slope you see the tops of the conical tents of Companies B and G rising up among the trees, producing a most picturesque effect. You can hardly imagine how pleasing to the eye is this intermingling of the new white tents and evergreens.

.   .   .   .

"I have sent in my application for leave of absence. When Colonel Terry signed the application, he said he hated to spare me (all the officers apparently feel in the same way, although there may be some exceptions among the men). It is extremely difficult to do one's duty and please all. There are a great number of shirks in a regiment, who feign sickness, to get rid of duty; these I must detect and report back for duty. Men, too, are such consummate fools about taking medicine. I have been applied to by men with pick-axe in hand or axe on shoulder, *for medicine.* When it is refused and they are sent back to duty, the chances are, they will be angry. It requires a little knowledge of human nature, at least, to get along smoothly."   .

"Camp Michigan, *December 22d, 1861.*

"My leave of absence has been granted, but only for three weeks, the same time that was given to Hamilton. My time is so limited I cannot join you in Cincinnati or any other place than Detroit. Thursday, the second of January, I must begin lecturing. I shall work hard and late in Ann Arbor. I hope to get a couple of weeks added to my leave. We have had brilliant weather for the last two weeks, but it is now cold and beginning to rain. Only ten days more, God willing, and I shall join you."

CHAPTER ELEVENTH.

WHEN Doctor Gunn's quota of lectures had been crowded into the space of three weeks, he returned to the army, taking his eldest son, a boy of twelve, with him into the field. Later, I joined them in camp at their quarters below Alexandria. The gal-·lops my husband had wished for in the Autumn, were now realized. Dr. Everett's horse was placed at his disposal, while I rode "Cam," and though I had little confidence in the doctor's horse, managed to ride him with sufficient courage to enable me, when mounted, to enjoy the delightful and picturesque views the doctor had so often and so glowingly described. This novel life was of short duration; a brief two weeks only were we together domiciled in a tent, when orders came to march the regiments to Alexandria for transportation.

It was in the early spring of 1862, that I saw the Army of the Potomac embarked on transports of every description, loaded to the water's edge with their human freight. Amidst that throng of troops, my thoughts were concentrated upon two, though my mind included the entire army that, alike uncertain of its destiny, steamed down the broad Potomac.

Alexandria was now more desolate than ever. In a few days I went to Washington, where for months I was surrounded by those who appeared to be antagonistic to General McClellan and his management. Some of these unfavorable criticisms were allowed to be reflected in my questioning letters to the doctor, which naturally called out from him spirited and characteristic replies.

"AT AN OLD REBEL CAMP,

"THREE MILES FROM YORKTOWN,

"*Wednesday Evening, April 10th, 1862.*

"I am now, since Mr. C—— left Camp Heintzelman, in a condition to write. Last Friday morning we marched for Yorktown; the whole army moved at different hours and by different routes, arriving in front of Yorktown on Saturday amid brisk and heavy cannonading, which was opened by the foremost batteries, and returned by the rebels from behind their entrenchments. The latter are thoroughly entrenched. We have heavy work before us. Heavy siege guns have been brought up, and soon the work will commence in earnest.

"It has rained constantly since Monday, and the weather has been cold even for Detroit at this time of year. Vegetation is much more advanced, peach-blossoms are fully out, but I have suffered more from cold than at any other time during the winter. I was ordered to establish a hospital in a house just in rear of our encampment, about a mile and a half from the enemy's entrenchments. I had just accomplished this when orders came to vacate because it was too much exposed.

"An old church half a mile in the rear was then selected. This I occupied but one day, as the surgeons concluded to get the several hospitals of our brigade together; and for this purpose we selected this Confederate camp, which was deserted when our forces began to accumulate at the point. They had no tents, but had made for themselves comfortable log-cabins. Of these we have taken possession, and they make us very capital wards.

"If, after the coming engagement is over, the wounded are sent back to Fortress Monroe, I may be sent there to take charge of the surgical wards. This I would like for several reasons: first, the hospital is a large and fine one, situated right on the shore of Hampton Roads; second, the service would suit me; and third, you could be with me." .   .   .

" BEFORE YORKTOWN, *April 18th, 1862.*

"To-day is received by Mr. C—— the letter which you wrote from Baltimore. He informs me that D—— told him your saddle was not brought to the boat; there has been some mistake, and you probably will have to go over to Alexandria to rectify it.

"I was aroused last night by musketry and heavy cannonading in the direction of our camp. Thinking our brigade might be in an engagement, we saddled and with our traps rode up to camp. We found all quiet, the skirmish being further to the left. There I found your letter and read it, in place of ministering to the wounded as at first I expected to do.　　.

"I am in haste and can only write you briefly.　　.

.　　.　　.　　I am well, though I was very lame and bruised for a couple of weeks from the accident which you have since heard about, but which I did not intend to disturb you by telling at the time. It was a narrow escape, but, thank a good God, I was spared."

.　　.

" BEFORE YORKTOWN, *April 20th, 1862.*

"To-day is Sunday, and my birthday. I will not tell you how old I am, for you are not fond of statistics.　　.　　.　　.　　I doubt my going back to Old Point; in fact, if we carry Yorktown and advance on

Richmond, I shall desire to go with the army, though taking charge of the hospital would be easier and more agreeable.

"We have been before Yorktown two weeks. Probably it seems to you we have been dilatory, but I assure you it is far otherwise, when one sees the amount of work already accomplished. We found the enemy fortified and as numerous as ourselves. Our respective lines are eight miles long; they, behind strong entrenchments. Roads had to be cut from Ship Point to Cheesman's Creek landing, six miles below, to bring up provisions and forage, and also the heavy siege guns we find to be necessary to carry the works of the enemy's batteries. The traverses for these guns had to be constructed, and principally in the night. Twenty miles of road have been made since we have been here, and the amount of work necessary to be done to build one of these batteries is enormous. We are now nearly ready to begin an assault, but the siege must be somewhat protracted. McClellan will, however, triumph; his plans must be successful, and then this will virtually settle the question.

"God bless 'Old Abe' for standing by and supporting McClellan when so many others at Washington are trying to slaughter him. To cripple General McClellan now, would be to protract the war. Don't talk politics with any one, but trust in McClellan, Lincoln, and a good God. We have generals all over the country, fighting well and truly (I would not detract one iota from the merits of any), but the campaigns have all been conducted on the general plan of General McClellan. Lincoln stands by him, and in spite of some wretched politicians, has given him a true support."

"BEFORE YORKTOWN,

"*Sunday Evening, April 22d, 1862.*

"I have been unfortunately situated since coming here about writing; during the two weeks we have been here I have organized and assisted in organizing three different hospitals, and have moved as many times. Much of the time has been wet and cold.

"Our supply of stationery is about played out! We have *one pen* left. I am reduced to foolscap, and as you will see from the variety of the envelopes I have used, that, like the others, I beg, borrow, and steal. Don't be alarmed for my morals; we all interchange this dishonesty, then laugh about it.

"You allude in your letter to McClellan's delay, and say that Manassas could have been taken last Autumn. I *know* better! I know what the army was last Fall, and I know that, had the attempt been made,

it probably would have ended in another Bull Run;
but if successful, it would have been so at the expense
of *ten thousand lives!* McClellan's plan was from
the very first to push the campaign as fast as the dis-
ciplining of the troops would permit in the West, and
by turning the enemy's flank, then compel the evacua-
tion of Manassas, without the loss of a life. The
history of the Spring has proved the sagacity of the
plan. The western flank is turned, and the advantages
there gained are being pushed, while Manassas is evacuated to fall back upon the Rappahannock, and form
there another line. McClellan then moves behind
them upon the Peninsula and they are obliged to fall
further back upon Yorktown and there concentrate
their forces.

"Before McClellan left Washington it was well
understood that McDowell and Banks with their *corps
d' armée* were to advance overland and occupy Gloucester Point opposite Yorktown, thus making capture
of the latter place and bagging the whole rebel force,
almost a certainty. But after McClellan left, political
influence detached McDowell and Banks at Gloucester.
Hero-like, McClellan, while he demanded from the war
department forty thousand men more, set about making roads, dragging up heavy siege guns, and will in
good time carry Yorktown; not by hurling thousands

upon thousands of human lives upon their works, but by a stratagem that will save thousands of our soldiers' lives.

"Fortunately, 'Old Abe' is not so corrupt as some of his advisers, and while they voted against giving McClellan the additional forty thousand, he stated to them that *McClellan should have the men!* Yorktown will fall! and with it will crumble the last hope of the rebels. Listen not to the quacks who criticise things as far above their comprehension as holiness is above the capacity of the devil!

"Lieutenant T—— did not understand what I said about going to Fort Monroe. Surgeon Cuyler, the medical director of the military district in which the Fortress is situated, solicited me to take charge of the surgical wards of a large hospital which was being organized there. He said he had selected a good physician, and he wanted a competent surgeon. I had had no previous accquaintance with him, but when introduced, he immediately recognized me as the Professor of Surgery in the University of Michigan, and at our second meeting proposed this plan to me. Dr. Cuyler made application to Dr. Tripler for the transfer. Dr. T——' told him if the hospital in question was made the depot for surgical cases he would effect the transfer. So the matter rests.

"If Yorktown falls, I would about as soon go on to Richmond, as to go back to Fort Monroe, although the surgeoncy of a large army hospital is a responsible and honorable post and one that any surgeon in the army would be glad to have offered to him. I shall accept, if it is again offered, but shall not seek it. The annoyances I have suffered have been of a minor nature, and from a minor source; still they were annoyances.

"Glynn, on the whole, is a good boy, but he thinks it hard that I won't allow him to go on picket, etc. He would go a little in front of the foremost, if I would let him." . . . . .

"CAMP WINFIELD SCOTT, *April 23rd, 1862.*

"Your letter is received and I am sorry you so readily take on the color of those about you. It is possible there may be those who honestly distrust McClellan, but the hue-and-cry originated with scheming politicians who began to fear his great popularity. I don't believe McClellan ever thought of the presidency, but these howling politicians will excite the army to take the matter in hand, and when the time comes give their vote together; the army has full confidence in him. What called him to the command but the manner in which he conducted the campaign in Western Virginia? The energy, decision, and rapidity of his movements, the success which attended them, was what directed attention to him when a great leader was called for.

"You wonder what induced McClellan to come here! Why, of course to meet the enemy in their last stronghold, after having by stratagem and battles driven them from all others. You allude to this place as a trap! It will prove a trap to the enemy only. Their outcry is that that portion of the army immediately under McClellan has accomplished no more. Why! they have been disciplined, and at the same time have kept at bay the grand army of rebels which was strong enough to have thrashed out all our Western forces, and which has been waiting for some flaw in our plans to march upon Washington.

"This grand army has been obliged to fall back to York River, through the splendid military concatenations of McClellan; and through the same genius will, in spite of all the aid which the miserable politicians give them in trying to cripple McClellan, be completely routed from their position also.

"Do not write any more of this nonsense; write *love* and I will do the same."   .   .   .

CHAPTER TWELFTH.

FROM the doctor's standpoint, neither the intensity of his feelings nor his language excited wonder in me, for soon I learned that what he said was verified. He (the doctor) was as anxious to get to Richmond as two prominent senators were determined that McClellan *should not!* The wife of one of these senators said in my presence, that she "lived in fear night and day, lest McClellan would gain another battle and *finally get to Richmond.*" Since then I have heard the doctor assert "that whatever were the merits or demerits of General McClellan, it was a significant fact that after his removal, there was no further harping about delay." And later he said "that the conservative young general deserved the greatest credit for first forming that Grand Army of the Potomac, which was the foundation for those to work upon who came after him."

"CAMP WINFIELD SCOTT, *April 24th, 1862.*

"Your letter of the twenty-second was received this evening.   .   .   .   If you knew how much

I have to do, how embarrassed I am by a thousand cares, the wearing anxiety that results from the oversight of the sick, you would indeed commiserate me. I am quite certain that under present auspices, I am heartily tired of the service. Dr. Clark and Mr. Howard came yesterday and were my guests to-night. They came to furnish comforts for those in hospital, and will wait until after the battle. .   .   .   .

"*Tuesday Evening, April 25th.*—This morning brought another letter from you, which came down from camp, having been overlooked last evening by the mail carrier.   .   .   . Men are now falling ill, and we have so little to do with. Tonight brought the first fruits of the committee from Michigan in the shape of bedding, etc. I hope soon to have the men comfortable once more, Dr. Clark has gone to Fortress Monroe to procure some luxuries for those who are ill. He will return tomorrow. It appears to do the men so much good to feel that the citizens at home have remembered them.

"You speak of the interest you have in my everyday life. I assure you I have felt very little interest in it lately, I have been so oppressed with care. The fare is poor; nothing in the way of bakery can be procured except hard bread, which I abominate. I have paid two dollars per bushel for potatoes and was glad to get them at that price. However, lately I have been able to get flour, and Charlie makes elegant fritters, albeit he fries them more than half the time in suet.

"Yesterday Dr. Clark breakfasted with me for the first time. We had some of Charlie's fried steak with plenty of gravy, potatoes, fritters, and coffee without milk! Dr. Clark wrote to his wife that it was the best breakfast he had eaten in a year! I told the doctor that sometimes Charlie fried the fritters in suet, but although they were good, they smacked a little of tallow, and were not so good as those we were now eating. Just then I looked at the cooking paraphernalia (we eat in the kitchen) and discovered a large piece of suet from which some had been freely cut, glanced at Charlie's face, which had on it a sort of suppressed grin, the truth flashed upon me, and I exclaimed, 'By George! the rascal has fried these we are eating in suet!' We enjoyed the joke quite as much as we did the breakfast.

"As I before mentioned to you, our hospital and consequently my own quarters are located in deserted barracks,—log-huts, some of them nicely built. Mine is about fifteen by eighteen feet square, almost as large as four such tents as my last one at Camp Michigan. There is no floor, but a large fire-place in which, as I write, burns a cheerful fire. In this room I have medi-

cines arranged on one side; in the center a table; in
one corner a rough bedstead, covered with pine boughs,
upon which, with my buffalo-robe and blankets, I make
a bed for Glynn and myself. In another corner is a
Secession army cot (formerly the property of Colonel
McKinney of a North Carolina regiment), which I
appropriated at the house we first occupied as a hospital and which we deserted as the shells of the enemy
flew directly on the house. This cot young Allen sleeps
on. I keep him with me to dispense medicines, write,
etc. Colonel McKinney was killed in a skirmish occurring about a week since, and is spoken of very highly
by the Confederate papers. You perceive the cot to
be quite a trophy. In the rear of my mansion, I have
another smaller one, where Charlie reigns monarch!

"Thus I have photographed for you a picture of my
rude but comfortable surroundings. I can fill but three
pages, having no envelopes, neither wafers, wax, nor
gum, so must fold my letter the old-fashioned way and
resort to surgical plaster for a seal."   .   .   .

"CAMP WINFIELD SCOTT, BEFORE YORKTOWN,
"*April 28th, 1862.*

"You ask several questions about McClellan's
movements here which I have already answered in a
former letter that you have probably received before

this, but there is one question which requires an answer. You ask why he came into this horrid, unhealthy, swampy country. 'Did he not know the miserable hole into which he was going to lead that fine army?' Of course he knew all about it from the maps of the topographical corps. I consulted one of them before we left Fort Monroe, and probably McClellan consulted them last Autumn.

"Necessity compelled him to move here upon this Peninsula, of the advantages of which the rebels availed themselves one year ago, and by means of which they whipped out Butler at Big Bethel in May last. You slander the country. It is as fine a level country as any about Detroit. Would you condemn a general for leading a fine army into the vicinity of Detroit if his object was to take the city?

" Our division happens to be encamped in a swampy place, because its position fell there. The line must be perfect, the place must be occupied, and it was the lot of Hamilton's division to occupy it. I repeat it, the country from here to Fort Monroe is the finest level country I ever saw. Hole! Would to God there were no worse holes on His footstool!

"You say it is with McClellan's expenditure and delay that people are dissatisfied. As to expense, those who dance must pay the fiddler; as to delay, I have answered that in a former letter. It is a set of implacable politicians who raised this howl; that they have succeeded in drawing into their wake unsuspecting persons is more than probable. My only fear is that Lincoln will not hold out against the political hounds who are pressing him. He has had McClellan's resignation in his hands for months, with the direction from McClellan to accept it whenever he distrusted his policy or ability.

"You ask if I think the siege of Yorktown will be as bloody as the battle of Pittsburg Landing. Probably not, if we regard McClellan's humane and scientific mode of warfare; and yet for this very act there are those who vituperate him."   .   .   .   .

"CAMP WINFIELD SCOTT, BEFORE YORKTOWN, VA.
" *Wednesday, April 30th, 1862.*

"I have read and reread your letter received this morning in order to make a long one out of it,   .   . though I hold that a letter should be the measure of its own length and not the paper on which it happens to be written. I mention its brevity only as being a disappointment to me.   .   .   .   .   .

"I am glad my letter in reference to McClellan pleased you. I shall be most happy to answer all your inquiries, but in two or three of your letters *you, your-*

self became the critic, saying, 'You must admit so and so.' Now . . . I do admit that I know nothing about military service; much less that high branch of it which involves the combination of extensive movements. Whether this or that would have been the better course I am no more prepared to say, than would General McClellan be to say whether this or that would have been the best way for me to manage that fatal form of measles which so afflicted the army last winter. However, I do recognize General McClellan's ability and training in the profession of arms.

"General Heintzelman, who was no admirer of McClellan, when he was made a major-general and assumed command of a *corps d' armée*, and was then for the first time made acquainted with the whole of McClellan's plans, says that 'they (the plans) must succeed; there is no chance of failure (humanly speaking). Perhaps the plans might have been less elaborate and still successful, but with a much greater expenditure of life.'

"Let these croakers go themselves, or send their sons and brothers into the field; let them leave the comforts of their homes and the society of their families; let them hurl themselves upon the breach; let them throw themselves upon the batteries of the enemy, and rest assured we shall hear less of expenditure and delay.

"No! . . . Ask as many questions as you please and I will answer them most cheerfully, but do not find fault with plans that tend to save life, to soothe lacerated hearts at home: do not criticise things that neither you nor I can understand. I approve your plan of not talking politics. I never allow myself to talk of such things now. After the war will be quite time enough for that." . .

"CAMP WINFIELD SCOTT,

"*Thursday Afternoon, May 1st, 1862.*

"Glyndon has just written to you, and as he has told his experience of yesterday, it becomes my duty to explain a little that you may not be quite so uneasy as you otherwise would be. The siege batteries are numbered; the heaviest (No. 1) is situated on the bank of York river, commanding the river front of Yorktown and Gloucester Point opposite. Below, something like a mile, lie several of our war steamers. Day before yesterday they had been firing at a steam-boat crossing between Yorktown and Gloucester Point. Dr. Clark and I went down to see the firing and I allowed Glynn to go along. There was no danger; the steamers being beyond range of the enemy's guns there was no return to their fire, and had there been, we were completely to one side of the range.

"Battery No. 1 was not yet completed, consequently there was no firing from it; masked by an orchard, the enemy knew nothing of it, and it had not yet drawn their fire. Yesterday G—— asked me if he might go down, and I allowed him the privilege. It was five o'clock; I was about closing my letter to you when Dr. Clark, who had gone out some two hours previously, came in and said that battery No. 1 was completed and they were getting range of their guns by a few shots upon the enemy, and that the shells from the rebel fortifications were falling all round the scene of our visit the previous day. I was alarmed, and asked if he had seen Glyndon there. He had not. In double-quick time I was in the saddle and on my way to the scene of action. I had hardly ridden a third of the distance, when I heard a shrill signal whistle, which I instantly recognized. Glynn, returning and seeing me, thus signalled. He was all excitement, and as he related his experiences, seemed supremely happy. I was infinitely relieved. The rest he has told you." .   .

"VAN ALLEN FARM, JAMES RIVER, VIRGINIA.
"*Wednesday Evening, May 7th, 1862.*

"My last note was abruptly broken off by an order to march. I trust you received it with an explanatory one from Dr. Everett.

"Well, to take up the thread of events, I got into saddle as speedily as possible, and after making slow progress through the mud, an aid-de-camp arrived, ordering us on with all possible speed to reinforce General Hooker and to clear the road of any and every-thing in the way, and push on! General H—— was fighting the enemy.

"Our brigade led the division, and our regiment the brigade. Soon another aid came back hurrying us on. General Kearney rode in advance to ascertain how the land lay. At ten o'clock he came back and halted us, telling General Berry to rest the men for half an hour, then resume the march without knapsacks, leaving them in charge of a small guard, and to run the men on for three miles at the utmost speed and go at once into action.

"The scene lay just this side of Williamsburg, in a thick wood where the enemy were fighting General Hooker from a rifle pit in front of strong works. They were driving him gradually back. Such was the first stern work the Fifth were called upon to do. We pushed on, and as we neared the scene of action, the road lay through a dense forest, and on either side of the way were the exhausted soldiers who had been in action, and were withdrawn for rest, while others still fought on. Cheers greeted our arrival, which were returned by our brigade with a yell that seemed fairly devilish!

"Reaching the field depot to which the wounded were brought back I turned in to aid in the exhausting work of the tired surgeons. Here General Heintzelman sat on his horse impatiently awaiting us. As I turned in, he said, 'Just in time, Doctor,' pointing to the field of my operations, and passed on across the road to give General Berry orders.

"Dismounting, I commenced my labors. It seemed I had hardly been engaged five minutes, when Captain LeFarren was brought back with the end of his nose shot off and his cheek horribly mangled; then in they came constantly—terribly shot and maimed, some dying as they were brought in. It seemed as though our regiment was being wholly slaughtered! The rain continued to pour, the garments of the men and the ground on which they lay, literally soaking. None of us had on a dry thread; my own water-drenched trousers had dripped into my boots until my feet were in a bath. On we worked until night overspread us, and still the rain poured, only darkness stopping the dreadful carnage.

"The nearest building was one mile away, no ambulances of our division had yet come up, and those of Hooker's were not able to carry one in twenty. A few were carried; those who had been shot in the arms, and could, walked; the rest remained on the ground all night in the continuous rain. Many died before morning, and all suffered terribly. When night came on and nothing could be done but to watch the poor fellows, I left Everett and Adams, rode back here, and went to work. At midnight wrapped myself in the robe which had been rolled up on 'Cam's' back all day, the fur soaking; and in it, with my wet clothes, laid down on the floor and slept till morning. I had eaten nothing since breakfast, which consisted of crackers and coffee. I arose faint and exhausted; sought a negro shanty where I procured some coffee and biscuit, and thus fortified, I again commenced work. At noon we had coffee and beef, an ox having been butchered for the benefit of the wounded and those who were working for their relief. By two o'clock we had all been tolerably well cared for. I then rode back upon the battle-field. Many were still lying on the ground at the depot, and many still continued to lie there until to-day, thus remaining out two nights after receiving their wounds.

" The weather had cleared and a genial sun warmed and dried the poor fellows. The dead of both sides thickly strewed the woods, presenting the most harrowing sight. Here and there was a familiar face. Unfortunate Lieutenant Gunning was shot through the head early in the fight. From this shocking scene I rode back to hurry up the hospital wagon containing my supplies, and found it detained by the quartermasters, who would order such useless things as supplies for the sick to remain behind to accommodate wagons containing quartermasters' stores. I ordered my wagon forward, and at night, Tuesday, it arrived.

"Glynn has been carrying lemonade to the poor fellows all day, and seems abundantly repaid by witnessing their grateful expressions. At noon, after completing the round at the barn (we have three houses and one large barn), one poor fellow called out to him, 'Boy, they have missed me. If you will bring me a cupful I will give you a quarter.' G——. replied, 'Do you think I would take money from a wounded soldier? No! but I will make, and bring you some.'

"This has been another day of hard work. We are shipping off the unfortunate fellows and shall probably get them all off to-morrow. So much for my personal experience. Now for the battle and result.

"The Fifth and Second Michigan and the Thirty-Seventh New York found and charged on the enemy; drove them back out of the rifle-pit and beyond, continuing to fight till night. About an hour after they entered the field, Birney's and Jameson's brigade came

up and also engaged in the strife. When too dark to
fight, all rested upon their arms till morning, when it
was found the enemy had retreated, leaving their dead
and all of their worst wounded (there are eight hundred
wounded prisoners in Williamsburg); then we advanced,
and as day broke, planted the Stars and Stripes on the
works, which are said to be very strong,

"The Fifth fought bravely and get good credit, I
believe. Colonel Terry was slightly injured by a ball
which shattered his stirrup; Colonel Buck was shot
through the thigh; Major Fairbank's horse was shot in
two places; several of the company officers are badly
wounded. The whole loss I have not yet learned.

"And now, I think you ask: 'Where was our boy all
this time?' I will tell you: and when I have told you,
you will wonder how I slept on that night after the
battle.   .   .   .   .   I found the field
depot too near the scene of strife at the time we entered it, to be agreeable, the shot crackling around us
on the trees. For this reason I sent Glyndon back to
a certain point on the road to wait till I should come
to him. After our forces had driven the enemy back
and there was less danger, I sent Allen to bring up
G——, but he returned without him. I then mounted
and rode back myself, only too glad to escape for a

while the sickening sights around me, but I too failed in finding him.

"Thus night and darkness closed over us, thirty thousand men in the forest around us, the rain pouring, and my boy missing! How do you think I felt? As I reasoned, I knew if he had obeyed me, he was safe, and I believed that he had obeyed; but still the question would arise whether his curiosity had not led him forward to the field, and if so, whether he had not been shot!—At this thought my heart quaked with fear; then to my comfort would come my confidence in his obedience. So I worked on till midnight, and, worn out, I slept.

"Early in the morning I sent a note to Allen to report to me, and if Glyndon had turned up, to bring him. When Allen came he reported the young man to be on his way; that he had come along in the morning while they were breaking their fast on hard bread, took a seat on the ground with them and helped himself as coolly as if he had not been gone. They asked him where he had slept. He replied, "With a darkey in the woods.' He had remained in the spot I had designated, or in its immediate vicinity, until nearly dark, then he thought it time to look out for himself. He would not go forward against my injunctions, but he had learned from some one that I had gone back to the hospital. It was then too dark for him to attempt to find it; so, casting about for a supperless bed, he fell in with General Berry's servant. With him he made friends, and as the fellow had a small shelter tent, a blanket, and a big overcoat of the general's in his keeping, they pitched their tent, built a fire; then, the darkey wrapping Glynn in the overcoat, they laid down together and slept till morning. G—— is a capital boy and has a generous heart. God grant that he may be a comfort to us in years to come! Now I have told you my participation in an affair that you probably know all about through the papers."

CHAPTER THIRTEENTH.

GLYNDON, with an abandoned pocket-case of his father's, containing a few instruments, and with some dressings, was ready for an emergency. A plucky soldier who had not yet received attention, allowed him to extract a bullet from his temple. He had just made the incision, when his father came along, and said (purposely evincing no surprise), "Young man, you had better make that cut a little longer." But the boy worked on a few seconds, grasped and brought out the ball!

By this time two or three doctors and some officers had come up and were amused spectators, while the young operator fished from his pockets what was required and finished dressing the wound. Then turning to his father, said, "There was another fellow I wanted to get at, but he was afraid!" After this he dressed many of the simpler wounds and was intrusted with another operation, for this achievement (of a boy of twelve) had made him quite a hero.

"IN CAMP BETWEEN JAMES AND YORK RIVERS,
 " ABREAST WEST POINT LANDING,

      " *May 11th, 1862.*

" Last evening I received several letters from you and am perched up on an ambulance to answer them. They are the first received since starting on this march; and since the letter from Van Allen's farm, this is the first opportunity I have had for writing. To-day we are permitted to repose on our march while some other portions of the army are on the move. We have just heard of the possession of Norfolk by our troops and the blowing up of the 'Merrimac.' We have also just heard some cannonading off to our left in front and in advance. It may be our vessels advancing up the James river.

" Before I left the hospital on the Van Allen farm, two rebel gun-boats came up the James and threw shells on our side of the river some five miles below us, then passed up the river, respecting our flag and not shelling us. We were agreeably disappointed, for we were shipping off our wounded men and had a train of some fifty ambulances drawn up around the hospitals. However, before the boats got abreast of us we had the ambulances, such as were loaded, drawn into a hollow out of sight. Perhaps the reason they respected our hospital flag, was the knowledge of our having some eight hundred of their wounded prisoners in our keeping at Williamsburg.

"A couple of hours later, as we were bidding adieu to the scene of our labors, two or three large men-of-war appeared in the river below us and commenced shelling the opposite shore; by this we knew they were our own boats. We could not wait to have them come up opposite, but hurried up to join our forces at Williamsburg. They started onward to Richmond. All the route hither from Williamsburg is strewn with broken wagons, several cannon and caissons, showing that their flight was to them, what Bull Run was to us. Many prisoners have fallen into our hands and many have skulked off into the woods during the fight, glad of a chance to desert.

"The papers we have seen, fail to do justice to Berry's brigade, for it was our timely arrival that saved the day. We are, however, to be righted in this matter, and an order has been issued for 'Williamsburg' to be inscribed on our banners. It is singular how trivial circumstances sometimes turn the whole tide of events; for instance, when we had received the order to hurry on and clear the road of everything that obstructed our passage, we, in obedience to that order, broke into somebody's division that was filing into our route from another road, cutting off a whole brigade. They were marching very slowly and we were hurrying on. They were indignant at thus being broken into.

"After marching on something like a mile we were met by General Kearney, and at the same time an aide came up from the brigade which was cut off, complaining that we had broken into their columns. General Kearney said, 'Ride back and tell the rear to halt till your brigade can join your column.' But after the aide had started, he evidently thought of the great necessity of haste and called to one of his own aides, 'Go back and tell them to let us come on, we shall soon be out of their way, for we shall take another road!' He then rode forward to the front.

"Soon after we came to two roads; no one had been left to designate which one we were to take, and General Berry was continuing on the main route. I remembered General Kearney's order to his aide, and turning to General Berry, said, 'General, I think you are wrong,' and repeated to him General Kearney's words to his aide. The general immediately halted the column, and after investigation took the other road, saying, 'Doctor, I thank you for noticing and telling me what General Kearney said, otherwise I should have been out of the way.' Had we been half an hour later we should have lost the day; and had I not taken in and repeated the remark, we should have lost more

10

time than that.   I had the satisfaction of thinking that
I did something that day to save the honor of our flag,
as well as to minister to those who defended it.

"Since writing the above, I have stopped to read
the 'Clipper' of the 9th inst., in which there is an
account of the battle of Williamsburg; and in the
account the division of General Kearney is mentioned
only to say that it arrived on the field just before night;
while the truth is, we arrived at half past two o'clock,
when the rebels had driven our forces back to within
two hundred yards of the operating depot, over which,
when I entered it, the bullets were clattering at every
discharge.   Our brigade immediately went into the
fight and drove the enemy back to a rifle-pit, and then
from it at the point of the bayonet, and continued to
drive them backward till dark, where they remained
resting on their arms until morning broke.   Such is the
true state of matters on the left wing, and in the official
reports you will see them so stated.   But enough of
this.   I long to get to Richmond.   .   .

"Since the battle I have obtained a pet colt for
Glynn.   He is two years old and has evidently been a
pet, and though unused to the bit is tractable.   G——
has ridden him several days, is much pleased, and may
well be, for it makes him quite independent.   He calls

him 'Dixie,' is now writing to you, and no doubt will tell you all about it." . . . . .

" CAMP AT SLATERVILLE, VA.,

"*Wednesday Evening, May 14th, 1862.*

" I have been ill for two days, and this writing in camp is no fool of a trick. When I am busy, Allen is equally so; and when not too busy to write, there are no conveniences for writing. While on the march every day, it is almost impossible, and aside from the fatigue, it is extremely difficult. I am now sitting tailor-fashion on my buffalo-robe, trying to write on my lap. Three times since I commenced, the candle has upset, throwing the sperm in all directions; once all over Allen's letter which he is (I presume from his impatience at the accident) writing to his sweetheart. Cramped from my first position, I have spread out flat! and will try this awhile. . . . . .

" This experience will apologize to you sufficiently, I think, for my not writing more frequently when on the march. I had no time Sunday. After Yorktown was evacuated I was working like a dog getting ready for the march. You don't—you can't begin to know the half of my difficulties. . . . . .
O! how my elbows ache! For this letter I deserve the greatest credit." . . . . .

"CAMP AT CUMBERLAND LANDING, VA.,

"*Friday Afternoon, May 16th, 1862.*

"To-day brought another letter from you. I hasten to answer it because we are lying by and I can write. Night before last the feat was accomplished under somewhat constrained circumstances.   .   .   .

"We marched to this point yesterday forenoon through the rain. I was wet and cold; slept last night as I did the night after the battle, with this difference, that my buffalo-robe was dry. Yesterday was much such a day as the Monday on which the battle occurred. We came here partly to obtain supplies, this being the landing where all our supplies now come. Look at the map and you will see the exact place, and will discover we are nearing Richmond apace. We expect another battle before we reach the city. God grant it may crown our efforts and do much toward quelling the rebellion!

"With regard to what our destination will be, of course nothing is known to us. You speak of it as a fact that General Porter will be provost-marshal of Richmond. How do you know this? General Porter, who was provost of Washington, is in command of a brigade only. General Fitz-John Porter is in command of a division.

"It is, I suppose, time that General Hamilton was

relieved of his command on account of his writing to General McClellan two very emphatic letters, as General Heintzelman paid no attention to his very just remonstrance against working the men of his division so hard while encamped in an extremely unhealthy place. General Hamilton will receive the hearty support of all the officers of his former division if he demands an investigation. I know not what was contained in General Hamilton's letter. It may have been the tone which was unmilitary, but to the fact that the location of the camp was highly objectionable, no medical officer in this division, I think, would hesitate to affirm.

"We shall probably move tomorrow, and several days may transpire when it will be difficult for me to write. Continue to write, for your letters are the only comfort I get out of this fatiguing dog's-life.   .   .

"I think G—— will get no harm by this kind of life, while it must enlarge his ideas. It strikes me that a sufficient reply to people who wonder that you should let him be here, would be simply to state that '*he is with his father.*' Glynn rides on General Berry's staff and is a fund of amusement to the officers, especially when riding in the rain with 'Dixie' up to his knees in mud, and the boy and horse almost covered by a mackintosh!

"Now to tell you how I got the pony. I paid five dollars to a little darkey who had captured it! Many horses and mules were picked up at Yorktown and along the road, this among the number. An order was issued from division head-quarters to turn over all such animals to the provost-marshal, but General Berry said 'Keep the little fellow; he can be of no use to Uncle Sam.' I think he is of the Virginia racing stock, is a fine walker, and though poor and undeveloped, is coming on nicely and with care will in time develop into a fine pony."   .   .   .   .   .

"CAMP TERRY, VIRGINIA,

"*Sunday Morning, May 18th, 1862.*

"This bright Sunday morning brought another letter from your dear hand, and this morning finds me answering it. Camp Terry is the same camp at Cumberland where we have been for the past two days and from which my last letter was written. We are, I suspect, to remain here a few days longer, I suppose for the purpose of allowing McDowell to come up from Fredericksburg. We are now completely in the rear with the exception of Hooker's division. The balance of the army is at, and between here and the White House, a point some five miles further up the river, where the railroad from West Point to Richmond crosses the Pamunkey. The roads are muddy and it is difficult to move over them. When mule teams get almost irretrievably stuck in the mud, the drivers' peculiar vocabulary is the most efficient thing that has yet been discovered in getting them out. The early foliage is beginning to appear and some of the spots in this vicinity are beautiful.

"I suppose the enemy will dispute our passage to Richmond at the Chickahominy. Much is said about capture; it seems to me dispersion is quite as effectual as capture. Once dispersed, the army can never be re-collected. Jeff Davis' frantic call upon the inhabitants to destroy their property will be unavailing to his cause, in fact it will injure it; for men who own a year's growth of cotton are not going to make such a sacrifice when it can avail neither them nor their government anything.

"I enclose the map which you sent me; it is the best one I have seen of this locality. The star that I have made, marks the operating depot; the black line indicates our brigade, to which point the Confederates had driven our forces back at the moment of our arrival. The house on James river marked 'Allen's,' to which I have prefixed 'Van,' is the position of the hospital where I was for two days after the battle. The circle to the rear of Fort Magruder was another place to which some thirty of the Michigan Fifth were removed and where I spent the afternoon of Wednesday and the morning of Thursday. I there had stolen from me the cot of Colonel McKinney which I prized so highly. . . . . . Keep the map for future reference." . . .

"*Tuesday, May 20th.*—I am by no means sorry you take so deep an interest in the battle of Williamsburg. It is evidently true that New York and Philadelphia papers are reluctant to award merit to any but New York and Pennsylvania regiments, and when, as in the present instance, they are forced to award to Western troops their due meed of praise, they also magnify their own state forces. As to the Thirty-Eighth and Fortieth New York regiments, they are in Birney's brigade and did well, but they did not arrive on the field until a full hour and a half after Berry's brigade had driven the rebels back from the rifle-pit.

"The loss in our division in killed and wounded is four hundred and twenty-six. Of these, three hundred belong to Berry's brigade, one hundred and twenty-six to Birney's brigade. Jameson's was not in the fight. Of the three hundred that belong to Berry's brigade, one hundred and fifty belong to the Fifth Michigan. These statistics tell the story.

"The request of Birney to allow the Thirty-Eighth
and Fortieth regiments to inscribe 'Williamsburg' on
their banner is brazen-faced assurance, while the desire
to inscribe 'Bull Run' is ridiculously foolish. What
regiment would wish to perpetuate the inglorious
retreat from this last-named field? But enough,
McClellan's headquarters are yet in sight of our camp,
though it is probable he will advance them soon." . .

"BALTIMORE CROSS ROADS, VA.,
"EIGHTEEN MILES FROM RICHMOND,
"*May 21st, 1862.*

"To-day I have received another most welcome
letter; and as we have as yet no orders to march, I am
seated to answer it. We have reached that point where
every one is uncomfortable; I, no more so, perhaps,
than others, but I cannot incur the hardships incident
to field service much longer if a resignation will relieve
me from them. The nights are always cold and very
damp, while the days are hot. If the weather is telling
upon my health, do not be alarmed, for it is only in
diminished weight and careworn looks that I am aware
that the climate and service disagree with me.

"There are other things which I cannot now explain, that make my position here uncomfortable.
The truth is that the administration of the medical

department of the army is utterly imbecile. The great mistake I made was in not applying for a brigade surgeoncy; a regimental surgeon is held responsible and his hands are tied. Medical directors, medical ditto of *corps d'armée*, and medical ditto of divisions are red-tape channels through which everything must go.

"There is not one ambulance where there should be ten, and to one regiment there are two little miserable sling carts only at my command. I can obtain no more, even for temporary use, except by following up red-tape through two or three medical officers; and since we started on this march, I have been unable to obtain them even by that means. Men fall sick and require transportation to be carried forward or back to some depot. It cannot be obtained; the men suffer and the surgeon is cursed by men who can't appreciate his embarrassments, and by some who *won't!*　　.　　.　　.　　.

"Ten Miles from Richmond,

"*Monday Evening, May 26th, 1862.*

"We marched over the Chickahominy yesterday, bridges having been constructed for that purpose, and we are now approaching swamps in earnest. This was our first Sunday's march, although other divisions frequently march on Sunday. There are now two *corps d' armée* on this side of the swamp. In crossing we found no opposition, and though some of the troops were assailed, there was no stand made by the enemy at this point. This march up the Peninsula, General Berry last evening pronounced to be the most scientific and skillful possible.

"Since the battle of Williamsburg the whole army has been within easy striking distance, *i. e.*, every part has been in supporting distance of other parts. Thus we have gradually moved up and are now working to the north side of Richmond, where we shall take possession of the railroad to Fredericksburg. This will enable McDowell to join us. Meantime, Burnside approaches from the south-east, Banks and Fremont from the north-west. Buell occupies the south-west. Thus if the army of McClellan does not press on so fast as to frighten the enemy to evacuate within the next week, the whole army at Richmond is completely surrounded, and sooner or later must surrender by their supplies being cut off, their escape thus being rendered impossible.

"Here you see the grandest development of the whole of McClellan's admirable plan. People have scolded about McClellan's delay; and now at this stage, the only thing that seems to me in danger, is that Mc-Clellan's portion of the army is almost too soon on the ground and may cause the escape of the enemy southward before Burnside and the southward forces are in position to prevent it.   But let us wait patiently for events as they arise.   .   .   .   .   .

"We have cold and comfort-dispelling rains, and until to-day, either marching or storms have prevented my writing to you or to any one else.   All feel that McClellan has at least verified one of his promises which he made in his address to his army in the Spring: that they would have 'hardships and privations.' · There is probably not an officer or soldier but feels a deep longing to be quit of this kind of life.   For myself, I often find myself wondering what could have induced me to leave the comforts that I did to encounter what I have.   It is quite possible we may have a battle before the city, but while this is so it may be quite otherwise.   My hope is that no battle may occur, but that the city may be so completely invested, as to compel its surrender.   .   .   .   .   .

"Enclosed I send a photograph of LeFarren's wounds; be sure and preserve it for me.   I wrote to you day before yesterday without having heard from you, and had I not schooled myself not to expect letters I should have been greatly disappointed; but to-day I have received three."   .   .   .

CHAPTER FOURTEENTH.

"Camp Ten Miles from Richmond,
" *Wednesday Evening, May 28, 1862.*

"I HAVE been marching and counter-marching, in heat, in cold, in wet, in hunger, in anger, in ignorance and in despair, at the beck and nod of others, until the thing is about 'played out'. I have. never felt so small, so insignificant, in short so *mean*, as I have since I have been a *thing* to be ordered about. Could I leave the service to-morrow with credit to myself, or rather if the people of Michigan would be satisfied, I should do it most assuredly.   .   .   .

"You say that Mrs. R—— complains that surgeons are never alluded to after a battle. No! why should they be? Poor benighted soul! did any one dream for a moment that a surgeon's field had aught of glory about it? No! The glory consists of carnage and death. The more bloody the battle, the greater the glory. A surgeon may labor harder, must labor longer (we continued to fight three days), may exhibit a higher grade of skill, may exercise the best feelings of

our poor human nature, may bind up many a heart as
well as limb, but who so poor as to do him honor?
There is no glory for our profession.

"We may brave the pestilence when all others flee;
we may remain firm at our posts when death is more
imminent than it ever was on the battle field; but who
sings our praise! Does the world know who the physicians were who fell at Norfolk when yellow fever
depopulated that town? Does it know who rushed in
to fill their places? And of those who survived, can it
designate one? Did they survive to receive fame?
Yet those men were braver than the bravest military
leader, for theirs was a bravery unsupported by excitement or by the hope of fame. No! there are none so
poor as to do us reverence. And, thank God, there are
few of us so unsophisticated as to expect it."   .   .

CHAPTER FIFTEENTH.

"Camp near Fair Oaks, Va.,
"*June 7th, 1862.*

"It is a week since the battle! and still we have made
no apparent progress. Matters seem to us here
on the ground just as they did then, and it requires not
a little patience to keep from fretting. This being so, I
do not wonder at the tone of your letter dated May
30th, the day after the battle. But try   .   .   .
not to be influenced if people do say McClellan is so
slow; that 'he is always a day too late'. I assert without the possibility of a truthful contradiction, that he
has *never yet been a day too late.*

"Six weeks ago Halleck fought the battle of Pittsburg Landing, which was similar in many respects to
the one we fought a week ago. Both were a surprise,
both were unfavorable to the Union cause on the first
day, and in both the Confederates were routed on the
second. After that, a battle was supposed necessarily
to follow speedily upon the first, but it did not;
weeks went by, and now we just hear that the rebels

have fled and Halleck is after them and has cut their line of retreat, it being a railroad, taken many prisoners, etc.

"Now, did not Halleck know better what he was about than anybody else?   Has not his time been well spent?   He has gained a greater victory than he possibly could have done by a battle.   So here, McClellan and his associates know their business and will fully perform their duty, and if there is delay there is a good reason for it, even if the world does not know it.   Who can be more impatient than I, to get out of this?   You could answer these cavilers when they open on McClellan, by quoting Halleck's delay .   .   .   .
Let these civilians leave ·their dressing-robes, their dining-rooms and couches and take the field!   Perhaps then it would be different.

"I often picture to myself the joy of our reunited home; the circle in which our children form their part of the grouping.   .   .   .   . I hardly know what kind of a letter this is.   I have been constantly interrupted since it was begun.   I close with a feeling of confusion which to me is unusual.   But I am clear on one point."   .   .   .   .   .

"Camp at Fair Oaks,

"*Tuesday, June 10th, 1862.*

"I wish you could give me the name of that Michigan Fifth soldier who mourned because the Fifth could fight no more! Judd is truly heroic. His nerval force, if I may so express it, gives such a support to his physical, that it enables him to sustain an injury with less shock than any man I have ever seen. · His brother Captain Judd, said to be equally brave, was killed. It was probably a mistake about Dr. Johnson being taken prisoner, for I have heard that he sent to the Sanitary Commission for supplies, having lost everything, even his personal effects.

"You say that the last battle has disappointed you, as we have gained nothing. In this you are mistaken. The enemy, finding we were closing up around them and getting ready to make regular approaches, made a very powerful and desperate attempt to break through our lines. They failed! Is this no success? But now we have advanced our pickets at this very point, and at others have advanced the position of the whole force. Everything is progressing.

"You ask why we did not make a dash upon Richmond while the enemy retreated! I do not know what McClellan's reasons were, but I can tell you my own impressions. The enemy is in strong force before us;

11

the obstruction to our progress, the Chickahominy, prevents our making a simultaneous movement; Porter's portion of the army is not yet across, nor would it be safe yet to abandon that point, for it would enable the Confederates to turn our right flank and cut off our supplies.

"It is possible that a dark night would have been successful, but it is equally possible that it would have ruined us. Now, what was McClellan's duty in these premises? One false step costs us our Nationality. Let those who bear the responsibility, judge for themselves. It is cruel to do otherwise. McClellan cannot escape the responsibility of this campaign, and it is wrong to constantly stir up dissatisfaction. You cannot possibly be more impatient than I am for the capture of Richmond, but it will do no good to fret about delays. There are no unnecessary delays.

"You ask about my every-day life. Charlie left me at Yorktown. Since then I have had no cook but the hospital cook, and if I had, I have nothing to cook! I assure you it is a hard life for one who appreciates a good dinner; but, *n'importe*, I trust I shall be able to stand it."

"Camp in Another Swamp,
"*June 13th, 1862.*

" For the last two days I have been engaged in the discharge of duties arising from a change of location. .   .   .   .   I find a little leisure to-day, and with it has come another letter from you; it is the one written after your meeting Dr. J——. He was fortunate in being with a comparatively small army and one that was fitted out at, and marched from Washington. Rules as to means of transportation and baggage were not so strict as they otherwise would have been. He was fortunate also   .   .   . But enough said on this point. I shall come through it all right.

.   .   .   .   .

" I anticipate hard fighting before we occupy Richmond, and then I anticipate a speedy termination of the *active* portion of the war. I don't believe our regiment or any other will be called into very active service after Richmond is taken. We are, as I intimated, in an unhealthy location. We are now to the left of the battle-field and in a swamp! I am half a mile to the rear, on pretty good ground, with the medical department of the several regiments of the brigade. It is at this point an operating depot ought to be established, should we have an engagement here, and yesterday for a few hours, one appeared imminent.

"I think McClellan will make an advance on Richmond soon; everything seems to indicate that he is nearly ready to make the first combined move in the game. What the subsequent moves will be will of course depend upon the resistance of the enemy. My own belief is that, after an advance, we shall be obliged to begin a regular approach by a system of parallels. If we find the city as strongly guarded by defensive works as it is represented, such undoubtedly will be the plan; but if not, then a dash may carry all before us. God grant we may be successful without great loss of life!"

"BEFORE RICHMOND,
"*Monday Morning, June 23rd, 1862.*

"I suspect that the Confederates are evacuating Richmond; at least we see evidences this morning that something of the kind is being done. They have retired from our front, and whether it is a strategic movement or whether it is the same all along the line, is not yet known here. God grant that they may evacuate! I had much rather such would be the case than that we should capture the city and twenty thousand prisoners by the loss of ten thousand lives.

"Now for the reason of this preference. Should we have a battle and capture the city and twenty thousand prisoners, and kill and wound ten thousand, that would make their loss thirty thousand. If they have one hundred thousand, that would leave them seventy thousand who would be in good moral condition. If, on the contrary, they *skedaddle* and the whole one hundred thousand get away, they will be so demoralized by the retreat that they won't be worth fifty thousand, while there will be the full one hundred thousand to feed, and clothe, and control. The probability, however, is, whatever the appearance may be, that they have *not run."* .

"CAMP AFFLICTION, *July 11th, 1862.*

"I am sitting in my ambulance, to which I have been almost confined for eleven days. On the first day of July I gave up and took to the ambulance. I fought as long as I could against it, but finally had to succumb. I sent in my resignation on the third day, but at this rate I shall get my returns about the first of August."

.　　.　　.　　.　　.　　.

The above paragraph is from a long letter, the last the doctor wrote from the army. It refers to the trouble he had in getting his resignation accepted.

———

I remember an incident Doctor Gunn repeated about the thoughtfulness of his boy at Harrison's

Landing, while he was confined to his ambulance for eleven days or more. Beef, it was almost impossible to procure. Glyndon learning that slaughtering was going on at head-quarters, proceeded to the spot, hoping to be able to get something for his father. I do not remember whether he arrived too late, or just what the reasons were, but he was unsuccessful.

Noticing a quantity of entrails which had been discarded, to which small pieces of liver still adhered, he took out his knife and cut as much as he could possibly carry in his hands. When he appeared before his father with the tiny bits protruding from between his fingers, the doctor said he could *have cried*, and fully appreciated then what his boy was to him. Glyndon cooked and served the savory meal, the first the doctor had relished for weeks, the sentiment and practicality enhancing its value and his enjoyment.

The following letter appeared in the "Detroit Free Press:"—

LETTER FROM DR. GUNN.

"We are permitted to copy the following extract from a private letter written by Dr. Moses Gunn. It will give the reader some idea of the wretched manage-

ment of the Medical Department of the Army of the
Potomac:—

"BALTIMORE, *July 14th, 1862.*

"I have been to Gettysburg, where I remained two
days. I was too late to do much surgery, but saw
many of the Michigan wounded, and dressed many of
their wounds. I dressed Colonel Flannigan's stump
twice; he is doing well.

"The battle was a most terrible one, and victory
wavered in the air before she finally perched upon our
banners. The loss on both sides was fearful! The
medical department was wretchedly managed. I have
never seen such inadequate provisions. Many a poor
fellow lay out five or six days before being brought in.
As I have often said, the Medical Director of the Army
of the Potomac has not capacity to administer its affairs,
and now he is so narrow and jealous in his views as to
prevent others from rendering him the assistance they
otherwise might.

"Medical Inspector Johnson volunteered his services in providing for the emergency, but Letterman
said 'All needful preparations are made, sir'; and this
when but a scanty medical corps was left behind, with
so small a supply of instruments as to necessitate the
borrowing of the same by the officers from one another.

"Only about thirty ambulances were left behind to transport the thousands of wounded, who were scattered over a space at least of five miles in diameter. For two days there were literally no provisions, and until the last four days no organization, and but an imperfect one now. It is simply sheer incapacity coupled with inordinate conceit to which this all is to be attributed.

"I am now going to the front where a battle is hourly expected. If it comes off, I hope I may be able to do some good; if not I shall return soon."   .   .

CHAPTER SIXTEENTH.

WHEN Doctor Gunn arrived in Washington he was
worn and thin, and a mere shadow of himself.
Glyndon, though not the rosy-cheeked boy he was
when he left Alexandria in the Spring, had endured
the hardships better. The change of climate and food
was invigorating. After a few weeks had elapsed, the
doctor returned to Detroit and resumed practice. He
once more established us in our home, where he enjoyed
his garden of fruits and flowers and a small green-
house that required little care and afforded him the
greatest satisfaction in seeing camellias and roses of
his own in bloom.

He had a superb greyhound, a lively and mischiev-
ous ornament on the place, whose ruthless disregard
for young shoots and buds brought down upon him
the doctor's vengeance, but still the hound roamed
unscathed. When dressed in a suit of G——'s or
W——'s clothes, he was the most ludicrous spectacle
one could well behold. E—— in one of her letters
relates her first experience on seeing him:—"I have

seen a large greyhound run in habiliments, and still survive! Yesterday my cousins came in and announced that 'Pike was ready to run.' This sport which the boys aptly call 'a torture of fun' came near killing me. The dog began to race, and I to laugh,—he tore up and down the street, and jumped fences, his costume flapping in the breeze. Finally, when disappearing over a neighboring gate, and in a second bounding back again with *a loaf of bread in his mouth!* I thought I was dying. But at this moment of collapse, uncle drove up and the responsibility of my future devolved upon him." . . . . .

The color of this hound was a light soft grey; he was beautiful and of gentle breed, but unfortunately *a thief!* The choicest joints, if unwatched, were spirited away; our bread, like that of our neighbors, ignominiously disappeared. When pastry was placed on the sideboard, the knave walked in, and when he walked out, battlements of pastry with embrasures, alone remained.

We were finishing our soup, when the alarm reached us that the more substantial part of our dinner was in Pike's mouth! We rushed to the scene of his struggles with a large hot turkey (we all wished it had been hotter), that burned him in his frantic efforts to drag it to the general hiding-place of his stolen treasures.

The doctor's tolerance seemed wonderful, but he was fond of animals and especially clement to this hound, though he said he sometimes felt like annihilating him.

In the plenitude of his affection for horses, the doctor permitted those that were intelligent to do responsible things by themselves. He had a young, high-spirited but perfectly reliable animal, possessing unusual instincts, the only drawback being that she was piebald! As an illustration of her gentleness and ingenuity, she was always allowed to take herself and the chaise to the stable. It needed some engineering to cross the platform that spanned the gutter. Sometimes missing her calculations, and finding she was not going to strike the little bridge squarely, she would stop, reconnoiter, back a few steps, veer towards the opposite side of the street, and by this *modus operandi* pass securely over.

Starting one day as usual (with the chaise), she discovered some obstruction in the alley. Halting, she appeared to consider a moment, then with head high in air took her way up Shelby street, turned on Fort, then down Wayne, entering the alley at the other end which opened upon that street. She had gone a distance of more than two blocks, watched by those who knew her, being conspicuous by her beautiful white mane and tail and stylish appearance,—albeit she *was speckled!*

The doctor had five nieces only; they belonged to one family, were his brother's children, and rejoiced in a superior mother. One of these nieces happened to be present during an initiatory undertaking of which she writes facetiously to one of her sisters:—

"   .   .   .   .   .   Uncle Doctor had resolved upon having if possible a comfortable as well as a perfectly fitting boot, and as a preliminary step proposed to take a cast of his foot. I wish you had been here the evening he appeared with a box of plaster-of-paris and announced to us his intentions. Although he had never (like a certain illustrious historical personage) performed elaborate toilettes in the presence of royalty, he did proceed to accomplish the act of taking a cast of his foot in the presence of his family, niece included. Aunt A—— did not enter with much zeal into the enterprise, but the children—two of them—were delighted when pressed into the service of supplying the delicate mortar.

"He secured his position at a comfortable angle, and all was going on smoothly we supposed, when suddenly springing to his feet he cried, 'By George! I can't stand this!' and like showers of hail, the fragments of plaster flew to the four corners of the room. My aunt was now as attentive as before she had been indifferent. We plied him with more questions than he could answer, but in a general way gathered that the tumult had been caused by *setting-plaster!* The débris of the disaster was removed and we subsided into our normal condition for the evening.

"A few days after this, Uncle came in, holding up rather triumphantly a perfect and shapely cast of his foot, that he had taken unaided in his office, and said: 'There is the result of a torturing experience; had I *shaved* my foot and ankle the other night, I should not have been *defeated.*'"

CHAPTER SEVENTEENTH.

GLYNDON'S companionship in the army, and a thousand other fond associations had endeared him to his father. During the last few weeks in the army he had been of the greatest comfort to his father, and he had now become useful and important to him in many ways.

The year before Doctor Gunn went to Chicago to remain permanently, he was called in that direction to see some one who had been injured on the Michigan Central railroad. During his absence of thirty-six hours, that fearful accident occurred, by which Glyndon was drowned! He had been seen to go down, and that was the last! We were in a bewildering state of despair, but there was no escape from our sorrow! Who could meet the doctor and tell him his boy was drowned?— His boy,—for whom he believed that no ambition would be too great, no achievement impossible! The blow fell with crushing weight upon him,—it was pitiful to see him struggle with his grief, and more pitiful were the sad circumstances he afterward encountered.

He said, "Never while memory lasts can I forget the hour, when searching hopelessly for some resemblance, I laid that poor swollen hand within my own and rubbed it (God knows how long!) until I found a *little scar*, that could alone identify my boy! I might have known his golden waving hair—but it was damp—and straight—and unrecognizable!"

It was the most oppressively hot day of that Summer that Glyndon went down to his boat-house, accompanied by Highland, a servant, to whom he proposed that they should cross the river. The man, timid and unable to row, refused at first, but afterward consented; he was tall, muscular and heavy, and the boy did all the rowing. Highland thus unoccupied, was more than anxious to reach the Canadian shore. Landing at Sandwich, he protested that he would never go back in the boat.

Glyndon then said: "Well, Highland, if you won't go back with me, wait here while I row out into the stream and take a little swim!" At that point where he jumped from his boat, the river had a strong and dangerous current. He was seen to once re-enter the boat and to dive the second time; then it drifted away out of his reach, and that was the last!

The following lines are taken from a notice in the "Detroit Free Press" of that date:—

"The unfortunate death of Glyndon Gunn by drowning, a brief notice of which appeared in our paper yesterday, requires more than a simple passing notice. He was at the time of his death, about sixteen years of age, and was, in many respects, a young man of remarkable promise. For originality of intellect, strength and vigor of mind and power of analysis, he had, perhaps, few equals of his age; and he was noted no less for his singular urbanity of manners and gentlemanly bearing towards all with whom he was brought in contact, than for his intellectual vigor. Such, indeed, was the maturity of his intellect, and the soundness of his judgment, that he became the companion of men far in advance of his years.

" During the recent rebellion he accompanied his father to the field, and was with him during four months of the Peninsular campaign. The officers and soldiers of Berry's brigade, more particularly the Fifth Regiment of Michigan Infantry, will remember the lad of then scarcely twelve years of age, who, riding upon his pony, made the campaign with them from Fortress Monroe to the front of Richmond, and subsequently, in their retreat to Harrison's Landing. He will be remembered by many a grateful soldier who will drop a tear over his early death, as the lad who, with unwearied exertion, contributed to the comfort of the famishing soldiers at the memorable battle of Williamsburg. . . . . .

"The river had peculiar fascinations for him. Possessed of remarkable mechanical genius, he had had constructed, after a model of his own devising, a beautiful little craft, and this it was which led him to the river, and to a sad and untimely death." . .

CHAPTER EIGHTEENTH.

AFTER the death of Dr. Daniel Brainard, the distinguished surgeon who had been so long identified with Rush Medical College, Doctor Gunn was tendered the chair of surgery, which having accepted, he came to Chicago to reside. At the inauguration of the new buildings on the North Side, there was a large audience present, showing the general interest felt in the institution.

The President of the College, Professor J. V. Z. Blaney, delivered the opening address, giving a brief review of the history of the institution, and speaking in the warmest terms of admiration and praise of its lamented founder, and late president, Professor Daniel Brainard. This was followed by a short, characteristic speech by the Hon. J. B. Rice (Mayor of Chicago), which was received with much applause.

Doctor Gunn then gave the welcoming address to the assemblage, which may have some interest after all these years, to the alumni and to others who were once his friends.

He said:—"In behalf of my colleagues, I bid you welcome! Welcome to Chicago, the Young Giant of the West! Welcome to Rush Medical College, and to these halls which we this day dedicate to science and to humanity!

"You compose the twenty-fifth class which has annually assembled here, on what has become classic ground, seeking after truth in medicine; truth ever simple and yet often elusive; which lies not unfrequently immediately before us, while with strained vision we attempt to pierce the dim and smoky distance to discern it; which from its very simplicity is often-times completely hidden from a search which looks for it enshrined in deep and difficult mystery only.

"Annually for the past twenty-five years, in search of this gem have your predecessors come, up hither; with what success let their individual history in the teeming north-west, with its cities, villages, and expanded plains, and its ever increasing population, and also during the late protracted and bloody war, tell.

"Twenty-five years! In the longest life an extended measure; in the history of human events, a pitiful period; and yet, in the early history of a city or a nation, how important! And if measured by what is sometimes accomplished, how the little quarter of a century seems to sink its fractional character and assume the dignity of the full and unbroken unit.

"Measured by her growth and achievements, Chicago might well rise to the full period of a century! What was she when the first little class assembled here under the auspices of the then infant college? An old military post on the extreme north-western frontier had but recently become recognized as a town. Westward stretched the rich and undulating plain, on to the Father of Waters. Eastward the great chain of lakes afforded communication with the older cities of the continent. The plodding team of the emigrant, and the mail of our venerable and common Uncle Samuel, transported as the exigences of the season and condition of the roads would permit, constituted the only means of communication.

"Nestling on either side of the bayou lay the infant city. No broad avenues stretched off for miles over the plain, but low upon the oozy surface of the original prairie lay the yet limited streets. Reared upon posts stood the young city, the whole aspect verifying the need which found expression at a later date, when the characteristic enterprise of the inhabitants rendered the idea not wholly improbable, to-wit: Issuing proposals and inviting bids for a young earthquake to elevate the site to a desirable altitude. No railway network stretched out to the boundless regions on all sides, bringing to a common center the more than Indian wealth of the country, and making here a granary for half the world. No temples of trade crowded compactly the streets, and upward towered for more ample accommodation. No tunnel, at once the wonder and triumph of art, penetrated for miles under the majestic lake to draw from its crystal fountain health and happiness for half a million.

"No medical halls like these we this day dedicate, invited such a class as we now welcome; and no Æsculapian orator had caught the spirit of place-glorification, which outside barbarians assert to be the sign diagnostic of a Chicagoan, and held forth to the first class here assembled with that peculiar and diagnostic modesty. .   .   .   .   . On the contrary, a small and unpretending building occupied the spot; a little class of twenty-two students assembled here, and while the primary faculty were honestly and earnestly and successfully initiating this great enterprise, they dared not dream of the magnificent future. To that first faculty I would here acknowledge, in behalf of the whole profession, our great indebtedness. But one of that little band remains with us, and he, honored among all, is our crown of rejoicing.

"But if on this ground has grown from a small beginning, a great city and a great medical college, so that as compared with the original, the present appears to be a full fruition, we shall find that change and improvement are not confined merely to city and college. The science and art of medicine and surgery has, during the period which we are contemplating, made such advances as to elicit the admiration of him who watches its history, and to excite the pride of its votaries. The student who sat under the first course of lectures in this institution, could he be transported over the interval without having participated in the advance of the profession, would find himself utterly bewildered and unable to understand much that he would hear in the course of instruction now given. While the whole scientific world has been pressing forward in pursuit of undiscovered truth, medical men have not been surpassed in industry and zeal, nor have the fruits of their labors been few or scanty.

"In chemistry alone a new science has almost been created. Old fields have been re-worked and new ones explored; and not content with the elements and organisms of the earth as presented in its great laboratory, swallowing up bodily the new science of geology, and illustrating that its evidences are but the result of chemical reactions in old earth's chronology, the chemist has pushed his investigations into other spheres and in his spectral analysis vies with the astronomer in the study of those remote fields. The domain and laboratory of chemistry is the universe!

"Within this period the microscope has mainly wrought out its great work, and histology now claims its own peculiar dignity. Under its ministrations, too, physiology and pathology have extended their bounds and refined their processes. Physiology then was dispatched in a few crude lectures, and these were usually given by the anatomist. The physiology of the nervous action had then to offer as its latest and brightest work the reflex-motor action of Marshall Hall, which the intelligent physiologist of the present day knows to be but a single phenomenon in the list of reflex actions. The reflex influence of impressions upon organic changes,—nay, the reflex influence of those changes upon other functions of nutrition; and the reflex influence of the normal processes of local nutrition upon one another; the influence of mind upon matter and matter upon mind are but the operation of the same law. An elaborate paper announcing the discovery of reflex secretory action of the nervous system was presented to the American Medical Association, at its session in 1857, by Prof. Campbell, of Georgia. Marshall Hall, himself, admitted the discovery, and hailed it as a twin companion of his own, thus publicly complimenting his young American brother.

"But it is within the knowledge of your speaker that the whole subject of reflex nervous influences, of which excito-motor and excito-secretory actions are but constituent parts, was taught as early as 1850 in the University of Michigan by the present incumbent of the chair of medicine in this institution, Professor Allen. In his teachings and writings, too, are to be found the only explicit and comprehensive exposition of the whole subject of reflex nervous action that has ever fallen under my observation. Fresh, then, were the experiments of Beaumont upon the stomach of the soldier, Alexis St. Martin, which, interesting and valuable as they were, have required the scrutiny of subsequent analysis to correct many of the first conclusions and to expunge not a few gross errors.

"Therapeutics, as a *science*, has almost been born within this period. While materia medica was as colossal (God save the mark!) then as now, the philosophy of the action of the remedies, not mere medicines, has claimed paramount attention, and general therapeutics to-day commands far more study than mere materia medica. Pharmacy, the hand-maid of materia medica, as taught and practiced to-day, would hardly be recognized by a member of the profession who had indulged in a Rip Van Winkle nap. Crude processes and gross preparations have been supplanted by delicate manipulations and the active principles of medicines. The doctor no longer bestrides his Rosinante with his pannier-like saddle-bags stuffed with the crude *materiel*, nor does the table in the sick-chamber look like an apothecary's counter. Organic chemistry enables the pharmaceutist to fill our prescriptions with efficient, concentrated and non-repulsive remedies.

"Practical medicine has, also, during the period which we are considering, undergone a no less marked change and improvement. A more general and at the same time clear, definite, and intelligent view, and application of nervous influence upon normal and abnormal action, and the use of such influence in allaying disease and promoting health; a more confident reliance on inherent recuperative power, and the ability to excite, control, and modify that power and marshal its forces, and command its aid in the cure of disease; a much more guarded resort to powerful and uncontrollable means and depleting medicines; a growing tendency to look to the general conditions of nutrition as a means of cure, as, for example, in the management of phthisis and kindred conditions of the system; the influence of pure air, cleanliness, and light, as seen in the management of hospital wards, and sick-chambers, in private dwellings—all these considerations mark the progress in medicine since the days when Eberle wrote, and the mass of the profession in this country followed his directions, or if differing with him, still relied as confidently as he on the mysterious power of medicine to combat and cure disease.

"Surgery, too, has felt the influence of the times. First in importance, as well as chronologically, is the discovery of a means of producing a state of complete anæsthesia, a discovery which was the dawning of a new era in surgery. Not merely the ability to perform operations without pain to the patient, or even to perform at will hitherto almost impossible operations, constitutes the limits of this discovery. The relaxation which attends full anæsthesia, is a condition of the system which is often-times most desirable and which was formerly sought to be established, in many instances, by a resort to nauseants, venesection, and to the hot bath. Unconsciousness is, at the same time, frequently desirable, and in this double effect are the power and influence of anæsthetic agents at once grateful to the patient and valuable to the surgeon. The honor of this discovery is American. Whether to Drs. Wells, Morton, or Jackson, individually, appertains the immediate credit, it is not my purpose to inquire; it is sufficient that it belongs to the period of time which marks our history, and that it is American.

"That department of surgery which appertains to the eye has also been marked with the most noteworthy advances. The ophthalmoscope, alone, has wrought great changes. It has opened up as rich placers as did the stethoscope of Laennec in another department, and at an earlier date. Still more recently, the laryngoscope has enlarged our means of observation in another field; while the endoscope, with still greater enterprise, enables us, almost,

"'With optics sharp, I ween,

To see what is not to be seen.'

"The late war has also afforded means for successful study, which have not been neglected, and the accurate observations in reference to the pathology of pyæmia and hospital gangrene, have resulted in such a development of their pathology, as to direct to a rational and eminently successful treatment, both prophylactic and curative. In all departments of our profession, progress has been the watchword, and in those branches which more nearly approximate the fixed sciences, and which, consequently, afford fewer opportunities for advancement, improvement in method, and refinement in process have been as marked and decided, as discovery has been in others.

"But I have not thus alluded to the achievements of our science in a spirit of vainglory. I would not underrate the labor and advance of any period previous to the last quarter of a century. I would not even attempt a comparison which might be deemed invidious, between any period and that which I have contemplated. Each century, and even each decade, has had its own success and glory, and extended along through the whole history of medicine, are the records of labor, some plainly saying to us, 'This is the way, walk ye in it'; others, like beacon lights, warning us off the rocks and sands of error. And so it must continue to be. As long as there is yet a truth to be discovered, many failures to a single success must occur. But for every success there is ample reward, though accompanied by a thousand failures.

"I have indulged in the line of thought which I have followed, rather to encourage and stimulate hopeful effort on your part. By so much as we have advantage over those who have preceded us, our successors may and probably will realize improvements upon us. Appreciation of ancient truth does not demand of us unbounded credulity. It does not require us to accept as truth all that is ancient, simply because it is venerable; neither does it expect us to shut our eyes upon the glory of the present because it has not the dust of ages upon it. There is a class of men, represented largely in our profession, whose veneration is profound, and leads them to see no good in the present, except that it was born in the past; who so constantly exclaim 'There is nothing new under the sun!' From such veneration, in the language of the Litany, 'Good Lord deliver us.'

"But, on the other hand, appreciation of modern discovery does not require us to sneer at the past because its measure was not full; nor should we make the mistake of regarding our own period as the culminating point in the history of medicine. That point will never be reached. The grand day of science will have no declining sun; but the glorious orb of truth will ever rise higher and higher, and shine with ever increasing refulgence, until the universe shall be lighted. When shall that be? When *all* shall be known; when we shall know even as we are known. Would you estimate the period by the lapse of ages? Attempt if you can to conceive of the amount yet unknown, and when your mind can begin to take in that conception, then commence to measure the day of science. We are yet but in the early morning, a morning to be succeeded by no noon, no evening, but by an ever brightening day.

"With this conception of the situation, with this

idea of the relation of the present to the future, there is no ground for indulgence in vainglory; for vain indeed would be any glorification which forgets for a moment the littleness of the present, when compared to the probabilities of the future. As our perceptions of temperature are relative only, so our estimate of the present state of science must be relative. It may be great compared with the past, but what is it when we look forward to the possibilities of the future! It is yet the day of small things, and our pleasure as well as our duty, should be to work earnestly, as opportunity offers, and opportunity is not rare; we can hardly miss it; our fault is rather in a disposition to select from the mass, than to avail ourselves of that which is immediately before us. Whatsoever thy hand findeth to do, do it with thy might! Work is and must be the motto and lot of every successful man; it is so *par excellence*, with the student in the science of medicine.

" There is no short high road to advanced learning; but by study, thought, experiment, and observation, must the race be won. Most medical men study more or less; they are also, as a general rule, good observers; a few experiment, but, alas, how very few seem to *think!* and I confess it has sometimes occurred to me that those who conduct large series of experiments seem to think the least. I have spoken of medical men because I am speaking to you who are to become such; but I would not be understood as criticising my professional brethren as peculiarly disinclined to reflect; this remark applies to all men.

"Mankind is prone to accept the *seeming* rather than to search out the real; to accept a received explanation rather than laboriously to criticise it. It is not enough to study, to observe, to experiment; we must do more; and in this connection let me impart this injunction:—*Think!* Whatever you do, *think!* Study, but *think!* Observe, but *think!* And especially, if you experiment, *think!*

"It is easy, by study, to possess yourself of the thoughts of others, to appropriate, assimilate and make them your own; but you may do this without ever indulging in the luxury of a thought of your own. You may observe extensively, and yet, like a crab, you shall even go backwards for not pondering well upon what you have observed. You may experiment till you draw down upon your devoted heads the persecution of a sentimental Bergh and his co-laborers, who are themselves examples of observation without thought, and yet never penetrate deeper than the simple fact or phenomenon which is the immediate result of your experiment.

"Therefore, I again repeat, *think!* Think for your-selves; contract the habit of thinking, and with the practice will come increased ability to study, to observe, and if you choose, to experiment. But while thought will not take the place of study and observation, it is the soul of both. Without it, either study or observa-tion is the Adam into whom the breath of the living spirit has not yet been infused. It is the ovum without fecundation, destined only to blight and decay. But perhaps I should be more explicit in this injunction. Men differ in intellectual power, and, in accordance with this general proposition, you are not all mentally equal. To one is awarded only mediocre powers, while on another are bestowed both brilliancy and profundity. Neither are you all equally advanced in education. To some, the advantage of free and generous culture has been abundantly given, while others are struggling in their course with the impediments incident to an im-perfect education. In medical advancement too, you will be found to be widely different. Some are but just entering upon their course, while others are well advanced, and are more or less familiar with all matters appertaining to medical and surgical science.

"It is evident that the ability to think correctly and advantageously upon the various subjects of your study and observation will vary with the different orders of intellect, and the varying degrees of culture. Still my advice applies to all. None need be so deficient, if at all qualified to pursue medical studies, as to accept all that he hears, reads, or observes, as truth so positive and unqualified as to need no other effort of mind than that involved in the act of appropriation. The merest neophyte, though incapable of calling in question anything that is presented to his understanding, should, by earnest thought, endeavor to detect the reason for whatever he hears, or reads, or observes. Not only will this mental process fix the subject of his thought, and constitute in itself the most perfect means of assimilation, but it will prove a method of mental training that will develop power and facilitate future effort.

"As the student advances in his course, and attains a standard of acquirement that gives him a stock of well established and undoubted truths, he should, in addition to the search for the reason of things, compare his results with these standard truths, and thus another step in advance is taken. His stock of the actual is constantly increasing; and not the actual only, but the reason thereof, and the relation which it sustains to other facts and phenomena. Prove all things, hold fast that which is good. Accept nothing because you hear it, or read it, or even *see* it. Subject all things

13

to careful mental analysis, and finally, believe, not because you have read, heard, or seen, but because it is recommended, *per se*, to your individual judgment. Let your religious belief be a matter of faith, but let me warn you against receiving your scientific creed on the same basis.

"Faith is an excellent quality in your patient, for oftentimes he will be obliged to indulge in the substance of things hoped for, the evidence of things *not* seen; but on your part it will be better both for science and humanity that you believe nothing, literally *nothing*, till proven. As students sitting at the feet of your Gamaliel, even though you may have good reason to distrust your own judgment, and feel greater, far greater, confidence in the author you read, or the professor you hear, still make the effort to go through the process which I have recommended, before finally deferring and believing. You will thus strengthen your own power and gradually acquire independence and accuracy of thought. You will acquire, too, the power of discrimination, the power of weighing and comparing before deciding. The medical man finds a great amount of conflicting, or apparently conflicting evidence, and like the jurist, he must weigh, compare and sift out, reject this, and accept that; all, too, in accordance with established law. Thus the law becomes purified by rejection, and amplified and perfected by slow crystallization. Our circle of knowledge is expanded and the domain of truth is enlarged.

"Another habit of thought should be cultivated, viz., the seeking after the *soul* of the truth. As there is a soul of goodness even in things evil, so there is an innermost kernel to all subjects, an element by which and through which they differ from all other similar subjects with which they might be confounded; it is in virtue of this element that truthfulness exists. A clear and definite conception of this element only will enable you to master a given subject; and so long as you fail to detect it, the real truth remains hidden from your view. A loose, general, and vague idea you may have, even as one sees an object through a foggy atmosphere, without being able to discern its exact form, its individuality. It is the fault of many minds to be satisfied with such a view, and to neglect the labor incident to the full defining of the picture. It may be that all effort will fail in some instances to bring out the details clearly; but the effort should, nevertheless, be made to attain a clear and definite perception of what I have termed the *soul* of the truth.

"To illustrate:—Volumes have been written, and more said on the subject of *inflammation;* all the phenomena thereof have been enumerated and the changes

rung on them.   Concise definitions have been attempted
and criticised; and by some it has been said that such
a thing as a correct definition of the subject was an
impossibility.   All observers, of any experience whatever, recognize an inflammation when they see it, and
yet many fail to discern in just what it consists.   Let
us now make an effort to obtain a view of some one
circumstance in reference to inflammation, by which it
differs from all other similar conditions.   It is not pain,
heat, redness, nor swelling, nor all of them that constitutes the condition under consideration, for any one
or even all of them may be present without the part
being in such a state.

" The blush which mantles the cheek of shocked
and offended modesty, when extreme, may cause it to
burn and tingle with heat and pain, while the actual
engorgement of the vessels supplies the redness and
swelling.   Blood may flow in greatly increased quanti-
ties *to* and *through* a part, invited to do so by an
increased activity of normal local nutrition, producing
even hyperæmia.   This may serve a temporary and
useful purpose. examples of which will occur to the
mind of any medical man; or, it may, if long continued,
result in hypertrophy of a part; but so long as the
local nutrition is only stimulated and increased in activity, so long as the advance and retrograde changes

exactly balance each other, there is no inflammation. But the instant that this active hyperæmia is attended by oppression and impairment of local nutrition, inflammation begins, and in this impairment or suspension it consists. Just so soon as normal local nutrition is again established, inflammation has ceased, even though active hyperæmia may yet remain. This is the key to the whole subject. *It is the soul of the truth.*

"Another illustration:—You attempt the study of *ulceration;* you read author after author; you watch the process at the clinic, and the probabilities are that you will obtain a confused idea of disintegration of tissue, mortification in miniature, and absorption, attended by suppuration. Confusion worse confounded! But careful observation of the process, in numerous instances, and correct analysis of what you observe and read will clear up the subject, and isolate the identical characteristic of ulceration. Disintegration of tissue in particles, or mortification in miniature is not ulceration, for, pathologically, mortification is the same whether in miniature or on a colossal scale. Suppuration, although a frequent attendant on ulceration, is not a necessary part of the process. By observing the ulcerative process you will see that tissue disappears, sometimes without crumbling away by mortification in miniature or even being attended by suppuration.

What has become of it? It is not volatile, and can not have vaporized; only one other method of disappearance is left, and that is by absorption; an absorption that destroys the integrity of tissue; and here we arrive at the isolated characteristic of ulceration, viz., *destructive absorption of tissue.* In this it consists and in no other process.

"Thus, you should *think; reflect* upon each and every subject which you enter upon, and endeavor to arrive at the *soul of the truth.*

"But there is one matter especially which I earnestly recommend you to carefully consider and endeavor fully and perfectly to comprehend. It is expressed in the answer to the question, What is disease, and how can it be prevented, alleviated, cured? I do not purpose to attempt an answer to this question at this time. That answer will be found permeating the whole course of instruction which you will receive in this college.

"But I warn you against regarding disease as a subtle essence which invades and permeates the animal being, to be charmed away by incantations or other spiritual means, on the one hand; or on the other, as a hydra-headed monster which, in various forms, enters the fair citadel, to be ejected only by medicinal potations, either great or small. Learn rather to look upon the human fabric as a delicate organism, for a time the seat of a vital force, which, springing from the throne of the Omnipotent, wrests matter from the action and sway of mere chemical affinities, seizes chemical laws and harnesses them to its own work; permitting them to have full and unrestricted action in one place, modifying and controlling them in another, while in still another they are bound hand and foot; and the elements, like the lion and the lamb, are made to lie down together in peace and harmony.

"This intricate and delicate organization is the seat of numerous functions all subservient to the existence of the whole, and playing upon one another by a system of direct and reflex influences, which in harmonious action, conserve the object of its creation—a *limited* existence. A derangement in any single function exerts its influence upon others, and thus, by destroying the harmonious action of all, tends to shorten even the natural limit of existence. *This is disease.* To learn to detect it in its primary and all its secondary lesions, and to correct it—to recognize the causes which produce it, in order to obviate them, is your mission. In that mission I bid you *God speed*, and in behalf of my colleagues, I pledge you our hearty coöperation and assistance."

CHAPTER NINETEENTH.

A FEW years after its inauguration, the new college was destroyed in the Chicago fire. Doctor Gunn's office was in the building. Among the things he lost, most valued, and that could not be replaced, was a cabinet of handsomely mounted anatomical specimens, the careful collection of years, and the manuscript of a work on surgery nearly ready for publication. His distaste for the mechanical part of writing, together with the now almost impossible task of again gathering his data, discouraged its resuscitation. He encountered many difficulties; among them his library was gone, his surgical practice was scattered and much of it lost; for a time it seemed that everything was lost! But his house was left, and there he established his office. Directly after the calamity, he said "I shall have to begin all over again and be a candidate for general practice." But reflection made him hesitate, and he finally concluded *not to enter* the general field.

Every one, who ever had any interest in it, is aware of the Faculty's struggles while in a temporary building constructed "under the side-walk" on Eighteenth street.   In a few years a still finer college than the one destroyed was erected on the West Side; later the Presbyterian Hospital, which adjoins the college building, and whose staff is composed substantially of the college faculty, was also established.   Doctor Gunn's early connection with, and great interest in this hospital would have given him untold satisfaction and pleasure in seeing it completed by the magnificent addition of the "Jones Memorial Building."   I am not anxious to attribute an undue share of influence to the doctor, but the colleges and hospitals with which he had been connected, had always engaged his best efforts, and his strongest energies were given to Rush College in its dark, as well as in its palmiest days.

One of his colleagues once said to me:—"The only thing I have against your husband, is, that he will not make notes of his surgical cases and occasionally publish those of importance."

In his address at the opening of the present session of Rush Medical College, Dr. Senn said of Doctor Gunn:—"He left no encyclopedia of medicine, but his little pamphlet of less than twenty-five pages contains more learning than volumes that many others have compiled."

Remembering that Doctor Gunn was not fond of the

mechanical part of writing, the following articles are probably all pertaining to his profession that have ever been published. They were sent to me by Dr Billings from the library of the Surgeon General's Office, through the courtesy of Dr. Baxter:—

ARTICLES WRITTEN BY MOSES GUNN, M.D.

PHILOSOPHY OF CERTAIN DISLOCATIONS OF THE HIP AND SHOULDER, AND THEIR REDUCTION. "Peninsular Journal of Medicine," Ann Arbor, 1853–4, I, pp. 95–100.

>> Reprinted with some additions in the same journal 1855–6, III, pp. 27–35.

>> Reprinted in pamphlet form, 1855.

>> Reprinted with further additions. "Peninsular and Independent Medical Journal," 1859–60, II, pp. 193–206.

>> Reprinted in pamphlet form 1859.

>> Second edition, printed in 1869.

SELECTIONS FROM SURGICAL NOTES. "Medical Independent," Detroit, 1857–8; III, pp. 67, 186, 257, 377, 469, 575.

SELECTIONS FROM SURGICAL NOTES. "Peninsular and Independent Medical Journal," Detroit, 1858–9; I, pp. 464-467: 1859–60; II, pp. 140–143.

Doctor Gunn was one of the editors of the "Monthly Independent," Detroit, 1857–8, III; and of the "Peninsular and Independent Medical Journal," 1858-9, I; and 1859-60, II; and was the author of numerous editorials in these journals, usually signed "G."

ADDRESS OF WELCOME TO RUSH MEDICAL COLLEGE delivered October 1, 1867. "Chicago Medical Journal," 1867, XXIV, pp. 499-512.

VALEDICTORY ADDRESS, Rush Medical College, 1870-71. Ibid, 1871, XXVIII, pp. 157-169; also reprinted.

SURGICAL CLINIC of Rush Medical College. Ibid, 1874, XXXI, pp. 560, 725.

DISCUSSION of Dr. Gross' paper on Syphilis. "Transactions American Medical Association." Philadelphia, 1874, XXV, p. 243.

CASE OF TRAUMATIC TETANUS, St. Joseph's Hospital. "Chicago Medical Journal and Examiner," 1875, XXXII, pp. 421-426.

ADDRESS IN SURGERY AND ANATOMY, delivered May 8, 1879. "Transactions American Medical Association," Philadelphia, 1879, XXX, pp. 479-493.

REPORT OF A CASE OF PURULENT EFFUSION INTO KNEE-JOINT. Ibid, 1879, XXX, p. 517.

TREATMENT OF FRACTURES OF THE SKULL, RECENT AND CHRONIC, WITH DEPRESSION. Read June 1, 1882. "Transactions of the American Surgical Association," 1881-83. Philadelphia, 1883, I, pp. 83-90.

THE DOCTORATE ADDRESS ON MEDICAL ETHICS. "Chicago Medical Journal and Examiner," 1883. XLVI, pp. 337–352. Also reprinted.

THE PHILOSOPHY OF MANIPULATION IN THE REDUCTION OF HIP AND SHOULDER DISLOCATIONS. "Transactions American Surgical Association," (1884). 1885. II, pp. 399–419; also in "Chicago Medical Journal and Examiner," 1874, XLVIII, pp. 449–468. Also reprinted.

THE UNION OF NERVES OF DIFFERENT FUNCTION CONSIDERED IN ITS PATHOLOGICAL AND SURGICAL RELATIONS. Address of the President, delivered April 28th, 1886. "Transactions American Surgical Association," 1886. IV, pp. 1–13.

Doctor Gunn also took part in the discussion of many of the papers published in volumes I, II, and III of the Transactions of the American Surgical Association.

Between Professor Allen and Doctor Gunn the closest personal attachment had existed for years. Dr. A—— once said to me, "I know more about your husband, than any one living, unless it is yourself, and possibly in some things even more than you." This remark led me to build hopes of at least one chapter, upon his knowledge. The reminiscences he would have given, he has not been able to furnish on account of a painful and lingering indisposition.

Aware of the incompleteness of these sketches without something from Dr. Allen, the only alternative is to include his brief synopsis of Doctor Gunn's biography up to 1876, contained in a volume of "The United States Biographical Dictionary." Necessarily some of these references will be repeated in my own allusions, and in the mention, by others, of certain incidents in his life.

"Moses Gunn, occupant of the chair of Principles and Practice of Surgery and Clinical Surgery in Rush Medical College, Chicago, a native of East Bloomfield, was born on the 20th of April, 1822, the son of Linus and Esther Gunn, both of whom were natives of Massachusetts, the Gunns tracing their ancestry through a long line of Scottish lairds into the depths of olden times.

"A very thorough academical education interrupted by an illness that wasted him to a shadow scarcely to be conceived of by one who now looks upon his robust and powerful physique, was followed by a course of professional study in Geneva Medical College, where he was graduated in 1846. He was accompanied on his journey to the West, by the cadaver of a huge African in one of his very innocent-looking trunks, which, however, excited the ire of the driver as being as heavy as a passenger.

"He arrived at Ann Arbor, Michigan, in February, 1846, and contemporaneously with beginning practice, commenced the first systematic course of anatomical lectures ever given in that State, before a class of twenty-five or thirty students. The course was repeated for three successive years, until the organization of the medical department of the University of Michigan, when he was elected professor of surgery by a very flattering vote, although there was strong and active competition,

"For three years he gave the lectures upon both anatomy and surgery, the annual course extending to nearly seven months. During this period, in addition to attendance upon a laborious and constantly increasing practice, he acquired an accurate and fluent acquaintance with the German language, which has now become almost as familiar to him as his vernacular.   .   .

"In 1848 Doctor Gunn was married to Jane Augusta Terry, only daughter of J. M. Terry, M.D.

"In 1853 he removed to Detroit, still retaining his chair in the university until his final removal to Chicago in 1867. In 1856 he received the honorary degree of A.M. from Geneva College.

"In 1857 he became senior editor of the "Medical Independent," a journal which made its mark upon the literature of the time, and, its mission being fulfilled, was consolidated with another medical periodical, of which for some time he was joint editor.

"In the winter he made a series of dissections and experiments with a view to determine what particular tissue opposes the effort to reduce dislocations of the hip joint. These experiments and dissections were repeated before the medical class of.that and subsequent sessions, and its results embodied and read before the Detroit Medical Society in the summer of 1853, and also published in the "Peninsular Medical Journal" in September of that year. From the following quotation the professional reader will at once be able to recognize the great practical as well as scientific value of this investigation, and it will also put at rest the question of priority which has occasionally been raised:—

"'The principle, then, I would seek to establish is this: that in luxation of the hip and shoulder, the untorn portion of the capsular ligament, by binding down the head of the dislocated bone, prevents its ready return over the edge of the cavity to its place in the socket; and that this return can be easily effected by putting the limb in such a position as will effectually approximate the two points of attachment of that portion of the ligament which remains untorn.'

"Some little idea of the industry and arduous labors of Doctor Gunn may be gained from the fact that whilst conducting a large and successful practice in Detroit, he visited Ann Arbor twice a week to deliver his lecture on surgery (having in 1854 been relieved from lecturing on anatomy), and in so doing, up to the time of resigning his chair in 1867, he had travelled a distance of upwards of fifty-six thousand miles.

"Aside from his lectures at Ann Arbor, his reputation as a skillful and accomplished surgeon had so widely extended that, notwithstanding the disadvantages of the location of the college in a small inland town, his clinics were thronged by patients, some from very great distances, and afforded many illustrations of severe and difficult operations.

"The first class that Doctor Gunn lectured to at that institution in 1850–1 numbered ninety-two, even this being deemed a remarkable success. The last class, 1866–7, he there instructed, numbered five hundred and twenty-five, probably the largest class assembled in the United States that year. It is not too much to say that to Doctor Gunn more than to any other one person was due this unexampled prosperity.

"In order to familiarize himself with the details of military surgery, Doctor Gunn entered the military service of the United States the 1st of September, 1861, accompanying General McClellan through the Peninsular campaign, and on several occasions rendering most efficient service. During a three weeks' leave of absence he gave fifty lectures at the university, conveying a vast fund of useful information to the students, a large number of whom were then preparing for the field.

"In the Spring of 1867 he accepted an earnest invitation to occupy the chair he now holds in Rush Medical College, it having been rendered vacant by the death of the distinguished surgeon and teacher, Daniel Brainard, M.D. He accordingly removed to Chicago where he has since resided. In this position it is perhaps sufficient to say that he has achieved marked distinction and high success. His reputation is now firmly established, and national, both as a practical surgeon and teacher. The present prosperity of Rush Medical College is largely due to his business energy, professional skill and personal popularity as a teacher.

"Doctor Gunn's success as a surgeon depends upon his wonderfully minute and accurate acquaintance with anatomy, combined with exquisite power of diagnosis, a cool head, steady muscles, and great mechanical

14

genius. He is never at a loss for apparatus, and invents models, off-hand, that would make the fortune of a patent-right seller. His instrumental paraphernalia, straps and splints, springs and bandages, always fit the variety of the species, and not merely the class and the order.

"As an operator he is bold and dextrous, handling the scalpel with the delicacy of an artist's pencil, and yet the strength of iron muscle; but withal never trusts to these, but guards against the chance of failure by careful attention to those really indispensable details which, being too often neglected, cause brilliant operations to be succeeded by ignominious results.

"As an instance of his energy and decision may be mentioned an incident personally known to the present writer, then a colleague. There was to be a faculty meeting in the evening. In the morning Doctor Gunn was called to a case of strangulated hernia, thirty-two miles away. Of course his attendance was given up; but promptly at the hour he was present for business. He had driven in his sulky over Michigan roads to the patient's residence, but the attending physician had not yet arrived; the case was urgent, and, assisted only by the patient's wife, he operated successfully, dressed the wound, consigned the patient to the tardy doctors he met at the door, and in eleven hours from the morning's start was quietly asking for the business of the evening.

"Personally, Doctor Gunn has the advantage of a fine figure and an *air distingué*. In lecturing, rapid, emphatic, mindful of his subject, clear in statement, giving confidence to his auditors of thorough mastership. In conversation, somewhat abrupt, occasionally abstracted, a reserve sometimes taken for hauteur (of which he possesses not a particle), he gains no popularity by seeking it, and labors under the too common hallucination that a man should be taken for what he is, rather than for what he assumes.

"If he had devoted his life to mere business he would have been a millionaire. If he had taken up the army he would have been a general, knowing no such word as fail, and never being caught in an ambuscade. Still in the prime of life, energetic, scholarly, having both brains and position, he has yet a noteworthy future before him."

CHAPTER TWENTIETH.

IN the winter of 1879 Doctor Gunn was dangerously
ill from pyæmia. It was a time of great apprehen-
sion; few if any of his brother physicians believed he
would recover. How kind they were—some of them
remaining with him night after night! Under similar
circumstances came like and later kindnesses which
will never be forgotten.

That perilous morning is engraven on my mind. It
was about day-break. I was alone with my husband,
when he said: "You will have to get the props under
me soon or it will be too late." I was almost paralyzed to find him cold and sinking. I gave him
brandy, but not as much as he needed; I was anything
but composed, but ran to the next room, rang the stable
bell, told the man to harness and go for Dr. A———.
When the doctor arrived, I knew he was alarmed, but
he quietly sat down by the bedside of his old friend,
and commenced giving him stimulants. It was not
very long before the doctor rallied. Turning to Dr.
A——— he said " Old fellow, I know you would have

hated to have me slip through your fingers!" then added, "The world is a pretty good place and I am not sorry to stay in it a while longer." Some kindly and affectionate remarks then passed between them.

Doctor Gunn's arm troubled him for months afterward, but by the latter part of February he began again to lecture. The first day he appeared before the class, the amphitheatre was decorated with flowers, and the doctor was welcomed with enthusiasm.

The following May, some physicians were about starting on a European trip, and he was urged to make one of their number. He needed the journey, in fact it was the very thing he most needed, but hesitated on account of a rash statement he had made to his wife, that he should never go abroad without her! This objection, however, was speedily overruled by her, and his arrangments were made accordingly. Dr. M——, who had frequently crossed the ocean, proposed this time trying the advantages or disadvantages of Cook's Tours, in which they all acquiesced. Some days later Mrs. H—— meeting Doctor Gunn on the street, she said to him, "Doctor, I hear you are going to Europe; shall you take Mrs. Gunn?" With a twinkle of his eye he replied, "O, No! *I am going for pleasure!*"

Before leaving, the doctor announced that however unattractive letter-writing was to him, he should write every Sunday, and think of his wife *all the time.* Another rash statement, possibly, but one which, in regard to the frequency of writing, he more than carried out.

"AT SEA, STEAMER 'GALLIA,'
"LAT. 44–35°, LONG. 44–8°, *June 1, 1879.*

"You notice we are about mid-ocean. It is Sunday evening, eight o'clock and after dinner. I am seated at the table in the cabin to write my first Sunday's letter. I suppose that you are now writing to me and that I shall receive the letter in Dublin, two weeks from to-morrow. . . . We have had a remarkably pleasant voyage thus far, nothing rougher than you and I experienced on the Gulf last year. Dr. R—— has been out to-day for the first time since we embarked; unfortunately he has suffered from seasickness, while the rest of us have been undisturbed in the enjoyment of our meals. The ship and her appointments are perfect. Wednesday, Thursday and Friday were clear days, to-day has been rainy. Yesterday I saw six whales; two of them spouted, and I realized the ideas given by the illustrations. To-day we have had service on board, read by the surgeon of the ship. Prayers were read for the President of the United

States; also for Albert Edward, Prince of Wales, and all the Royal Family.

"We have a large load of passengers; among them Rev. DeWitt Talmage, accompanied by his wife and daughter, whose acquaintance I have made and find them agreeable people. There is also a Scotchman and his wife from D—— who started from home accompanied by a daughter who was to make the trip with them. She was engaged to be married this coming Autumn. Her fiancé came as far as Chicago to bid her good-bye, but instead, while in the city procured a license, married the girl and took her back to D——. The mother, naturally, was quite indignant at their haste and says she gave him a bit of her mind. I said, 'So you gave him a foretaste of the mother-in-law?' 'Indeed I did,' replied she.

"I have indulged in a good bit of gossip for me. . . . I thought of you when you were probably praying for me in church, making allowance for difference in time, when at your dinner, etc. My mind is scarcely ever absent from you, but still I am enjoying every moment, and anticipating much pleasure. Probably we shall land at Queenstown on Thursday or Friday next, and remain in Cork till Monday. I shall add to, and finish this letter before landing, that it may go with the first mail to London and then to the United States. You will get it about the twentieth."

"*Monday Evening, 2nd.*—I wish I could telephone and keep you daily advised of my movements. Another day on the whole favorable, head winds, and some sea, but nothing to disturb the passengers, most of whom are now seen at the tables. Opposite to me reading sits Mrs. W—— from Chicago; at my right, also reading, sits Dr. R—— who has fully recovered from his sea-sickness. .   .   Both Mr. and Mrs. Talmage are agreeable in conversation. Mrs. T—— tells a darkey story capitally.

"At noon to-day we had made three hundred and forty-two miles, in the last twenty-four hours, and are at Lat. 47–8° and Long. 36–54°. I tell you this, so that you can pick out our position on the map. We expect to land at Queenstown Thursday afternoon."   .

" *Wednesday, 3:30 P. M.*—Four and a half hours over one week at sea, and all has gone well. Tell M—— I have seen six whales, and two of them spout! Last evening we had a concert gotten up by volunteers for the benefit of some Sailor Orphan Asylum in Liverpool. It was amusing enough but hardly of supreme artistic merit. We are now within four hundred miles of Cape Clear, have had head-winds all the way, except four or five hours one day, when we derived a little benefit from our sails. Still we have made about three hundred and fifty miles every twenty-four hours, and our party has all been well excepting Dr. R——.

"The tables are very well filled, and, as many of the passengers have become acquainted, the evening dinner, which lasts about an hour and a half, is a lively, noisy scene, not unlike an evening party, where all is a confusion of voices. The fare is varied and excellent, but although I have been well, and have had a voracious appetite, it is getting monotonous, and I shall not be sorry to get on land again. The same routine of sleeping and eating, and very little reading will not prove continuously entertaining; card playing I detest, so that exhaustless source of amusement to many on board is unavailing to me. A mail bag is being made up for Liverpool; I finish this to be forwarded from there."　　.　　.　　.

"QUEENSTOWN, *June 6th, 1879.*

"We arrived here last night, or rather this morning at 1:30, and were met by our conductor who had rooms provided for us at the Queen's Hotel and breakfast in a private parlor this morning, and O! how exceedingly funny is this intensely Irish town; beggars who blarney and beg all in the same breath. I have seen but little of the town. I write now to get in an additional letter as the foreign mail closes at twelve.

"Yesterday, our last at sea, was rainy, and as no observation could be made at noon, and as we were approaching the coast in a fog, it was to me a matter of some interest, at least; but when at last our proud ship put her nose right in the passage between the Irish Cliffs and Fastnet light, which loomed grandly through obscurity up in the mist, I felt a warm admiration for the brain which piloted us across the trackless deep.

"We go to Cork to-morrow and remain there till Wednesday. I am sitting in the parlor of the Queen's; at a table opposite, a very pretty Irish woman with banged fore-top is also writing; she politely offered me a pen as I sat down to the table. Think of it! although we stayed twenty-four hours in New York, we slept in Ireland on the twelfth night after saying good-bye to you in Chicago." . ,. . . .

"CORK, IRELAND,
"*Sunday Afternoon, June 8th, 1879.*

"By my second letter, which undoubtedly will be received with the first, you will see we landed in Queenstown ahead of the contemplated time. However, we were met, though at midnight, by Mr. Cook's agent and guide, *i. e.*, both in one person, and by him conducted to our hotel where he had secured rooms for us. The advantages of travelling in this way we have chosen, were manifest here, as one or two at least of the many passengers who landed at the same time and place, have not been able to get a room. Ours being secured in advance, we had none of that strife which the others were obliged to encounter. Friday and Saturday forenoons were spent in Queenstown. The harbor is beautiful, and the town, which is planted on a succession of terraces on the side of the bluff, is a strange combination of charming difficulties and remunerating views. But, O! the Irish of it! I feel that I can hardly speak without getting off something *wid a brogue in it.*

"Yesterday afternoon we came here and are lodged at the 'Imperial.' An Irish hotel is of course like the English in type and it is odd enough. I cannot stop to describe or criticise, but as yet, to me, the type is not agreeable. Everything is excellent, but *the way of the thing* is not quite acceptable; perhaps it will become so.

"I have just lunched on some cold mutton that fully realized my idea of English mutton although it was raised, killed, and cooked in Ireland! I told you the other day the beggars were at hand on all occasions; one must have a pocketful of pennies to bestow upon

them. Their appeals are very droll. The other day
on leaving the hotel, I was accosted by one of the male
persuasion whose petition was, 'Plaze, sur, giv a thrifle
to a poor ould man wid a throuble in his bones.' A
little further on a vigorous middle-aged woman ap-
pealed thusly: 'God bliss the grand gintlemon!' To-
day a barefooted woman with a babe in her arms crossed
the street to intercept our passage with: 'For the love
of God, giv a copper to buy bread for the childers!'"

"I went to church this morning, but, I fear, not to
pray, but to see the old church of St. Ann's, otherwise
'Shandon,' and to hear the chimes. Yes, I have heard
the Chimes of Shandon! I have looked at 'The Bells
of Shandon,' have climbed the tower and looked out over
the ancient City of Cork. The bells are sweet and the
church plain and poor, but the poem rang incessantly
in my ear as from the tower of Shandon I looked out
over the Lee. The river Lee is very beautiful from
Queenstown all the way (about twelve miles) to this
place.

"Yesterday on a boat excursion, on the river from
Queenstown, a beautiful Irish girl, with a clear com-
plexion and a lithe and slender figure, neatly dressed
in a long, close-fitting cloth coat, with a bit of a hand-
kerchief peeping out of her breast pocket, came on
board at one of the landings. Her beauty and her

quiet and modest behavior, quite took young C——
and old G——! off their feet! We were standing
together as the boat approached the wharf, and added
to the above outline we saw just upon a level with our
eyes a neat foot in a well-fitting boot unobscured by a
train. A walking suit enabled her to move with ease
and grace, while we admired at a respectful distance.
We indulged in our amazement till the vision disappeared at one of the landings, and then we recalled a
story which a quaint old New Hampshire member of
our party told on shipboard. It ran thus: A wife
whose husband was obliged to travel in Pennsylvania,
on bidding him good-bye said, 'John, when the ankles
of the Dutch girls begin to look slender to you, *it's time
to come home.*'

"This morning as we wandered about, we thought
and said, how nice it would be to have our wives
here to enjoy this with us. Indeed I hardly see anything without wishing I had you here to see it with
me.   .   .   I am feeling well, have
had no unpleasant symptoms as yet, and if you were
with me, I think my cup of happiness would be full.
To-morrow our conductor comes on again from Queenstown with a second edition of our party who are to
arrive in one of the Inman steamers. I understand
there is *one woman* in the expected addition.   .

"On Tuesday we shall visit Blarney Castle; on Wednesday start for Killarney. M—— and I discussed this morning the advantages of this mode of taking a tour. It is an easy way, we are relieved of everything, no tickets to buy, no servants to fee, in short we have nothing to do but enjoy ourselves and encounter beggars. How much fun W—— would get out of these Irishmen! I can't remember a hundredth part of the queer things I see and hear.   .   .

KILLARNEY, *Tuesday, June 12th, 1879.*

"Here at Killarney I have just finished my dinner, which was at half-past six, and as we are six hours earlier than you, I suppose you are just over your lunch. It still seems strange to find myself in Ireland. I can hardly realize that nearly one quarter of the distance around the globe separates us. My last letter was from Cork, which place we left yesterday morning at nine o'clock, in the rain, and at eleven-thirty were at Drimoleague where we took a stage. Fortunately the rain had stopped and we all chose the top of the vehicle, even the woman ! which I have forgotten whether I mentioned as being the only one in our party.

"Well, the trip was surprisingly beautiful to Bantry on Bantry Bay, where we lunched. From there we skirted the head of the bay to Glengariff, the great, barren, rocky mountains which we had climbed and the spurs of which we were now crawling around, looming up on the one hand, and the picturesque bay on the other, both forming a landscape which combined the beautiful and the sublime. Arrived at our hotel on the shores of Glengariff harbor we found a lovely situation. At our feet we had the waters of the harbor, with their rocky inlets and shores, while on the opposite side towered grandly up barren, rocky peaks which formed a magnificent chain of mountains. The day had been one replete with pleasure, it was a red-letter day in our experience. When I looked upon this scene, which I have only touched, for I cannot attempt a description, I thought as I almost constantly do, 'Why cannot my wife be here to enjoy this with me?' But a truce to vain imaginings.   .   .   .   .   .

"This morning broke grand and bright, and when I looked out of my window the sun was gilding the tops of the opposite mountains, while we were in the shade. After a good breakfast we mounted a wagonette which carried eleven persons besides the driver; three good horses constituted our team, and we started off in fine spirits. Our course lay up the magnificent mountain range which we had seen before us. At the height of thirteen hundred feet we passed through a tunnel to the other side of the mountain. The scenery is beyond description. These mountains are barren rocks either entirely without vegetation or covered with heather. Great rocky ledges loom up in grandeur while we crawl winding along and around their sides on a road as smooth as the boulevards and a hundred times harder. These roads are simply perfect. I have not seen a rood of bad road in Ireland.

"We lunched at Kenmare, and as this is at the foot of the range on the other side, we had to begin a similar ascent over a very similar formation and to an equal height, passing through another though shorter tunnel and then descending gradually till we reached the lakes of Killarney. To the east of this spot the country seems greatly improved, speaking from an agricultural point of view, while to the west and south from this point over which we have just travelled the mountains are the highest in the island, one peak, which we had in view a greater part of the afternoon, being three thousand four hundred feet high.

"I cannot speak of the lakes. I have seen so much I can hardly tell you any thing, but will try to do so Sunday when I write again. Of to-day's trip I can only say, it surpassed all my dreams. I have been in a constant state of wonder since starting out this morning. It will take time to assimilate and reduce to order all these new impressions.   I have seen enough to-day to last a lifetime.   I am in a sort of dazed condition, which I thought to clear up by writing to you, but have run on about these scenes that have engrossed my attention and am not much better settled in my feelings.   .   .   .   .   I hope to find a letter from you in Dublin on Monday evening.   .   .

KILLARNEY, *June 15th, 1879.*

"My last was written after my arrival here on Thursday evening; since then we have had two glorious days, and now after attending the Episcopal Church here, and having since then lunched, I am in my room to keep my promise good for writing.   .   . My family are arranged on the mantel just at my right. .   .   .   .   I seem to have been gone three months! and yet it is only three weeks!   I have wished for a telephone to give you my experience with electric speed, writing is so slow.

"We have been especially favored regarding weather and yet we have passed only two days without some rain.   On Friday we visited the ruins of Aghadoe, made the pass of Dunloe, where at the entrance stands the cottage of Kate Kearney, lunched at a little island at the head of the upper lake, passed down the lakes and in the lower one visited the ruins of an old Abbey

15

on Innisfallen island, and the ruins of Ross Castle. The day was perfect and the scenery simply grand. I cannot describe it in detail, for it would take too much writing.

"Yesterday we went to the ruins of Muckross Abbey which are well preserved and are extremely interesting, did several islands and Lord Kenmare's park, and just got home to dinner. Two days of sight-seeing found me very tired last night and I slept well. We lunched yesterday in a romantic spot just about the time you were at breakfast. I thought of you while I was lunching, and calculated the time and derived pleasure at the thought. I have collected photographs of such points as interested me most, and of the lunching place of yesterday.

" To-morrow we go to Dublin, but it is not necessary to write this, for we adhere to our schedule very closely, so you can follow us accurately if you wish, making allowance of six hours in our favor, *i. e.*, we dine six hours in advance of you, at six-thirty, which would be at twelve-thirty, with you, your lunch hour; when you are lunching, our afternoon has passed and we are dining. It is now three-thirty; while I am writing you have had breakfast and are reading 'The Sunday Times,' which I hope to receive in about two weeks. To-morrow evening on my arrival in Dublin I hope to get a letter from you. I have just paused to calculate when you will get your first letter from me, and find you cannot receive your first news after my leaving New York before next Friday, June twentieth, almost four weeks after my departure from home. How long the time seems! . . . God bless you. . .

"LONDONDERRY, IRELAND, *June 19th, 1879.*

"Here we are in the North of Ireland, and that we are far north you may realize when I tell you that when I awoke this morning the sun was shining in my room; looking at my watch I found it lacked fifteen minutes to four. I realize it in another way, namely, in that I am obliged to wear my overcoat continually. I would not live in Ireland for the whole of the island! Perhaps that is rather extravagant, but it expresses my present feelings so far as temperature is concerned.

"We came to Dublin on Monday, and on that day and on the following, in which we had to *do the city*, it rained continually; our stay there was most unpropitious. Yesterday we had good weather and a pleasant journey north along the shores of the Irish Sea to Dundalk, and across the country to this old city. Tell W—— to read up the siege of Londonderry. It is walled, *i. e.*, the walls and gate-ways of the ancient city yet remain, though the town has grown far beyond them.   It is yet a small city and could not have contained more than three or four thousand at the time of historical interest.

"We did the city last evening after dinner (an advantage of our long days) in order to go on to Port Rush this morning to breakfast, and to have more time to give to the Giant's Causeway.   Your letter and the enclosed introduction from Dr. Gross to Sir James Paget was handed to me in the museum of Trinity College, Dublin.   I am much interested in all about me, but I am also thinking of home.   .   .   Write three times a week if you can.   .   .   .   .

"INVERSNAID, *June 22nd, 1879.*

"Here in the Highlands of Scotland on the shores of Loch Lomond with the cloud-kissed heads of Ben Ledi and Vorlich in front of me I sit down to hold a few moments converse with you.   On the mantel are arranged as in Killarney, my family pictures; but more than four thousand, yes, six thousand miles intervene between us.   I can hardly yet realize that I am in the old world.

"My last was written at Londonderry on Wednesday morning.   After a vile cup of coffee we went to Port Rush to breakfast; and after this most refreshing pastime, to the Giant's Causeway, some eight or nine miles distant, passing the ruins of Dunluce Castle, but did not venture to explore them, as the only approach to the ruins was over a narrow wall spanning a deep chasm; the wind at the time blowing so fiercely it would have been dangerous to attempt the passage. At the Causeway we took boat to a couple of caves worn deep in the rock by the waves of the ocean running into them for a distance of two hundred feet or more, quite as far as any of us were disposed to penetrate; then to and upon the Causeway which is indeed wonderful and interesting. Then lunch at the Causeway Hotel and a drive back to Port Rush, a rainy evening, a fire in my room, a good night's rest, and bright morning on Friday, and then by a pleasant rail trip to Belfast, at which place it began again to rain.

"Belfast is large and populous but presents little to sight-seers. By evening boat we arrived at Glasgow, where we stepped upon Scotch soil. Glasgow is a very large and solid city, with much that is interesting. I will not attempt an enumeration, only mentioning a Cathedral which boasts the finest ecclesiastical architecture in Scotland, and the Hunterian Museum, which being anatomical and pathological will not interest you. Here we found the cleanest and most comfortable hotel we have yet encountered. The landlady, who in this kingdom is *the personage* of such an establishment, is an American; the furniture was all of American make, and the table service, each piece decorated with the stars and stripes and the cross of St. George, the staffs of which were crossed and tied with ribbon. We fared well and our American hostess was pleased to make us comfortable.

"At five last evening we took rail to Balloch at the foot of Loch Lomond, and then steamboat to this place, where we had tea at nine o'clock. At ten-thirty, although the evening was both cloudy and misty, I read the time on my watch out-of-doors; had it been clear, I think I could have read it at eleven. The weather is atrocious and robs us of much that is attractive in the scenery. The tops of the mountains are obscured by mist.

"It is Sunday, a lazy day, M—— and C—— are indisposed to go out and R—— seems to be of the same mind, leaving me to stay in or go out alone. I cannot bear to lose any of this scenery, but much is lost on account of the weather. . . . To-morrow, Loch Katrine, Ellen's Isle, the Brigg of Turk and on to Edinburgh." . . .

"KESWICK, ENGLAND, *June 25th, 1879.*

"Here in the lake district of England, in the vale of Keswick, the most charmingly picturesque spot I have yet seen, I am lodged in a fine hotel that looks out over the village, river, and upon a semi-circular range of hills or low mountains. On Monday by open stage we went across to Loch Katrine, passing over the intervening mountain range, past the shores of a lakelet on the opposite shore of which, Helen MacGregor was born, this being the domain of Rob Roy. At Stronachlacher, took a little steamer for the foot of the lake, passing Ellen's Isle and the spot where Fitz-James first espied her; then by stage through the Trossachs along the shores of Lochs Achray and Vennachar, over the Brigg of Turk to Callander; then by rail to Stirling, where we visited that ancient castle of early Scottish history. I cannot stop to describe the Castle, or the extensive view from its battlements, but will bring photographs, also a sprig of ivy which I reached out and plucked from Queen Mary's Look-Out.

"The same evening we reached Edinburgh, which I wish I could take more time to describe. It is one of the most beautiful capitals of Europe; its peculiar location on a group of hills, separated by deep ravines, forms a landscape and background that is most picturesque. Looking down from the ramparts of the Castle or looking up from the lower parts of the city at its heights, it is equally impressive. Calton Hill, occupied by the Royal Astronomical Observatory, affords an extensive view. Descending the hill in one direction, you approach by walking, Holyrood Palace the ancient abode of Scottish royalty, where Mary's room and bed-room are shown, also the apartments and bed of Darnley; many interesting things are seen here. The Castle and National Gallery also claimed our attention yesterday. . . . . .

"Last evening we came to Melrose; this morning visited the Abbey where, at the end of several centuries, the ruins of its elegant architecture still remain. At Abbotsford I sat a moment in Sir Walter's chair, in the library which looked out over a vast extent of meadow reaching to the Tweed. From this interesting spot we went to Dryburgh Abbey where the genial poet was buried. Then by rail to this place.

"It is now eleven, I have just come in from a visit to Southey's grave in a quaint old church-yard, passed his former residence, and now after a hard day's work I am tired but determined to write you this sketch before sleeping. . . . We sail for home on the sixteenth of August; you can write to me as late as August first, but send that letter to Liverpool in care of the purser of the 'Bothnia.'" .

LONDON, ENGLAND, *June 29th, 1879.*

" We arrived last night in the greatest city on the globe, and to-day (Sunday) I have spent in trying to get the main points in the topography of this unlimited labyrinth. I am tired although I have not walked much; the omnibuses run everywhere, on top of one is the best place to see to advantage and to get acquainted with the city. This mode of sight and conveyance is extremely advantageous. . . . . .

"My last was written at Keswick. One day was spent in an excursion, the next, in a journey to Furness Abbey, after which we came yesterday to London. We had a special car which was *shunted* (that's the word used here for switching) on to different trains as we struck the various lines. At last, one hundred and ninety-three miles from London, we struck the Midland Road and one of the fast trains. Our first run was seventy-four and a half miles, in one hour and twenty-five minutes; some of the time we made a mile in forty-five and forty-six seconds.

" Well, we have been in Great Britain twenty-five days, and have had rain every day but two! Still we have dodged the showers, and have had a good time. To-morrow begins the work of *doing* London! and I have learned enough to-day, to show me how imperfectly the task must be done in the time alloted. One thought is ever present with me; that is, the distance between me and all that I hold dear.   .   .

" LONDON, July 2nd, 1879.

" Your letter of June fifteenth was received on Monday morning.   .   .   .   .   While I was dressing on Tuesday morning, there was a knock on my door and the boy handed me your letter written on the sixteenth, after receiving my first missives from across the water.   I was delighted not only at receiving a letter from you, but at the speedy passage made by the mail which brought you my letters, so much in advance of my calculations.   Ten days from the time I wrote my letter in Queenstown, you had it in your hands!

" The letter which you wrote in reply was mailed on the seventeenth of June and was handed into my room in London on the morning of July first, making fourteen days.   It seems incredible that you should have gotten my letter so soon.   I wrote it after my first breakfast in Ireland in order to get it in the mail that closed at twelve o'clock.   At three o'clock two of us were on the heights of Queenstown looking at the mail-boat that took our letters out to the steamer which was on her way to New York.   We watched the movements with interest, knowing our letters were on their way to Chicago, calculated when you would receive them, etc.   .   .   .   .   .

" I have now been in this great, noisy, crooked city three days and am bewildered with the numberless historic associations which we encounter on every hand. Westminster Abbey where the tombs of monarchs and nobles of olden time are shown, itself venerable with signs of age and decay, seems to oppress and confuse one in its intricacy, at least it did me, and I found myself trying to take it all in, and realize the fact that centuries rolled between *then* and *now*.

" To-day I have been to the Tower where are shown suits of armor worn by Henry IV, the Duke of Suffolk, and Robert Dudley, Earl of Leicester.   I noticed one suit of armor said to have been presented to the wearer by Queen Bess! at any rate there is visible on the breast an inlaid likeness of the stately Queen, high-necked ruff and all.

" I saw the spot where Lady Jane Grey was be-headed, but alas! she was only one of a multitude who suffered a like fate on the spot.   Anne Boleyn's crown rests in the case which contains those of the present Queen and Charles II.—But enough of this; to me it was depressing, and I fear it will be so to you.   .   .

.   .   The National Gallery disturbed me with so much of beauty and its opposite, actual ugliness.   The trouble is, there is so much to see and so little time to see it in. . . . . Dr. P—— who has been abroad some weeks, joined us in London, and will go on with us to Amsterdam." . . .

CHAPTER TWENTY-FIRST.

DOCTOR GUNN'S natural propensity to throw off trouble and look at the bright side of life, induced him often to say: " Enjoy your rose but don't look round for the thorn." Thus he commences one of his letters:—

" I think our roses have really as few thorns as any one's, and I am sure that we may keep our fingers off of them if we only try. . . . At this untimely hour, five o'clock in the morning, I am writing to you from Amsterdam,—this genial old city of the Dutch. Breakfast is not ordered for us until nine o'clock, therefore I prefer writing to you before going out. When we awoke yesterday morning and got on deck, we were in the German Ocean, the south end of which we cross in going from Harwich to Rotterdam.

" About nine o'clock we could make out the low coast, which soon came more plainly into view, and as we entered the mouth of the Maas, or as you probably will find it on the map, 'Meuse,' the dykes and low-backed fields made a picture which fully realized my idea of Holland. Along the dykes there appeared to be a road (it was undoubtedly a road), as wagons were occasionally passing thereon. Long rows of handsome trees and almost as many windmills, with their long, ponderous wings slowly moving in obedience to the wind, with here and there a cottage, gave picturesqueness to the scene. The river was dotted with vessels of all descriptions from the little Dutch hulk to the fine, large, India-bound ships. Schiedam, where the famous gin is made, was soon before us, and by ten o'clock we reached the city of Rotterdam where we disembarked, lunched, wandered about, visited two picture galleries, where we found some fine paintings, dined, and then by cars came on to this city, arriving about eleven o'clock.

"Our party was greatly augmented at London by both gentlemen and ladies; the addition of the women, I think, will add something to the trip. Before reaching London we had only one! but her husband stuck so close to her, the rest of us had no chance *to peep*. Four of the women are travelling alone; two of them went over in the Gallia, and I had become slightly acquainted with them. .   .   .   . They are solid in a metaphorical sense, but not in a physical one.

"Well, here I am almost at the end of my sheet, and as I know nothing yet about this city, can say nothing. To-morrow we shall go to Antwerp, stopping at The Hague to see some pictures; much is proposed that often is hardly worth seeking after.   .   .

.   .   So far we have had constantly bad weather, the only days entirely without rain being at Killarney; and I begin to fear we shall have bad weather all the way round. But we have dodged the annoying showers, and have not suffered much discomfort. It is now half-past eight, and the bells, a chime, are striking the hour close by. With a few words more I must close and get ready for breakfast.   .   .   .   .

BRUXELLES, BELGIUM, *July 9th, 1879.*

"Yesterday evening on our arrival here, I found your letter of June 21st; this morning, another was brought dated two days later.   .   .   .

My last was written Sunday morning at Amsterdam. As we had only Sunday in this quaint, interesting and curious old city, the day was devoted to it, instead of to church. We took a carriage and drove about visiting several points of interest. Amsterdam has been called the 'Vulgar Venice,' but he who calls the city vulgar, makes a sad mistake. It has a commercial grandeur that is wonderful! it may not have the poetic associations of the town of the Doges and Council of Ten, with its 'Bridge of Sighs;' but it has wealth, thrift, cleanliness and beauty. The residences of the wealthy are on well-kept streets, rich, lofty, and substantial, while they, and the promenades, and the canals, are all so clean, and the unique picture of the whole so charming that, despite the cold, damp weather in which we saw them, we were delighted. Quaint old gables, steep and plain, with here and there one highly carved and ornamented, with black or almost black doors opening upon steps, with rails and trimmings polished as high as labor could reach, characterized the dwellings, which stood prominent along the streets. We visited the Royal Palace, saw its paintings and statuary, three different museums containing paintings, the Zoological Garden, and diamond polishers who, being Jews, were hard at work on Sunday. I saw the man diligently at work who cut, or rather polished the Koohinoor. I went to bed tired.

"On Monday we came to Antwerp by way of The Hague. At Antwerp I went on board the steamer Trenton and saw Surgeon Bloodgood, who appeared delighted to see me. Bruxelles is beautiful—evidently fashionable and gay. I have just learned that J. C—— from Chicago is here. I have been very busy to-day, will call upon her this evening. To-morrow we go to the battle-field of Waterloo! there is nothing to see but it is the thing to do, and *we do it.* Rain! rain! incessant rain! only two days without, since we landed.

.   .   .   .

"WIESBADEN, GERMANY,

"*Sunday, July 13th, 1879.*

"I dropped W—— a postal from Cologne yesterday morning just as we were starting up the Rhein. We arrived here last evening at nine-thirty, having had, to our surprise, a fine day; that is, only one shower during our dinner. I had formerly dreamed of the Rhein as a most romantic piece of river scenery, but of later years have so often heard it referred to as no finer than the Highlands of the Hudson, that my expectations were somewhat toned down. In this mood I encountered the reality. Well! the half had not been told! To compare the two, seems absurd,—as well compare the anatomical perfections and beauty of a leopard, with the grace and beauty of a greyhound! The Hudson has a few miles of grand and wild scenery. The Rhein has nothing so wild, but it has six times as much; a great portion of it wild, and all so highly cultivated with the vine that when crowned with the numerous old ruins about which cluster so much of historic romance and mythical legend, it leaves the Hudson far in the background.   Castle and crag here and there present bold and stern reminders of the career of the robber feudals, with now and then a bit of sweet and touching romance; while the Lorley or more properly the Lurlie, calls up the familiar legend, which has been so distorted upon the stage.

"Well, here in Wiesbaden I have just attended an English Church, where Victoria and the Royal Family, Kaiser Wilhelm and the President of the United States were all remembered in the ritual.   How odd it seems to be here!   It is raining, my window is open, and I look out on a beautiful small city while you are one quarter of the way round the globe to the west, and are just sitting down to breakfast."   .   .   .

"HEIDELBERG, GERMANY, *July 14th, 1879.*

"I wrote yesterday from Wiesbaden and was disappointed at the non-reception of a letter on my arrival Saturday evening.   To-day in Heidelberg, I found your letters of June 26th and 27th with the enclosed from T—— written on June 29th, giving a description of their journey, similar to yours they wrote you from Manitou Peak.".

"*Tuesday, Fifteenth.*—Have just returned from the Schloss or Castle which is Heidelberg's lion!   It is the most extensive and, on the whole, the most interesting ruin I have yet seen.   I cannot go into details, only to say that there are garden terraces, trees, towers, gables and a drawbridge over the moat, and that in the vast and solitary chambers is the architecture of past ages.   All combine to make this one of the most interesting of ruins.   Among other things, it contains in a well-preserved condition, the great tun which is said to contain, I believe, eighteen thousand barrels; it is also said to have been three times filled with wine.   A flight of stairs leads to a platform on its top, where can be danced a double quadrille!

" From the Castle walls we overlook the town, and in the distance catch a glimpse of the Rhein, into which the Neckar below us flows.   Behind rise the heights of Kaiserstuhl, while on the opposite side of the Neckar we behold the vine-clad sides of All Saints. When I stood there and looked out on all this beauty, I thought   .   .   well, in a word, I wished that you were here.   God grant we may some time take this journey together!   It is raining again and I am gloomy.   .   .   .   I get comfort in the thought that I am on the last half of the allotted time for the journey."   .   .   .   .

" HOTEL SCHREIBER, RIGI-KULM, SWITZERLAND,

"July 19th, 1879.

" Here at the top of the Rigi, five thousand nine hundred and sixty-five feet above the level of the sea and four thousand nine hundred feet above the level of Lake Lucerne from which we made the ascent on the inclined railroad, I sleep to-night, and go to Luzern to breakfast in the morning. Dr. P—— is also here and we hope to get a clear sunrise, though it is extremely doubtful.

" I last wrote you at Heidelberg, writing on Tuesday evening my Wednesday's letter.   I agreed to write you every Sunday but have written twice weekly instead. .   .   .   .   We stopped over in Strassburg, for in order to hear the clock strike, we were obliged to wait until afternoon, and lose the train that would bring us into Schaffhausen in seasonable time.   Next day we came to Schaffhausen, stopped at a most delightful hotel, situated directly in front of the falls of the Rhein.   On the next day, Friday, came to Luzern, stopping at Zurich two hours, instead of all night, thus catching up with our programme.

" To-day we have lingered in a most delightful locality, with the Alps in front of us, and this peculiarly beautiful sheet of water at our feet.   Nine miles by steamer brought us to Vitznau, and then the elevating railroad to this immensely elevated point on the top of one of the Northern Alps. I hardly can contain my enthusiasm, so charmingly beautiful is the picture upon which I have been looking to-night.

"It is dark, and I write my Sunday's letter now instead of to-morrow, in order to have it mailed from this mountain. It is higher in the air than I have ever been before and the grandeur and picturesqueness of the view I only wish you could see. Monday we take steamer to Alpnacht and then stages over the Brunig Pass. I am some feverish to-night, possibly from excitement. My arm was again opened during the last week.   .   .   .   .   I feel that my letters are meagre affairs, but I am always hurried, my heart is full of the scenes around me and equally full of regret that an ocean is between us."   .   .

" INTERLACHEN, SWITZERLAND,
"Wednesday, July 23rd, 1879.

"My last was from Rigi-Kulm. Sunday was spent on Lake Lucerne going to Fluellen at the head of the lake, passing some very fine points and the Tell Platz where, according to the legend, Tell sprang on shore and shoved the boat out into the lake. Monday we took boat to Alpnacht, then carriages to Brienz on the north shore of a lake of the same name, crossing which we stopped at Giessbach for the night. Our carriage route was over the Brunig Pass, from which at a post-office stop, I dropped a line to W——. . .

" The scenery over the pass was simply sublime! Imagine yourself creeping up and still up along the side of the mountain, at times effecting a turn in order to accomplish a zig-zag movement, then up and up a mile or two of travel and you look directly down upon the path over which you have just come, perhaps some five hundred feet below. At last the summit of the pass is reached, and you begin a similar descent, catching constantly magnificent views of snow-capped peaks, warm, sequestered nooks, where the peasant was pasturing his herd or making hay for winter's use. Now a mountain torrent is seen rushing down the mountain side, leaping often hundreds of feet at a single plunge. Thus one beautiful fall was in sight for more than an hour; our view being altered only by the varying altitude from which we beheld it, in our back-and-forth, zig-zag course down the mountain. At last when nearly down to the level of the lake, we pass beneath the overhanging rocky side and emerge into the valley, embark on the lake, cross, and catch sight of a fine hotel located upon a little plateau some four hundred feet above the surface of the lake. This we reach by a new inclined railroad which has been in operation only one day.

"The view from the hotel is charming, the waterfall leaping in a series of cascades down to our very feet from nine hundred feet above us. The window of my room looked out upon the fall, and the roar of the rushing water lulled me to a night's repose. Before this at nine-thirty, came the illumination by Bengal lights. I had heard much of this illumination, but had failed utterly to conceive of its great beauty. It is useless to attempt a description, but when I see you, I hope to be able to give you an approximative idea of this picture which I shall carry with me to my life's end.

"To-day the rain has prevented our going to Grindelwald; we were obliged to postpone the trip until to-morrow. I had gotten to the fourth page of this letter, when P—— came in and proposed an extra trip to Lauterbrunnen. The rain had somewhat abated, and we had a lovely afternoon, seeing in addition to the fine mountain scenery, a waterfall where a small brook bounds over a precipice and falls sheer, nine hundred and fifty feet, breaking into a white mist before reaching the bottom. Well! I cannot write all, but must wait to tell the rest *in propria persona.*" . .

"LAUSANNE, SWITZERLAND, *July 25th, 1879.*

"On my arrival here last evening, I found your letter of July seventh, just nineteen days old. At Interlachen, where I wrote you last, I received two! .

"Now to take up the thread of my travels:—My excitement and enthusiasm are awakened at every turn. On Thursday we went to the Glacier of Grindenwald where we entered a grotto cut for three hundred feet into ice, clear, and blue, and old, how old I cannot tell, but perhaps formed a century or more ago. The drive to Grindenwald was magnificent; the walk to the glacier was fatiguing, but with the use of my alpenstock I accomplished a walk that you would wonder at as much as I did myself."   .   .   .   .

"Friday it was Bern and the bears! which are a humbug. 'Old Grizzly' in Union Park would eat them all at one meal. The organ in the Cathedral, however, was a, wonder. I never heard an organ, nor organ playing before! Yesterday we stopped at Freiburg to hear the organ there; it was grand. Had I not heard the one at Bern the evening previous, I should have been astonished; but on the whole, I think it superior, and prefer the organ at Bern.   .   .   .
Again I cannot enter into details, but may entertain you with them when I see you. We arrived here to dinner. I go to church at eleven o'clock, and this

afternoon shall wander over the town.   I enclose a printed list of our party, with a brief commentary on each."   .   .   .   .

"LAUSANNE, *Sunday Evening, July 27th, 1879.*

"I wrote you this morning and now, alone in my room, have been reading over your last, received here last evening.   .   .   .   I forgot to mention in my letter this morning a surprise at Bern. Coming out of the dining room, I heard my name pronounced.   Turning, a lady held out her hand to me. It was none other than Mrs. W—— who said she had seen you not long before she left.   It did me good to see a Chicago face.   She left three weeks after us.   I shall finish this at Chamouny in the face of Mont Blanc. Till then good-bye.   .   .   .   .

CHAMONIX, *Wednesday, July 30th.*

Monday we embarked on Lake Leman and landed at Chillon, inspected the famous castle, saw the dungeon of Bonnivard and the ring to which he was chained, and the other sights of this renowned prison! Re-embarked for Bouveret and then by cars up a most rugged and romantic valley to Martigny, from whence the passes over the St. Bernard and Tête Noir start. Spent the night here, visiting the old ruin La Batiaz in the evening. Up next morning at half-past five, visited a noted gorge and waterfall, back to breakfast at eight; then by carriages over the mountains via the Tête Noire down into the valley and village of Chamonix, Mont Blanc rearing his hoary head of eternal snow grandly up before our delighted vision. The day was simply beautiful and unusual, no cloud to mar the uninterrupted view of the mountain.

"I have now returned from a trip to the Mer de Glace. At nine this morning, mounted on a mule, commenced in company with a large crowd, the ascent of the mountain, on attaining the summit of which we looked down upon the 'sea of ice.' Our mules were then sent down into the valley to re-ascend on the other side of the glacier as far as possible. Then with shoes armed with hobnails and ourselves with alpenstocks, we placed ourselves in charge of guides, who piloted us across the glacier; our course for an hour or more taking us up a rugged path over boulders brought down in ages past by the ice flow.

"Afterwards along a path hewn by the edge of the mountain, the abyss on one side, the perpendicular rock on the other, safety however being secured by an iron rail fastened to the rock, of which we could seize hold. In time we met our mules; then down, down, to the valley and a two or three miles ride brought us to our hotel at three o'clock, having made the trip in six hours.

"Dr. Grey of Utica is here with his son; he crossed the glacier with us; the last I saw of the genial doctor was on looking back,—I beheld his guide grasping him with both hands, and tugging him up the rugged path. He has not yet arrived and it is four-fifteen. We have another glorious day. To-morrow to Geneva, which will be turning towards home. Home! how blessed!   .   .   .

"PARIS, *Sunday, August 3rd, 1879.*

"I wrote you last from Chamouny just after my mountain and glacier trip. Next day by a tedious and warm diligence journey we arrived at Geneva, where I found four welcome letters from you.   .   .

.   .   We remained only one day at Geneva, a beautiful little city from which we have in clear weather a fine view of Mont Blanc, more than fifty miles away. This evening, from the lake, the mountain glowed with a deep pink tint, just as the moon with a like roseate hue climbed slowly from the horizon along-side the majestic and glowing mountain. It was a sight never to be forgotten.

"Yesterday we came by a dusty and hot rail-jour-ney to the city brilliancies of Paris! We arrived by moonlight and lost much of the attractiveness which the activities of the day would have given, but we gained all the weird effects that moonlight lent to the scene. We know nothing yet about the city, for it is too warm to move about much before evening. We remain here six days; then on to London, and then home. I am not a little excited by all I behold around me, but still I long for home. If you were with me and I were not obliged to hurry on so rapidly, I think I should be content to stay indefinitely; but as it is, I begin to tire of the work—for it amounts to work. I was amused by the account of your visit to R——, describing M——'s misadventure. Tell M—— I shall never dare to make him a present for fear some 'Mick' will rob him."   .   .   .   .   .

"PARIS, *Wednesday Morning, August 6th, 1879.*

"On Sunday, which was a *scorcher*, I wrote what I fear you found an unsatisfactorily short letter; this may prove no better. The fact is, with fatigue and excitement, I can hardly attain even my usual small degree of patience for letter writing. You know how I dread the mechanical part of writing; if I could *talk* letters, you would receive long ones daily.   .   .

"This morning as I lay in bed, thinking of the actual labor of sight-seeing, I shrank from it and thought how glad I should be to get home once more. The simple fact is, this doing a place in a given time is a grand humbug, unsatisfactory and fatiguing. I realized this. more at Versailles, where amid sights and glories that would have required days, it had to be compressed into a few hours. It is true I *have seen*, but how little I have brought away with me is fearfully apparent. Madame de Maintenon's residence at Trianon,—Petit Trianon, where poor Marie Antoinette danced on the threshold of a volcano, — the palace, now filled with historical paintings illustrating the glories of France, I have looked upon, but how I longed for days to contemplate and admire! The paintings surpass anything I have yet seen, excepting those in the Louvre, and the gardens, laid out on a scale of magnificence, are something to excite wonder as well as admiration. Indeed, when I look upon these surroundings, I can appreciate how a Frenchman feels when he cries out, 'La belle France!' It is a glorious nation, this French people, with a past that ought to make them rejoice in their inheritance.

"On Monday we drove about the city something in the following order:—Place de la Concorde, Champs Elysées, Arc de Triomphe, etc.; yesterday, the Bois de Boulogne, and so on through the programme. To-day will be the last of the prescribed drives, when we shall have a few days to ourselves, then on to England, and then home.   .   .   .   .   I am writing before breakfast, and as the hour is at hand, must close, and after breakfast must begin the tread-mill of sight-seeing! I am just beginning to see some of the disadvantages of these *convenient tours*."   .   .   .

" GRAND HOTEL, BRIGHTON,
"Sunday, August 10th, 1879.

"No weary and worn mariner ever longed for port and home more than I have since receiving your letter on Wednesday last, in Paris. I had already begun to weary of continual motion. Yesterday, although the rest of the party except Dr. H—— of Boston remained in Paris, I came on, or rather started for London, but found I could lay over here at one of the most celebrated watering-places in England.

"To go back:—On Wednesday we accomplished the last of the three day's 'excursions.' Thursday I looked all over Paris to find a pair of spurs like those I bought in Washington, but with no better luck than I had in London. In the afternoon it was the Siege of Paris and Hotel de Cluny. Paris is beautiful and attractive, but I, unfortunately, am wearied of so much hard work in sight-seeing, and am confused by its rapidity. Paris undoubtedly is not a divine city, but to see its wickedness one must seek it, it is not thrust upon you. In London, on the contrary, it is paraded, and even protected by the police.

"You see by the cut of the building on this sheet, that it is a fine hotel, with only the street between it and the sea. Fronting south and looking out upon the channel, we have before us a fine extent of beach, and this morning before breakfast I watched the bathers in the surf. Last evening I saw the Aquarium, said to be one of the most complete in the world. This afternoon I go on to London, and before the week is out I hope to embark for home.   .   .   .   My Summer has indeed been a novel one, a strange succession of new sights and impressions."   .   .

"GRAND HOTEL, BRIGHTON,

"Sunday, August 10th, 1879.

"I have just written you a letter which I have sealed and mailed, forgetting to enclose the promised Paris programme. I should like to accompany this letter. I will write you again from London on Tuesday, in order that you may have a letter a day or two in advance of me. I shall sail from Liverpool four days after I mail my last letter from London."   .   .   .

"LONDON, *August 11th, 1879.*

"I wrote you yesterday from Brighton, and came on to London this afternoon. I have written two, and sometimes three letters a week, to make them narrators of my movements. Writing letters under the circumstances, is no easy thing to accomplish. I fear this correspondence has not been satisfactory. I know it has been hurried. Sometimes I have arisen at unholy hours! and sometimes I have written late at night, to fulfill my promised quota. .   .   .   This morning I found four letters from you, mailed on the 24th, 28th, and 29th of July. I opened the last first in order to get the latest news." .   .   .   .

"LONDON, *August 12th, 1879.*

"Another letter of July 30th has just been handed to me. You have been most prompt in writing, .   . which I thoroughly appreciate. M—— said to me this morning, 'I now feel as though I was almost home again.' But the two weeks, at least, which must elapse before we are at home, seem longer to me than did the time when, at Chamonix, we first turned back on our journey.

"Yesterday I spent at Kensington Gardens; in the evening, at the Haymarket where Rose Eytinge, well supported, played to a beggarly house. .   .   .

This afternoon I shall go to the British Museum, Regent's Park and Zoological Gardens. On Thursday we start for Liverpool via Stratford-on-Avon and Warwick. On Saturday we sail; this will be the last letter I can get to you before sailing. I will telegraph you from New York."   .   .   .   .   .

"S. S. BOTHNIA, OFF S. W. COAST OF IRELAND,
    "*Nine O'Clock P. M., August 17th, 1879.*

"I am seated in the saloon of our unremarkable steamer to gratify your wish to have me write a letter to *bring with me!* Well, to begin. Promptly at three o'clock P. M. yesterday, the lighter took us off to the steamer, which required half or three-quarters of an hour. Arriving on board, I inquired for letters, but found none! I was more than disappointed! But in the course of half an hour, I was greeted by the announcement that a package which the lighter brought when she came with us, contained the much longed-for letter from you.   .   .   .   .   .

"At six o'clock precisely, we flung out the Stars and Stripes and put our wheels in motion. At two o'clock this afternoon we steamed into the Cove of Cork, or as it is now called Queenstown, to receive the London mail and a few additional passengers. We were on board the same steamer, and lying in the same

17

place, and for the same purpose as on the seventeenth of June when we had watched the Bothnia take to the United States our first letters. Now from the steamer we looked up at the eminence from which we then had regarded her, but how different it all was! Then we sped off our letters and had our trip before us; now, the trip completed, we were impatient of delay, every moment seemed an hour, and we longed to be on the wing. I at least was anxious to annihilate space. As on the occasion of the quick passage of our letters, I hailed it as a favorable omen of our passage to you.
.　　.　　.　　.　　At last the mail and passengers were all on board, then we steamed into the Channel, and now at this hour, are well out to sea, off the extreme south-west coast of the Green Isle.　　.　　　.

"*Sunday, August 24th.*—Just one week ago I wrote you off the south-west coast of Ireland; now we are eight hundred miles from New York, and shall not, at best, be able to reach port until Wednesday noon. Before that time, no doubt, you will be anxiously watching for the arrival of the Bothnia. The boat is slow, the winds constantly ahead, and some of the time fierce; consequently we have had a tedious as well as a rough passage. Monday it began to be troublesome to those who could not stand the motion. Tuesday and Wednesday ' Joseph ' was heard from on all sides!

The tables which were crowded on Sunday, were now sparsely enough occupied, and those of us who were able to be on hand had plenty of room. R—— succumbed at once, and never appeared at table or on deck, until yesterday (Saturday). C—— took his meals on deck, and did not particularly relish them; he reappeared at table, however, on Friday. M——, P—— and I, do justice to our meals.

"Three days of fine weather have given us better progress. I have not missed a single meal; in fact my happiest moments (although the fare is not very good) are at the table. The motion of the ship made my head feel badly, but my stomach was proof against its influence; however, three or four days are quite enough for me at sea. I have grown impatient over the slow old boat, wretched weather, abominable table, and nothing to while away the time. It has seemed that I must drive on faster, but how impotent are such desires! I have been almost as much demoralized as I was during those last ill and miserable days in the army. . . . I will wire you as soon as I reach New York." . . . . .

On landing in New York, it was a matter of congratulation to the doctor that he was not doomed to a hotel on the European plan. When sitting down to breakfast at the "Fifth Avenue," with a cantaloupe in front of him, he again congratulated himself that he could consult his menu, and give an unlimited order without contemplating "items."

He arrived home in high spirits, had forgotten the "slow old Bothnia," the whirl of travel, the fatigue of sight-seeing, the surfeit of paintings, etc., and was overflowing with recitals of his new-found, Old World, experience, and said, " We must go over in a year or two. I want you to hear the Bern organ! that, alone, is worth crossing the ocean for! "

CHAPTER TWENTY-SECOND.

IN the following *Olla Podrida* from numerous anecdotes which I have heard the doctor relate (some at his own expense), are a few which I venture to repeat.

He had rendered some surgical service to one of his confrères belonging to another school. Still partly under the influence of ether, his brother doctor said in a confidential tone—"Gunn! you are not such a fool, if you do wear long hair."

In regard to his hair, he often threatened to cut it off or *shave* it, and it required all his wife's diplomacy to prevent its sacrifice.

This recalls an incident of his earlier professional days:—Dr. P.——, an old resident physician of Detroit (a retired army officer), was singularly opposed to the connection of non-residents with the University. Outwardly courteous, there was a latent antagonism that led to an unwarrantable and undignified attack upon the then only non-resident, in one of the papers, in which this paragraph appeared:—"This erudite Professorial Apollo drives a parti-colored horse with white flowing mane and tail, up and down the avenue, and curls his hair with curling tongs!" To which Doctor Gunn replied, " 'The head and front of mine offending' is a parti-colored horse! My venerable critic, much to my regret, is right in regard to the diversified color of my horse; but for the objectionable kinks in my hair, Nature, alone, is responsible, and I can hardly pluck it out to mollify him."

There had been a sharp controversy between the "Peninsular Journal" and the "Medical Independent," before Doctor Gunn became editor of the latter. A complimentary contemporary noticing its editorial changes, among other comments says:—"We thought when seeing Professor Gunn's name upon the cover of the 'Independent,' that resort had been made to the ordinary custom in *military* practice, of turning captured *guns* upon the enemy from whom they were taken, and we opened the book rather expecting some *home shots*. But we were mistaken, and found the gun had been christened 'Peace-Maker!' Henceforth we opine the war is ended."

The doctor in reply says:—"Whether we shall deserve the honorable title of 'Peace-Maker' the future will alone determine." In this connection Dr. Gunn in his Salutatory, gives his opinion on the subject of controversies:—

"SALUTATORY.—With the present number, the subscriber assumes joint proprietor- and editorship of the Medical Independent; and before retiring behind the editorial 'we,' he wishes, even at the risk of incurring the charge of egotism, to appear before the fraternity and his readers, in the first person singular.

"From the sixth number, the Independent has been involved with a contemporary, in a controversy, which has partaken largely of a personal nature. This controversy has been regretted by many, including warm adherents of the journal and members of the profession at large, and has frequently prompted the inquiry, so often provoked on other occasions, 'Why *will* Doctors quarrel?'

"The harmony of the legal profession, forensic as it is in its practice, is cited as presenting a striking contrast to the quarrelsome proclivities of our own. While, from my relation to both parties, I refrain from interference, I remark in reference to the general subject, that the answer and explanation lie patent upon the surface of facts presented in the contrast. From the nature of the practice, men destitute of ability and acquirement cannot rise in the legal profession. In whatever specialty the aspirant may engage, merit alone will advance him. The opinions of the counselor are to be tried by those of counsel enlisted in opposing interests. The persuasion and logic of the advocate, are met by their like. Legal opinions and logical deductions are to be weighed in the scales of impartial justice, and persuasive or peremptory eloquence in the influence it exerts, registers a just estimate of its force. Hence, in the law, men soon find their true level, and standing competitors feel themselves peers. Mutual respect, confidence and harmony are the natural results.

"With the medical profession it is widely different. In practice, the acquirement and skill of competitors are not brought in contact. Medical practice is a broad field, in which truth and falsehood, education and ignorance, refinement and vulgarity, dignity and buffoonery are often competitors for patronage, and not infrequently the worse leading the better in the strife. The public are not capable of judging medical doctrines nor medical men; hence the crudities, the vagaries and the delusions which infest not only the public, but at times even the profession itself. It is not unjust to say that all these find lodgment in all classes of society, not excluding the most cultivated and intellectual.

"Such being the case, it is not strange that in the ranks of legitimate medicine, where may be found men of almost every grade of endowment and acquirement, competitors should frequently chance to be men unworthy, morally or mentally, of each other. Nor are the consequences more strange: distrust, jealousy and contempt naturally follow, and where these qualities prevail, bitterness soon reigns. Misunderstandings, misinterpretations and aversion to explanations are frequent, and thus when controversies arise, they are apt to assume a personal and bitter character.

"In the existing state of the profession, such controversies are not altogether unproductive of good. To be deplored they certainly are, not alone from the attitude in which the public beholds us, but also from the fact that they cultivate a spirit, which, from the peculiar nature of matters already explained, is but too prone to manifest itself. Still they are not destitute of good results. Entertaining these views, and perhaps not deploring controversy as deeply as some of my medical brethren, I shall, notwithstanding, strive to avoid its tumult. I shall not be the aggressor in personalities, but will manifest, should occasion require, even a laudable forbearance in this respect, and trust that the hand thus fraternally extended, may meet with a response prompted by fraternal hearts.

"Books, writings, public teachings and existing evils are, I conceive, legitimate subjects of criticism, and in the discharge of editorial duties, I should deem myself highly culpable in shrinking from their full performance. Adopting as a motto, 'Full and exact justice to all men,' I will zealously labor in the editorial field, for the true interests and progress of medicine."

Later on, when the "Peninsular Journal" "poured out of its editorial Pitcher" some of these aggressive personalities, they were cleverly answered by the doctor.

A well known physician of Michigan, thoroughly familiar with the circumstances, has furnished the following paragraphs with regard to the founding of the new medical journal :—

"It is difficult if not impossible, at this distance of time, and after the radical changes in the mode of thought of the medical profession, to appreciate the new era which the establishment of the 'Medical Independent' hailed.

"A few years previously a colleague of Professor Gunn, in the Medical Department of the University, had pronounced an address before one of the medical classes which demanded in no uncertain terms, advance to a higher plane of professional thought and endeavor.

The leading dictum was: The Science of Medicine should be looked upon and studied like all other sciences, and that portion which did not stand the test should be mercilessly discarded. The doctrines of the address provoked much of acrid controversy and serious comment among the medical societies.

"There was at that time living in Detroit an accomplished and brilliant young physician, Dr. L. G. Robinson, who at first was strongly inclined to look upon the author as almost if not altogether a professional heretic. Swayed by this feeling he introduced to the Detroit Medical Society a series of resolutions demanding of the medical faculty of the University whether or no they indorsed the 'paradoxes and dogmas' contained in the address. Without entering into details, it is sufficient to say, that within a brief period, Dr. Robinson himself announced his full adhesion to the, at that time, novel proposition that medical science is not exempt from the crucial test of Baconian induction. It may be noted, that a few years after, the author of the disturbing address was elected President of the State Medical Society of Michigan on the issues therein provoked.

"In full accordance with these principles, an effort was initiated to have the Medical Department of the University removed from Ann Arbor to Detroit so that students could be taught practically as well as theoretically. To this result the 'Medical Independent' lent its support, but as yet this desirable object has not been effected. Nevertheless the establishment of the 'Independent' proved a most powerful factor in awakening the profession of the state to a wider and profounder comprehension of great underlying principles. It sparkled with contributions from the leading writers, observers, and thinkers of the state. When ultimately it was merged in the compromise journal which succeeded it, a neutrality was secured which placated the Ann Arbor coterie, but with a loss to the profession of the ablest organ of its highest thoughts and its supremest deserts "

In looking over the pages of the "Independent" the following excerpt from Doctor Gunn's comments on a surgical case is taken as giving a perspicuous idea of his general views with regard to the value of so-called medicinal treatment, not only in external but also in internal disease—doctrines not then generally accepted, although now almost universally prevalent:—

" The above case affords a striking illustration of the evil effects of ill-applied and profuse medication. There is not, in my mind, the least doubt that recovery would have followed entire abstinence from medicine, and the continuation of generous diet. The free suppuration which followed the inflamed condition of the wound, was exhausting in its tendency, and called for supporting treatment; it received the reverse; the prostrating effects of the medicine favored the formation of pus, and thus, in addition to its direct tendency, contributed to exhaust the patient. It was a direct and absolute agent for evil. There was no indication for *medicine;* yet how few have the courage to say as much to a patient!

" 'I felt some hesitancy in putting forth that book.' The distinguished author of ' New Remedies ' spake thus in reference to this work. The reason assigned for this hesitancy was, that he feared that he was encouraging the disposition manifested by the profession to administer, and the people to take too much medicine. There is no doubt as to the fact, there is too much medicine swallowed. There is also no doubt that physicians prescribe too much of the same article, and too little of that which pertains to diet and regimen. They rely too implicitly on the supposed curative properties of medicines.

"The reason of the disposition alluded to by Dr. Dunglison, and which he feared he was encouraging, lies in an altogether mistaken idea of the relation

which a medicine bears to a disease, and to the recuperative process. I unhesitatingly make the assertion,
that medicine never *cured* disease—that there is no
direct relation between a medicine and a disease—that
there is no mysterious *curative tendency* in any medicine. There is only one curative tendency, and that
lies in the organism—it is innate with the being—it is
a necessary part of its existence and undoubtedly is the
same force which tends to preserve it, and presides over
its unceasing changes—it is everywhere present in
organic life—it heals over an abrasion in the plant and
closes up a wound in a man—it enables the drooping
flower to revive and bloom afresh, and the crowning
work of creation to arouse and throw off a syncope.

"The means of calling this curative force into action
are manifold, but a cure is effected *only through its
agency.* The most that a medicine can do is to arouse
it to action in some instances, and favor its operation
in others. There is no direct relation between an inflammation and the lancet, or tart. antim., or verat. vir.,
or cal. and opium; yet any of these agents may not
only be useful but absolutely indispensable, by so
affecting the system as to favor the operation of this
venerable but much ignored ' *vis medicatrix naturæ.*'
We bleed for acute pleuritis, yet who will say that
there is a *direct* relation between the lancet and the

disease? A recovery follows, but who will say that the loss of twenty ounces of blood *cured* the inflammation? It simply so *impressed* the system as to favor the curative effort of nature—an effort that will oftentimes be successful without aid, though at others imperatively requiring it, and failing in its absence.

"The antagonism between quinine and an ague, would seem to realize a direct relation between a medicine and a disease—in other words, the idea of a specific; but a strong mental emotion may accomplish the same result. An old pioneer in this state suffered for many successive years from an ague, which quinine finally failed to cure. Other remedies, also, were at last powerless, and in spite of all medication, each alternate day brought its paroxysm of chill, fever and perspiration. Pursuing his way along a woodland path one day, his ague surprised him an hour earlier than usual. Hurrying home as fast as his shivering, chattering condition would permit, his progress was suddenly interrupted by the appearance in his path of a huge black bear. For a moment the two stood gazing at each other, the man perfectly paralyzed with fear, after which the bear trotted off, leaving the patient minus the chill, with the sweating stage fully developed, without the intervention of the fever. The disease was effectually broken up, and there was no return of it for several years. What was the relation between a dose of living black bear and the ague? Direct? or indirect? Did it operate as a specific? or, through the *impressibility* of the system?

"Within the past few years many undoubted recoveries from pulmonary phthisis have resulted from the free use of *oleum jecoris aselli*, with and without brandy, and with appropriate regimen. Do such results indicate a *direct* relation between the remedies and the malady? Fat beef, butter and good ale will succeed as often, and the explanation is to be found in the physiology of nutrition, and the pathology of the disease. And in this connection may be expressed the belief, that if the various forms of cancer are ever cured, it will be through influences brought to bear upon the function of nutrition.

"Divest medicine of the idea of its *mysterious* relation to disease, and the seductive charm which leads to its continual administration is lost, and much less will be exhibited. When the object is to restore suspended or impaired functions, or to alter and improve the process of nutrition, by supplying or withholding certain elements, and so ordering the regimen as to derive the greatest possible good from such elements, medication will become definite, certain and moderate.

"If the object is to effect a given result by operating on the *impressibility* of the system, medication will be so conducted as simply to produce a desired effect, leaving to nature the real *curative* work. Too much medicine is administered by continuing its exhibition too long. It is comparatively easy to learn when and how to commence giving medicine, but hard to learn when to leave off—so hard indeed that some men seem never to learn the lesson. There is no course more injurious to the real benefit to be derived from medicine, than the blind and unphilosophical exhibition of remedies *by the clock*. Doses should be repeated, or not, according to the effect produced, and not according to the time which has elapsed. But I forbear, and while I express an abiding faith in remedial measures, confess to a growing dread of hyper-medication."

18

CHAPTER TWENTY-THIRD.

UNFORTUNATELY for Doctor Gunn, a book entitled "Gunn's Domestic Medicine" was largely attributed to him. One day when he received one of these "infernal letters," as he called them, asking about his book, Dr. A—— who was present remarked facetiously, "Gunn, you ought to have a royalty on that work! half the people who buy it think it's *yours*."

During a convention of the American Medical Association in one of the southern cities, standing on the gallery of one of the hotels, was a group of medical men. A physician standing apart with Dr. H——, of St. Louis, pointing to the doctor, asked, "Who is that?" "Why, it's Gunn! don't you know him? he always wears some d—— odd thing on his head, but he is a capital fellow, and I will introduce you."

Peddlers in any form were his aversion. One of these itinerant fiends had just handed in a package, when the vender was surprised before half way down the walk by his package, which came whirling after him. On the fly-leaf of one of his books is written,

" Bought of the Author to get quit of him." With inward amusement, evidently at the recollection, he said:—"To-day in my office was the smartest book-agent I ever saw! at least the fellow discovered how to manage me. He knew just what to say, and how to say it. The very last thing I wanted was his book, but he *talked* and I *subscribed!*"

Occasionally when on horse-back, he was the subject of speculation. Riding slowly one day in the vicinity of three small "Emerald Islanders," the pluckiest accosted him:—"Say now, Mister, ain't yez a doctor?" Second rough Emerald with disgust:—"Can't ye see he ain't no doctor? fellers don't look that way when they're *doctors!*" This equivocal compliment was followed by the third, who, staring with wide-eyed wonder and equally puzzled in his diagnosis, shouted after him:—"Mister, why the h—— can't ye *tell* a feller?" This rough incident perhaps needs extenuation, but I can never forget the way the doctor told it, and,——

" I *laugh* that I may not *weep*."

Doctor Gunn was exceptionally kind to children under his surgical care. He was greatly interested in a young patient, Winifred D——, who usually came to his office and frequently brought him flowers.

A bisque basket of lovely design, filled with the choicest roses, was sent to him one Christmas morning. Admiring the beautiful gift, which bore no name, he said with feeling, "It must be from my little *flower patient.*"

A child that had been cruelly burned he worked over for more than two years; she was a small philosopher. Though her beauty was destroyed she counted it as nothing and was always cheerful and happy.

A thoughtful friend sent me the following article by Dr. Rachel Hickey. In connection with the doctor, she mentions this unrepining and unfortunate little sufferer:——

"In our profession we meet some of the best men in the world, those who rival women in tenderness and patience, yea, excel many of them, and yet lack no manly trait. Such was the lamented Dr. Moses Gunn. I came in daily contact with him when I was head nurse at the Presbyterian Hospital for three months.

"Among our patients was a burned girl, Annie P——. This great, busy, skilled surgeon would allow no one but himself to dress little Annie. Every afternoon punctual to the minute, he would make his appearance, sometimes in his riding-suit, looking like a prince of Arthur's Round Table. His proud, perfectly erect carriage, his beautiful white curls, his riding boots and spurs were the admiration of all. Annie looked for his coming as the event of the day. She ran to meet him, took his hand, and they chatted together as two children. When the material was ready he would take her on his knee and say, 'Now, little Annie,' in such a tender, cheerful way that it made a lasting impression on me. Once he forgot and spoke in her presence of some little operation he intended making. At her cry of terror, he folded her in his arms and comforted her as few mothers could have done.

"He was just to women, just and nothing more. If they did well he gave them full credit; if they were inefficient he made no secret of the fact. It has been the custom at Rush, our oldest and wealthiest medical college, and the one with which his name is associated, to have questions sent down during a lecture, to be answered by the professor at its close. One of the slips sent to Dr. Gunn read:—'What do you think of women in medicine?' The answer was something as follows: —'Gentlemen, a few years ago, I should not have hesitated for a reply. I was spending a month or so north, trying to get rest and change to prepare myself for the winter term here, my private practice and my not easy duties at the County Hospital. My feelings are not to be described when I was informed by letter that my assistant at the hospital for my coming service was to be a woman. I was furious. If I could have seen the Commissioners I would have resigned instantly. I knew some of my cases there were to be difficult and interesting, and I did not want their success hazarded by placing them in a woman's charge. But I could do nothing at such a distance. Time cooled my wrath a little. On my return, I decided to see that woman and make her conscious of her inability. But, gentlemen, I never had such an assistant before; I never have had such an one since.' He referred to Dr. Mary E. Bates, the first woman to serve at this hospital."

CHAPTER TWENTY-FOURTH.

DOCTOR GUNN was the soul of punctuality, you could count upon him to the minute; his work was arranged and mapped out; even when in general practice he was seldom late to dinner. This point of punctuality brings me to an amusing though by no means an exceptional circumstance. We were having a very good time at dinner when a written message was handed to the doctor to "Come in haste." He pondered it a moment, then lifted up his voice:—"*How in the name of all that's holy do people manage to get bones in their throats at such unseasonable hours?*" With drollery his daughter replied, "Papa, probably if they had known you were at dinner, they would have *managed* to get the bone in afterward." This ludicrous remark, taken together with his own, raised a peal of laughter, amidst which with a broad smile he left the table and responded to the call.

The doctor's orderly habits, like his punctuality, were observed in his home, He disliked getting accustomed to finding things in new places. In a

jocose, half-earnest way he would assert:—"If I could,
I would have every piece of furniture in this room
made to fit some place and have it fastened there. God
be praised that no one can turn the *bed* upside down!"
He responded with as much alacrity to the ring of a
small rising bell as if a life depended upon it. He
seldom failed to hear this summons; if he did, I informed him in less than a minute, that the bell had
rung! Starting up from a sound sleep he would say
with alert, anxious avidity, and a boyish freshness
which was both amusing and attractive, *"Why didn't
you tell me sooner?"*

Sometimes I drove with him when he made professional visits on the borders of the city.   I had learned
to be prompt; yet he would invariably say on these
occasions, "Be ready   .   .   .   don't keep
me waiting."   The pleasant, cheerful way he pronounced the diminutive for my name, was in itself a
sufficient incentive never to keep him waiting.

One day on the outskirts of the city he left me to
act as hitching-post—not a coveted position. I usually
required the horse, or horses to be tied, so that in case
anything *should happen*, I might be at liberty to jump
out.   On this particular occasion I concluded that
driving would be less monotonous, but discovered, soon

after starting, a ditch on either side of the road which deterred me from attempting to turn round. His call finished, he came out and discovered his horses, vehicle and hitching-post half a mile from the spot. The only way he could reach them was by walking over the muddy road. After hearing my story (I wondered he was not cross!), he said good naturedly, "I think hereafter I shall trust to an inanimate post, that will not serve me the trick of driving *half-way* to Englewood— *to find a good place to turn round.*"

Doctor Gunn's mechanical ability was exhibited in various directions. Many of his surgical appliances were made according to his own ideas of excellence or convenience. Some of these instruments he originated, and others he improved. For a number of years he had tried in different cities, both at home and abroad, to replace a pair of light spurs. Being unsuccessful, he asked W——, his eldest son, who inherited some genius in the same direction, to design and carve a model from which a pair could be cast. W—— made and carved the design, but his father, wishing some little alteration, concluded to make another model himself. These spurs when finished were heavily plated with gold and when not in use were kept on the doctor's dressing-bureau, and are now souvenirs of inestimable value.

Desiring a model for some purpose, he called his colored man into his office, and without further preliminary said:—"Alex., I have noticed that you have a pretty fair-shaped leg; sit down and let me take a cast of it." The man had lived with the doctor eighteen years, and had great confidence in him, but not entirely comprehending, said:—"Doctor, I'm puffectly willin' to put my leg or any thing else to your sarvice, so as only you don't *cut it off*." The doctor laughingly: "No, Alex., we won't do anything so bad as that. I should feel worse than you would to have you lose a leg in my service."

A number of years before this another member of his family was temporarily made a martyr to his cause. He was on his way to Marshall to make some operation on the eye. I accompanied him to visit an old school-friend in the interval. He was young and ambitious of success. When well on our journey he said: "Let me put a little belladonna in your eye." He had an insinuating manner which usually prevailed. The drop, if not too much, certainly was not too little; it produced a dazed, unmanageable vision, making everybody in the car look queer. This I communicated to the doctor with some alarm. Taking from his vest a tiny mirror, with a glance which I did not then fully understand, he said "Look!" adding, "It is nothing; the peculiar sensation will soon pass away." I looked! and was sufficiently horrified to please him, but he never again (to my knowledge) experimented on me.

I remember his relating with amusement an incident of his earlier practice:—A bright woman from the country came to consult him about a minor operation and where it should be performed. His answer was, "You had better come to the office, my time is too valuable to go into the country for so small an operation, unless you are regardless of expense." She came to his office. The operation was nearly finished, when she noticed that he was waiting. Looking up with great apparent concern, she exclaimed, "Doctor, what *is* the matter?" "Nothing, my good woman; don't worry, I am obliged to wait a moment." Humorously, she retorted: "O! I don't mind, only it is such a pity that a man should be kept waiting by *any woman* when his *time is so valuable as yours!*"

I noticed in one of the doctor's journals a paragraph written by him, thirty years ago, when tracheotomy was considered a more doubtful and far less successful operation than it now is. He says:—"There is perhaps no operation which is more dreaded than tracheotomy.

The class of patients who require it, the gravity of the cause which demands it, together with the uncertainty of vascular distribution, all conspire to make the operation one of the most vexatious in the whole range of operative surgery."

He was called in consultation nearly eighteen years ago, to perform tracheotomy on a child that was supposed to be dying. The physicians informed the parents that the success of the operation was extremely doubtful, and that the child might die under it. The father despairingly asked Doctor Gunn what possibility there was of saving his little daughter. "About as much," he replied, "as there would be of drawing the Opera House at a lottery." It was a moment of intense solicitude, but the result was quickly ascertained, when the doctor joyfully announced "We have won the Opera House!" This incident was told to me by relatives of the family. For weeks the child was prostrated, but recovered, and now rejoices in being a beautiful young woman.

At one time the doctor was devoted to astronomy, and had fitted up on his grounds an observatory with a fine telescope. He had been up several times watching the sidereal heavens, when just before sunrise, he rushed in and exclaimed, excitedly, "I have seen Mercury! Copernicus died without the sight!" One of his greatest pleasures, was showing to his family and friends the stars and planets. Some were fortunate in beholding Saturn in the period of his glory, when the planet "like a magnificent golden ball was engirdled by its ring of golden light." Young people visited the observatory, ostensibly to view the heavenly bodies, but their speculations were speedily merged into the more earthly interests of their own.

Sometimes on clear moonless nights, when we were on the gallery, he would point out radiant stars that vied with Venus in brilliancy. Each new acquaintance made with these glowing worlds seemed to bring us nearer to the vast glittering panorama which filled our minds with wonder at the ethereal splendors and ennobling works of God.

Most of his leisure hours were spent in reading French or German. He spoke German well and fluently, but, taking up French later in life, he never quite compassed its colloquial velocity. At the Grand Hotel in Paris, giving an elaborate order in French to a waiter who spoke fair English and to whom orders had always been given in English, the astonished garçon did not refrain from saying, "Monsieur le Docteur speaks well ze French!" The doctor said to me in a low, amused voice, "Had the fellow known how long I planned the sentence before reeling off the words with so much volubility, he would have been less surprised."

The doctor's fondness for roses has been mentioned; he always brought me the *first* and the *last* rose of the season. He had an inexpensive and easily managed green-house in Detroit perfectly adapted for raising flowers; while his conservatory with which he wrestled in Chicago, was both expensive and troublesome. It enabled him, however, to protect and preserve some fine plants which had been transported from Detroit, among them *one* that was endeared to us by former fond associations. A beautiful rubber-tree, also, grew to an immense size. The doctor gave much of his individual attention to this conservatory, but it was finally abandoned and converted into something more generally agreeable and available.

Every few years he made additions and alterations in his house (an old one), which he likened to an "absorbing sponge." It required some ingenuity to improve the house, but he succeeded in making the interior home-like and attractive, much more attractive than the external appearance of the dwelling. He was fond of watching mechanics engaged about their work on the premises, and would contemplate the laying of a brick wall with as much interest as he would a fresco. Sometimes he would correct workmen when they were

going wrong (who should have known better than he);
a few may have been annoyed, but the majority who
understood that he watched to see their skill, and not
to criticise, were pleased.

Doctor Gunn gloried in self-respect, if I may use
the term, but he was not vain; he never made himself
unnecessarily conspicuous in public places. He facetiously would say:—"If you will bring your celebrities
to me, I will *look* at them, but don't expect me to *run
after* them."

A friend once said to him:—"Doctor, why is it you
so seldom visit your patients, or attend your clinics
when on horse-back?" adding—"you never look so
well as you do in a riding-suit." His answer was:—
"In the first place it is not the thing to do; in the
second, spurs are inconvenient in an operating-room."
He never went to either of these places wearing
riding-boots, unless it was to give me the use of his
other horses.

He was fond of dinners and social visiting, but
abhorred large parties, for which, he said, "He had to
dress just as he was *ready for bed.*" He combined
strength and tenderness, and although sometimes impatient, still had great forbearance. His home was the
most attractive place to him, and it was singular that
upon the festivities of Christmas Eve he entered with

more intense enjoyment than any member of his family.   On these occasions, directly after dinner his boyish effervescence commenced, and if we were delayed, he would call up to us cheerily, "*Come, bring on your bears!*"

His appreciation of a good story was proverbial, and though he would laugh heartily over what was simply broad, he had an utter contempt for any thing that was low or degrading.

Mrs. L——, a warm and intimate friend, in some recollections of the doctor, says:—

"I remember he would express himself strongly on some subjects; but his honor and caution in speaking of people was a trait I shall ever hold in the highest esteem.   His charity and gentle judgment of human nature, and silence on many occasions when censure seemed justifiable, proved to be more than prudence, and must be construed into kindness and not austerity.

"He upon one occasion wrote a letter introducing to a high official, a lady of his acquaintance.   She met with a courteous reception from the gentleman, who upon reading the letter, said:—'O yes! I know Dr. Gunn well; he is a famous surgeon; I had the honor to

shoe his horses in Detroit when we both lived there.'
Then followed an eulogy truly genuine. The hearty
enjoyment of the doctor on hearing a recital of the
interview, was gratifying, and I may here add, that
the generous reception of the situation by the official,
was only equalled by such honest words of appreciation
and praise as would come from one whole-souled man
to another.

"Dr. Gunn was a good story-teller, and enjoyed his
own *bon mots* as much as did his listeners. He was
very clever in telling a story at his wife's expense
(though one could see how thoroughly she satisfied
him). On one occasion he was about repeating an incident that some Chicago friends related to them on a
homeward trip together from New Orleans; when Mrs.
G—— said, 'Doctor! there are two versions to that
story.' 'Yes' he replied, 'I am going to tell mine.'
And continued:—

"'Directly in front of our Chicago friends at the
other end of the sleeper, sat a man and woman who regarded us with interest, the woman with unflagging
zeal. At length, turning to her husband, in an audible
whisper she said, "John, do you see that old fellow with
gray hair?" "Certainly, what's the matter of him?"
"Nothing, only he has just been getting married!"
"Why, what makes you think so?" "*Think! I know*

it! that's the way men always act to their *second* wives."
Looking sharply at my wife he said, "Well! I wonder
when the old fellow was about it why he didn't marry
a young woman!"   Our friends were on the borders of
lunacy in suppressing the fact from John, that the
"old fellow" had never but *once* had such an opportunity.'   With a quizzical glance the narrator then
turned towards his wife and joined in the uproarious
laughter that followed.

"I remember one evening when some friends were
about leaving that an allusion was made to his wife's
size.   I recall the irresistible twinkle of his eye, and a
significant way he had of rubbing the side of his nose
when about or after telling anything comical.   'Small!'
he repeated, 'Well, she is all I can manage; and I
sometimes feel like little Heber C—— when urged to
go up to a young colt! "Heber," said his brother, "why
don't you go up and *pat* the little fellow?"   "Because I
had rather not."   "Why! you are'nt afraid of a *little—
bit — of a colt like that*, are you?"   "Well—yes—I'm
pretty 'fraid.   I tell you, Charlie, the *littler* they are,
the *kickier* they be!"   To this story the doctor's laugh
added keener zest, and I thought his hearers would
never get out alive."

CHAPTER TWENTY-FIFTH.

IN referring to our tour abroad—one of the pleasantest journeys in our lives, these recollections may
be of small import to others, but are full of interest to
me. It would be an act of supererogation to attempt
to inform any one concerning such a tour, yet the
differences, or more probably the similarities, in the
individual experiences of such a journey may be appreciated. For this reason I have ventured to give a
brief *resumé* of some details of the tour as penned by
the doctor to his children.

In March, 1881, two years after Doctor Gunn's first
trip to Europe, we went over in the Waesland, an old
Cunarder that had been spliced and strengthened,
making it the best of the Belgian steamers in the Red
Star Line. The doctor writes to W—— : "There were
but ten passengers on board, the boat most comfortable,
our state-room large, and the table excellent.   .   .

"The first Friday out, our fore-topmast, though
made of iron, was broken off by the force of the wind
and lost!   .   .   .   We landed at Antwerp

just two weeks after leaving New York, heavy head-winds and a rough passage having prolonged our voyage.

"Antwerp is interesting, from the Musée Plantin down to dogs or milk-carts, or the Flemish peasants in gay attire who nimbly walk the streets in wooden shoes. Everywhere in this old town are reminders of Rubens; here are his best paintings as well as some of his worst. We were attracted by one of his pictures in the beautiful Church of St. Jacques, in which are represented portraits of himself and all the members of his own family." .   .   .   .   .

The next five months found us traveling over a part of the ground that had before captivated the doctor; and in addition, through Italy and Austria. He writes: "Over a garden of a country we reached Bruxelles, not to see her 'Beauty and her Chivalry' but to find one of the most delightful cities in Europe, a small duplicate of Paris." .   .   .   .   .

In the picturesque town of Heidelberg, at the pleasant Hotel de l' Europe, we were lodged. The doctor again enjoyed visiting the Schloss and showing me the old magnificent ruin of fortress and palace com-bined. I recall the picture while standing in one of the towers that looked down on the red roofs of the town, when he referred to Longfellow's description of the castle, and cannot refrain from giving a few lines from it:—

"High and hoar on the forehead of the Jettenbühl stands the Castle of Heidelberg. Behind it rise the oak-crested hills of the Geisberg and the Kaiserstuhl, and in front, from the broad terrace of masonry, you can almost throw a stone upon the roofs of the town, so close do they lie beneath. Above this terrace rises the broad front of the chapel of Saint Udalrich. On the left stands the slender octagon tower of the horologe, and on the right a huge round tower, battered and shattered by the mace of war, shores up with its broad shoulders the beautiful palace and garden-terrace of Elizabeth, wife of the Pfalzgraf Frederick.

"In the valley below flows the rushing stream of the Neckar. Close from its margin, on the opposite side, rises the mountain of All Saints, crowned with the ruins of a convent, and up the valley stretches the mountain-curtain of the Odenwald."   .   .

The doctor again writes:—"From . Cologne, by steamer, we went up the Rhine; the legendary castles and crags, the fortresses, old ruins and abbeys enhance the glory of the Rhine.   .   .   We stopped over at Remagen, a small town connected with the wonderful legend of St. Apollinaris, where, opposite St. Martin's (now St. Apollinaris') Church, the ship containing his holy relics 'suddenly stood still!' . .

. . We took a carriage to the celebrated spring and saw the extensive bottling establishment that exports millions of bottles of Apollinaris water to the United States every year." . . . .

The doctor was not much given to seeking after palaces, but in this weakness he was lenient with me. He was interested in the Royal Palace at Stuttgart, and in two suburban retreats belonging to the King of Wurtemburg. These villas were reached by a delightful drive over the Eastern Hills.

In his next letter he says:—"From Pisa to Genoa, the last half of the distance skirts the sea-coast, passing through innumerable tunnels, ever and anon coming out upon the loveliest sea views of the Mediterranean. Genoa is a peculiar old city; we drove some distance to the Campo Santo, which must be seen to be appreciated. The expression given to marble in the sculptured groups here, is indeed wonderful." . . . .

Speaking of the Old Pinakothek, in one of his letters, he says:—"There are more pictures here than we could contemplate properly in a year. There are at least an hundred of Rubens! Your mother scolds about his paintings, but I usually find her lingering in their vicinity." . . . . .

In Munich, when going to and from the Maximilianeum, and when crossing and re-crossing the bridge at the termination of the Maximilians-Strasse, the doctor called my attention to the "Iser rolling rapidly," and if I remember rightly, there was a school-boy declamation on the spot.

He further writes from Venice:—"We left our heaviest baggage at the Hotel Des Quatre Saisons, until our return from Italy, which when we reached it was anything but 'Sunny.' Our first stopping-place was Verona, one of the queerest of queer old towns, with an amphitheatre as interesting as the Coliseum at Rome.

"On our arrival in Venice it was novel to be met at the depot and from thence conducted in a gondola through the Grand Canal (their boulevard) to our hotel, where for the first hour your mother never moved from the window, but watched the graceful and dextrous gondoliers as they shot the pointed prows of their gondolas past each other with scarcely the width of a knife-blade between. . . . . .

"When we reached Milan the exposition was in full force, to which we gave half a day. Silks and velvets were the great novelty to us,—large, soft, yellow skeins, from the fibre as it is unwound from cocoons to the perfected fabric in every shade. The Cathedral, near the Hotel de Ville, we often visited, and drove, as every one does, to see Leonardo da Vinci's fresco of the 'Last Supper' on the walls of an old suppressed convent, now used as cavalry barracks. The painting is unattractive and defaced.   .   .   .   .   .

"Como was the end of our rail journey, then by steamer to Menaggio over as picturesque a body of water as there is perhaps on the globe. Here in delightful rooms overlooking the lake, we saw the snow-capped mountains opposite and at their feet counted six different villages. When we arrived at Hotel du Parc, which is in a suppressed monastery at Lugano, the scene was almost as beautiful as the last."   .   .

A detour was made to Bern, where in the morning we saw the bears which the doctor had called humbugs, . and said that Old Grizzly, the hermit of Union Park, could take in at a mouthful. In the evening we heard the organ. There were no strangers that day in Bern to make up a purse for the organist; the T——'s had accompanied us from Lucerne. Mr. T—— and the doctor therefore carried out the enterprise.

Who that ever entered that dim Cathedral in the dusk of a summer night, can forget the hour? Unlighted — save by a solitary lamp that cast its melancholy rays over what seemed a spirit, evoking from the organ a low rippling murmur, weird cadences, —that now and again resolved themselves into purest melody—then plunging into chaos and surging along until launched into that wonderful "Storm" electrifying the listener when reaching the climax of warring elements! Now comes a partial lull—then the distant, reverberating thunder—the wind—and the rain-fall.

Sweet, clear, and full rises the vox humana! one unaccustomed to this stop, almost believes it to be the note of a real human voice, penetrating through and above the storm! Sitting as we were, in that sombre old Cathedral nearly alone, it was an hour for inspiration; such an hour comes but once into a life-time. Yes! It *was* worth crossing the ocean for!

From Naples the doctor writes to C——:—"We have just received your first letter dated almost a month ago.   .   .   .   It was forwarded to us at Venice, then to Rome, and finally reached us here. We came to Naples on the 29th ult. and shall return to Rome to-morrow. Yesterday was fixed upon for an ascent of Vesuvius, but a heavy rain prevented, and all this morning the weather has been unpropitious; consequently we must leave Naples without looking into the crater. The old drone has steamed and smoked lazily since we came, much to my disgust, but last evening he deigned to light up several times and three times shot up brilliantly, but in the course of an hour went to sleep again.   I fear I shall get no more manifestations from the old rascal.   .   .   .   .

"On Monday we went to Pompeii, which is fascinating in its terrible calamity.   Tuesday we took a long drive—in a carriage large enough for the whole family—and wished many times you were all in it.   .   .   .   .   We have not more than half 'done' the Museum, which has claimed a portion of three days.   .   .   .   .   From our window we overlook the bay—distant Capri—a portion of the city, and up at his moody Volcanic Majesty.   It is a grand and charming outlook.

"A strange city is Naples, where elegance and squalor not only jostle one another but are completely interwoven on all sides.   The squalid indulge in oranges and filth at the same time; beggars pester you at every turn and parade their misfortunes with a tender commiseration, while another class of pests seek to render you some unrequired and undesired assistance, and then claim a recompense.   .   .   .   .   But enough of this. I will finish this letter at Rome."

.   .   .   .   "I will not attempt even an epitome of what we have done and seen in Rome, the vast center of magnificent ruins, antiquities and art. . . . . Yesterday we dined with Randolph Rogers and his family. . . . . At his studio saw his wonderfully beautiful Lost Pleiad, and Nydia with which you are familiar. Either of these sculptures will immortalize his name." . .

Later, to W———:— . . . . "We were joined by the T———s in Rome and went together by carriage over the unrivalled St. Gotthard. It was a three days' journey; the second day we arrived at the 'Bellevue,' a large, clean hotel just outside the village of Andermatt, more comfortable than any we have yet encountered on the Continent." . . .

The doctor was anxious to reach the Rhone Glacier but no diligence had yet been over the Furca pass. He was informed that by driving within five miles of the glacier the remaining distance could be walked! The next morning we were provided with guide, wine, lunch, etc., and with our three faithful horses started up the mountain. Reaching the summit we found a small station beyond which we could not drive. Here we halted, and consulted as to who would go on. I was not ambitious to walk ten miles (the distance there and back) over patches of snow, but Mrs. T——— said "I am going" and pluckily followed her husband.

There was not a soul at the station; it was closed, but the driver had brought a key that opened a shelter for himself and horses. I sat in the carriage. In front from a deep gorge, towered peaks of Alps; above, below, everywhere were Alps! The stillness and solemnity was appalling! the spot was completely shut in save a path along the mountain where, hours after, I intently watched the coming of those who had gone that way. Waiting five or six hours alone, every conceivable catastrophe had gone through my mind that might happen to them or to me.

For two hours I had scanned the path; the driver had also been looking. His eye accustomed to mountain sights and distances discovered a speck; at first it appeared stationary; then it seemed to move, gradually it advanced and soon assumed the shape and proportions of a man. The men were all tall! I wondered which one it could be of the three. When the driver finally called out—"It is the Herr Doctor! *I know him*,"—I think words never sounded sweeter, than this man's "*Herr Doctor*."

Leaving the others to follow more at their leisure the doctor had hurried on. At the Glacier they found a man and a boy, who had seen no one but each other for six months! They were in charge of a hotel but had little in the way of a substantial repast to offer the pedestrians. When the others arrived, the lunch (nearly all of which remained) was speedily dispatched and in half an hour we were on our way down the mountain at such a pace that if an accident should happen an escape would be miraculous. We drove furiously through Andermatt just as the lights began to glimmer in the cottages. We were back,—and the doctor had seen the Rhone Glacier!

He writes from the Hotel de France, Vienna:—"We arrived in Vienna by way of the Danube, which is more tortuous and more turbulent than the Rhine— equally beautiful with the Austrian Alps in the distance and the castles, chateaux and convents on its banks overlooking its blue waters. We find the Austrian Capital interesting, particularly the rooms in the old Hofburg once occupied by Maria Theresa, and furnished as she left them. The crown jewels are beautiful, and numerous, and interesting in their association and traditions. There is a glamour thrown round them, that is enhanced probably by the romances of that Imperial House. . . . Dr. H——'s letter to his relatives, living at Heitzing, one of the suburbs, near the Imperial Chateau of Schönbrunn, has given us an opportunity of meeting an attractive family. One of the daughters (a young girl of engaging manners and personal beauty) accompanied us yesterday through the imperial gardens of Schönbrunn.   .   .

.   We have twice dined with Dr. W——, a young physician of Chicago, who is here for an unlimited time.   The second dinner was served in approved style in a handsome room that commanded a view of the Schotten-Ring, a pleasant point in the Ring-Strasse.

"To-day we were interested in the Fête Dieu! The retinue in the procession immediately about the emperor was composed of magnificent horses mounted by fine specimens of men, both men and horses richly caparisoned.   .   .   .   .   .

"At the Rigi we were snowbound and left with disappointment at getting no view.   .   .   .   .
Dresden we reached by the Elbe.   .   .   .   We accomplished a long drive in and about Prague, which we found ancient and strange."   .   .

"We have been three days in Berlin.   Our room at the Kaiserhof is large, with a balcony, where we sit and look out on the Zietenplatz.   .   .   .   To-day we have been to Potsdam, visited the Old Royal Palace so identified with the immortal Frederick.   While at Sans Souci we were allowed to wander about what was once his beloved and charming retreat in unmolested pleasure.   We shall go again in a day or two."   .   .

CHAPTER TWENTY-SIXTH.

URING our stay in Berlin, the Minister of the
United States, Andrew D. White, one of the most
accomplished and charming of men, invited Doctor
Gunn to be present at a "gentlemen's dinner party"
given for the Rector and Professors of the University,
some Foreign Ministers, and others interested in educa-
tional matters. The dinner was presided over by Mrs.
White, with the ease and grace for which she was proverbial, and was further made attractive by the conversation and humor of a number of the following scholarly and distinguished men:—

Dr. Hoffman, Professor of Chemistry, Rector of the
University; Professor Mommsen, Roman Historian;
Professor Peters, Zoologist and Director of the Natu-
ral History Museum; Professor Wickelhaus, Physics;
Assistant Professor Hewitt, Cornell University; Pro-
fessor Zupitza, English and Anglo-Saxon Literature;
Professor Weber, Sanscrit; Professor Helmholtz, Phys-
ics; Baron Von der Heydt; Von Schlözer, German

Minister at Washington; Curtius, Professor of Greek; Scherer, Professor of German Literature; Mr. Coleman, Secretary of Legation; Mr. Frederick D. White; Mr. Heuner, Private Secretary to the American Minister; M. Rangabe, Greek Minister, formerly Minister at Washington; Professor Wattenbach, History; Professor Geiger, Modern History; Dr. Nachtigall, African Traveller.

Writing to C—— from Paris, the doctor says:—"For reasons that have never been discovered, some friends, who had been there, advised our going to the Hôtel Dominici! We arrived in the evening, went there and remained one night; the next morning (Sunday), came here to 'The Grand.' From our rooms we look directly across on the New Opera House, which has become very familiar. It has many faults; though magnificent in some respects, it is in others, disappointing. . . . We have been to Versailles and the Trianons; shall go again on Thursday. . .

"Your mother has just informed me that a struggle is going on in her mind between the importance of "Historical Associations" and *wearing apparel!* She is sure the "associations" will ultimately get the better of the *clothes!*" . . . . .

Later he writes to W—— :—"According to my programme, this was to be the last day in Paris; or rather this was the day to journey from here to London. But we shall now remain until the fifteenth, in order to be present at the National fête which celebrates the republic—the Fourth of July of the French republicans. It occurs on the fourteenth, and for the last week Paris has been getting ready for the event. It is to be a grand show, but I suppose like all other similar fêtes, there will be no opportunity of seeing anything because of the multitude of people.

"The time for our sailing is drawing near—only about five weeks now. We must begin to calculate about letters.   .   .   .   I want to get out of Paris, for your mother, like all women, has gone mad over the shops and wants me to buy and bring home the city!"   .   :   .   .

The doctor writing from London to W—— and M—— says:—"It falls to me this time to write you the weekly letter. Our Congress is now nearly over, Tuesday next being the closing day. We have had a very successful meeting and have been hospitably received and entertained.   .   .   .   .   About three thousand doctors and surgeons congregated here from all parts of Europe and America. London re-

20

ceived us with open arms.   Receptions and excursions have been of daily occurrence."   .   .   .

"*July 17th.*—It is a quarter to ten in the evening; with you it is about four o'clock in the afternoon.   .

.   .   .   Well, we are now in the largest city on the globe! and I assure you it is in every way a grand old city.   Paris is bright, beautiful and gay—London is dingy, solid and reliable.   In the way of beauty too, London need not be afraid of her brighter neighbor.

"The Parliament Houses, St. Paul's and old Westminster Abbey are not excelled in Paris, while Hyde Park and Kensington Gardens in some respects are really finer than the Bois de Boulogne.   But the two cities cannot be compared, so different are they.   I like London, its vastness has a charm for me that I cannot describe but constantly feel.   .   .   .   .

"On the whole, we have had a very good time in this great city, but I shall be glad to get back to that *model of modesty*——Chicago!

"It is my intention to remain here until the tenth of August, in the meantime making a little trip to Warwick and Stratford-on-Avon.   Then go to Edinburgh and take a short tour in Scotland, after which we shall reach Liverpool in time to sail on the eighteenth.   .   .   .   .   .   I hope we shall soon all be together in the old snuggery on Calumet avenue.   .   .   .   .   .

"It is delightful to travel, but when one leaves a part of his family behind, the pleasantest part is, after all, the getting home again.   I shall be glad to come to anchor on my own ground by the first of September, hopefully sooner.   Don't expect anybody but your mother and me—for I could never *manage a dog!*"   .

.   .   .   .   .

We had been some time in London, which seemed to have neither beginning nor end, when the International Medical Congress assembled.   The transactions that came to my knowledge were conversaziones at South Kensington Museum, Guildhall, and some garden parties.   Sir James Paget gave breakfasts every day during the sessions to which he invited many of the foreign members.   Doctor Gunn had the pleasure one morning of sitting at the right or left of Lady Paget, enjoying her conversation and a superior cup of mocha at her hands.

The Baroness Burdett-Coutts was "At Home" to the Congress;—A "Garden Party" at Holly Lodge, West Hill, Highgate.   For this occasion the doctor engaged what in the rather inelegant parlance of to-day would be termed a very "swell" turnout!   Unfortunately we hardly saw—and certainly did not enjoy

the extent of our magnificence, for just before starting
the rain poured down in torrents and all our attention
was given to getting ourselves in and out of the
brougham at both ends of the journey.   In this deluge
we drove *four miles* to Holly Lodge!   On arriving,
one or more functionaries, in liveries of blue velvet and
gold, met and conducted us through an arbor of vines
outside for a moment under umbrellas, up steps leading
to a veranda, and from thence to rooms where the
"garden party" had assembled.

We were announced and received gracefully by the
amiable baroness and her handsome young husband.
The rooms were filled, but not crowded, excepting one,
where a sea of heads was visible, whose mouths were
giving their undivided attention to choice game, Veuve
Cliquot and Johannisberger.

The lodge and its appointments were perfect.   After
a time we stationed ourselves at one of the windows,
and through the mist and rain discerned rather imperfectly the magnificent extent of lawn and fine old trees,
and speculated upon the beauty of Holly Lodge on a
clear day.   We were shortly joined by Dr. M—— and
his daughter; after condoling with each other on the
unpropitious state of the weather, we proceeded to the
now partly deserted dining-room and found seats where
our predecessors had stood, and soon, like them, were

giving our "undivided attention" *to paté de foie gras,* and —— other delicacies!

We preserved a vivid remembrance of that rain, the garden party—the Baroness Burdett-Coutts—and her handsome "Young Husband!"

CHAPTER TWENTY-SEVENTH.

W E almost flew on one of the fast trains from dingy London to beautiful Edinburgh. Thirty years before, the doctor had ordered from Edinburgh a handsome Highland dress. He now hoped to get a piece of the Gunn plaid, but was obliged to have it ordered from a manufacturer and sent over.

The motion of the Britannic was so apparent without a sea, that we longed for the Waesland many times before reaching New York. The custom of making more elaborate preparations for the last dinner of the voyage obtained as usual. We were a few hundred miles out of New York, the passengers in a happy frame of mind, the tables set, and the dinner in progress, when suddenly we struck a ground-swell, or it struck us, when with a crash, the glass and china were precipitated to the cabin floor! The after-effects of a storm at St. Thomas (wherever that may be) had reached us. The tables were re-set, this time with racks; the rolling of the steamer was now stupendous!

and all were becoming anxious to get wedged into their chairs for greater security. The wonder was, how we got through that dinner! but in spite of the colossal rocking it was the merriest meal we had on board.

In the morning the ocean was apparently smooth, but the deceptive undulating waves told a different story, and if possible, the motion was worse than the night before. Gradually we got out of the swell, reached Sandy Hook after lunch, got aground in the lower bay, and reached New York late in the afternoon.

The first of September saw the doctor again ready for work; he always said he expected to die in the harness. He was extremely fond of travel and deplored the necessity that kept him so constantly employed. Later he was anxious to view the midnight sun and anticipated this pleasure in 1888, but *that journey* was denied him.

I had just finished this sketch when a little diary the doctor had kept of this tour was discovered by M—— and put into my hand. How strange that I had never seen it and that it had been overlooked so long! I chanced to open at an entry made in London on Tuesday, July 26th, 1881. The mingling sensations produced upon reading this memorandum I cannot well describe. The doctor had never seemed averse to accompanying me on any of the many shopping expeditions in the different cities, beginning as far back as Brussels. Looking through the leaves I was surprised to see how much time he had devoted to me in *shopping!* According to his amusing minutes the random statement that "Historical Associations" would ever get the supremacy over "*Clothes*," was undoubtedly one of my delusions. We had been in Paris only five days (corresponding to his diary), before the shopping mania began.

"*Tuesday, July 5th.*—Napoleon's Tomb in the morning — Siege of —— shopping in the afternoon!

"*Wednesday, July 6th.*—Shopped with my wife in the morning—Lost umbrella in the afternoon.

"*Thursday, 7th.* — No shopping — Grand day — Second visit to Versailles and Trianons—Seeing fountains play.

"*Friday, 8th.* —Morning — Louvre; Afternoon— Bois de Boulogne and Jardin d' Acclimatation.

"*Saturday, 9th.* — Hotel de Cluny — Shopped at Grands Magazins du Louvre—lunched at Palais Royal.

"*Sunday, 10th.*—A day of rest—*from Shopping!*

American Church in the morning; Boulevards—Bastille and Notre Dame in the afternoon.

"*Tuesday, 12th. — Shopped!* with Mrs. G——. Went to Opera in the evening.

"*Wednesday, 13th.—Hot! but not too hot to Shop!!*

"*Thursday, 14th.—Last day in Paris—hot! but Shopped!!*—Dined with Dr. K——. Went to Hippodrome."

From his memoranda after arriving in London there were several days of interrupted sight-seeing. Then appears the following:—

"*Tuesday, July 19th. — Shopped! — Tower — Shopped!!*

"*Wednesday, 20th.—Shopped!!!*—Horrors!!

"*Thursday, 21st.*—Westminster Abbey—St. Bartholomew's; Registered as member of Medical Congress—Then Shopped!!

"*Friday, 22nd.*—Parliament Houses—Royal Aquarium, Westminster.—Shopped on the way home !

"*Saturday, 23rd.*—Zoological Gardens—had some trouble in getting Mrs. G—— away from Jumbo!

.   .   .   .   .

"*Monday, 25th.—Shopped!*—The Mall—St. James Park—and Piccadilly—Doré Gallery—Alhambra in the evening.

"*Tuesday, 26th.—Shopped!!* to get diamonds reset and cards engraved; Horrors!!—I could fit out an expedition to the Antipodes with less *fuss* than my dear wife uses in getting a card engraved."

I never realized how uncongenial this all must have been to him. Sometimes I had gone alone, but generally he had accompanied me, never saying he would prefer something else and never making me uncomfortable. The only means I had ever had of knowing what a bore my shopping had been to him, was this humorous escape-valve in his little diary.

CHAPTER TWENTY-EIGHTH.

DOCTOR GUNN had the liveliest interest in his clinics but always came home from them tired. When he had no very ill patient, nor important nor dangerous operation in view, he was cheerful and ready to extract enjoyment from his surroundings. Unpleasant subjects of any nature he banished as quickly as possible from his mind, never allowing these vexations, nor professional annoyances to be shared by those about him.

There were necessarily many occasions when he was preoccupied, then, if interrogated, he would say, "Wait a little; don't talk to me just now, I am thinking."

I remember so well one evening his troubled look; he paced the floor, and then exclaimed, "What are a lawyer's anxieties to ours? They fight for money, for honor or for dishonor, as the case may be, and some one wins! We fight *disease*, but no one wins when the battle is against the decrees of the Almighty."

I remember his remarking in a social way to a physician, "I never can, though I often wish I could, divest myself of anxiety and responsibility in dangerous, or more especially in troublesome cases; they keep me in a painful state of concern." The other replied—"You should not let them, I never do." After we left, the doctor said, "Yes, X—— looks young, he is without a wrinkle; no doubt trouble of that kind makes as little impression upon him as water would on a duck's back!"

It would be inexpedient, nor could I speak of Doctor Gunn in a professional way, except in quotations from others. Some one writing of him said:—"He was 'a giant' in the profession, known far and wide, . .
. . celebrated as much for his clean and honorable conduct toward those in his profession as for the rapidity with which he diagnosed all cases brought before him. His profound, rapid judgment was considered something wonderful; all who knew him remember him first for that."

A colleague says of him:—"By looking at a patient he could almost instantly advise the best course to be taken in the treatment. He was the best man to consult with I ever met. When I was in doubt which one of several plans was preferable, I would ask Dr. Gunn what he thought of it, and quick as a flash he would almost invariably answer. I cannot account for a man's intellect being so clear and quick in its perceptions. But perhaps that for which he will be longest remembered locally, was his high regard for the profession, and for each member's duty to the other. He was never known to give an adverse criticism on any physician, to the patient. If he had anything to say he said it afterwards to the man himself."   .   .

"Dr. Gunn's practice of nothing but surgery for twenty years in Chicago, made him a recognized authority. The graduates of Rush Medical College can testify to his superiority as an instructor. His delight was to have a class crowd round the table and hang over his shoulders when he was at work   .   .
.   .   His discourse was as full of jokes as it was of information; he always had some incident to relate, whereby a knotty Latin term or a particular point could be made to hang in a student's mind.   .   .   .   .
His profoundest thoughts were entwined with something original and entertaining as naturally as was the mingling of gray in his beard. The stories he employed to illustrate and assist in his demonstrations, will be quoted by the instructors at the college for years to come."   .   .   .   .   .

Dr. J. B. Herrick, who was graduated in 1887, gives his impressions of Doctor Gunn from a student's standpoint:—

"A few words concerning Professor Gunn as he appeared to the students of Rush Medical College, may not be amiss. We all thought him a noble specimen of physical manhood. His tall, erect, well-rounded and well-knit frame, his white curling locks, his keen, blue eye—all made him a conspicuous figure. And when added to this, we noted his firm, quick step, his energy in action showing the Highland blood that coursed through his veins, his scrupulous nicety in appearance and dress, even to the minutest details, we could readily understand why he was the prominent personage, whether in the drawing-room, in the arena at his clinic, or in the sick-room; and why it was that he was looked upon as the master—as the one who commanded, by all with whom he was associated.

"Many of us, at first, misjudged the man and the surgeon as we saw him at his Tuesday and Saturday clinics. We sometimes thought him harsh and over-bearing, but we gradually learned that he was born to have authority, and that underneath the apparently arbitrary word or action was a warm and honest heart. He had no nonsense in himself, he did not like it in others; and his words of reproof, like his scalpel, often caused pain by the wound so freely made; but they were sure to do good and in many cases to work a cure.

"Viewing him as a surgeon, we could not comprehend the certainty of his rapid diagnosis and his equally certain and rapid operation. At times we accused him of carelessness in the one case, and 'cutting and slashing' in the other. But our censure soon changed to wonder and admiration. His keen, disciplined eye detected at a glance the irregularity, change of contour, loss of function in the part—things which we could but faintly perceive after careful study. And we saw that where other surgeons toiled with laborsome and painstaking carefulness, feeling every step of their way, he, trusting to his very accurate knowledge of anatomy and wide experience, worked with a boldness and rapidity that were marvelous.

"He always took the 'short cut' in his surgical operations, for with him it was the safest. We have seen him make the complete operation for hare-lip in five minutes. The manner in which he extirpated tonsils, cut for stone, opened abscesses, etc., was a never-failing source of enjoyment to his student audience. Before one fairly realized that he was ready to begin, he seemed to be through; and yet he was not tempted to undertake an operation which would, perhaps, bring renown for its brilliancy, while it could not benefit the patient. Often as we saw the large tumor enter the clinic, our younger pulses beat a little more rapidly and the blood tingled in our veins with expectancy. But we were frequently disappointed in our hopes of seeing a brilliant operation, for he was always honest with his patients, and never held out to them false hopes for the sake of temporary applause.

"Much more might be said of him did space permit. He was a clear, enthusiastic, and practical lecturer; he had always on hand a fund of humor and good-fellowship; he was kind and indulgent in speaking of the mistakes of other physicians. The students always liked him for his promptness and punctuality. At the exact minute for clinic or lecture, he entered the arena. Many a time have I seen him stand with watch in hand, impatiently waiting for the moment to come when he could enter the amphitheatre and be at work. 'I would make a poor *waiter*,' he once remarked.

" We scarcely recognized his greatness when he was among us. Yet now that he is gone, the loss we have sustained comes to us with its painful reality, and we realize as we never did before, that our friend and teacher was a prince among surgeons,—in very truth a great and noble man."

Professor Norman Bridge writes: — "My first knowledge of Doctor Gunn was in 1866–67 when I attended his last course of lectures at Ann Arbor. Probably his impression upon me was similar to that of every other young man who has entered his class as a pupil. He seemed the embodiment of the brilliant surgeon; his presence, his way of lecturing, his methods of reasoning on any subject under consideration, but especially his promptness, and accuracy of diagnosis, his rapid and strikingly effective way of operating, all tended to impress one with his mastery.

"Before and since, I have seen other surgeons surprised, baffled, and foiled at some step of an operation, but I never saw anything in him approaching such a condition but once, and this was due to the breaking of an instrument. This was at Ann Arbor; when operating at one of his clinics, for stone in the bladder, his sound broke square off leaving part of the instrument in the bladder. An assistant was holding the sound when the accident occurred, and excitedly whispered something to Doctor Gunn, when the latter took hold of the instrument, to assure himself of the state of things, promptly withdrew the part he held, threw it upon the floor vigorously, and withdrew into the ante-room for another sound with which he finished the operation. It never seemed possible for

21

him to make an error in diagnosis, or a mistake in an operation.

"After coming to Chicago and especially after knowing him thoroughly in Rush College, the same effect of his personality was often noticed upon students and younger members of the profession. He was personally admired by a large number of young men; many of them, there can be no doubt, emulated his prompt and effective professional ways, to their great benefit as surgeons.

"Every young man of ambition is some time or other struck by the ways and character of some man whom he comes to admire, either instantly or gradually. That man becomes his ideal or model for emulation, and he can no more avoid in some way and to some degree imitating that model as it appears to him, than he can help thinking; and this influence not infrequently gives a bent and direction to his own growth and character, that ends only with his death. So every man of power, and peculiar worth who comes in contact with the thoughtful part of the rising generation, is, in his ways of thinking, and doing, and feeling, in this manner, continually transmitted to others, as a stream that only ends with his life, often not till long after his death.

"Doctor Gunn was marked in such influence; the

quality that he transmitted was undeniably most wholesome and most valuable. But notwithstanding that most young men with whom he came in contact admired him greatly, there were others who stood somewhat in awe of his stateliness of bearing, which had perhaps a suggestion of austerity that tended to keep them from familiarity. And if not his bearing, his prompt, sharp way of dealing with mistakes and shortcomings of students who failed to do the best they could, engendered in this class something like fear.

"He was so prompt and positive about things, and often so radical that he was frequently not credited with the warmth of personal nature he actually possessed. He held positive views about most subjects that had engaged his thoughts, and was not accustomed to shade the expression of them to suit or comfort any one; as a result, his words often struck hard and were always remembered, sometimes with feelings not altogether comfortable, but generally with admiration for the direct way they were spoken.

"In the work of medical teaching and in the work of a medical college, Doctor Gunn was, as in his private affairs, singularly honest and upright. He had positive ideas of what should be taught, and how a college should be conducted, and his conceptions were of a high order. It made no difference, that the measure he advanced would injure the financial prospects of the college, and probably therewith, his own; if the object was demanded by the final best interests of the public and the profession, as he understood them, he was in favor of, and gave it his constant and consistent support.

"He hated imposture, and was always irritated when he thought the college might, by any act or event, be placed in the position of appearing to pretend to do something it did not do. He would never take advantage of a technicality in any business, professional or secular; a moral obligation was always superior to a written one, because he seemed to feel that it was more likely to be neglected and its violation was more despicable, from the ease with which it could be accomplished.

" His habit of punctuality was carried to the utmost. I never knew a man who had this trait of character in so high a degree; he would not be a minute late at any personal appointment; especially was he prompt at his public professional engagements. Not only was he at the college in time for his lecture, but he, unlike any other medical teacher I have ever known, was usually standing just outside the lecture-room door, waiting for the stroke of the bell that announced him, when immediately, he was at his post to begin his lecture. He was quite as prompt in closing his lecture at the expiration of his hour. I have seen him, more than once, stop speaking in the middle of a word, and many times in the middle of sentence, when the gong proclaimed that his time was out. No brother teacher ever had occasion to accuse him of robbing the man who followed him on the programme, of any lecture time.

"In his professional life he illustrated a quality, the great worth of which is emphasized by its occasional absence on the part of surgeons and doctors—I mean the quality of seriousness. The business of surgery was with him always a grave one; it never descended to triviality. In his surgical operations there was always the air of sober business; there was no random talk or joking on the part of the surgeon and his assistants—a thing unfortunately too prevalent in this day of deliberate surgery and great freedom in the use of anæsthetics. As a result his operations were not only perfect in their accomplishment, but completed in the shortest possible time consistent with thoroughness, to the great comfort and safety of his patient.

PROFESSOR ETHERIDGE, whose visits to my husband I so well remember, when the echo of their voices and sometimes their cheerful laughter would reach me, says:—

"During the many years that I have been Secretary of Rush Medical College, I have now and then received letters that came under no written or known rules of management. My own judgment I so far doubted that I would visit Doctor Gunn, to ask how to reply to such communications. The one thing I was infinitely impressed with, was his quick, and always extremely judicious reply. Sometimes I doubted his judgment in these answers, but my return letters contained the replies he suggested, and ultimately I found that he was right.

"In matters of college policy he was decided and conservative. The more important the matter, the quieter he would remain in a faculty meeting while it was under consideration; but when he spoke, he was careful, deliberate, and forceful, always impressing me with his graceful thought, great wisdom, and strong convictions.

"If I ever wanted any new thing adopted in college matters, I felt morally sure of success if I could convince him of its wisdom, and secure his coöperation. Whenever he seconded an enterprise, or a new idea, it at once received an indorsement and impetus that ensured its success. On the contrary, if I encountered his decided opposition, I was generally willing to carry the new idea out and bury it. His voice was always in favor of the best and highest ideas in matters of medical education. He favored any scheme that would give to medical students greater facilities for acquiring technical knowledge.

"A great impression was made on my mind by a remark he made to the graduating class of 1869. You know he was so often epigrammatic in what he said. One day a student sent down a written question to him: 'What is a doctor's best road to success?' He at once replied with great earnestness and solemnity :—'Young man, your best road to success is to *deserve to succeed!*' The quietude that could be *felt* which followed this wise utterance, indicated that *that* class of students felt the truth contained in those words.

"With him to make up his mind was to act. He, often in doubt as to others' intentions, was a long time in concluding, but when he *did* conclude, it decided his line of action. On the contrary, when his mind was quickly convinced of hostility, he was so prompt to act that he often made matters brief.

"It was seldom that any one caught a glimpse of his inmost heart. One day he uttered a remark showing his great love for boys. He always loved boys and was full of kindly charity for their thousand-and-one foibles and foolishnesses. He seemed to have an abiding faith in the outcome of a well-brought-up boy who might, at the time, be going very badly. As he and I were driving along one day, we saw a policeman leading along under arrest a boy of perhaps sixteen years of age. He threw up his head and in an unutterably sad tone remarked: 'Such a sight makes me heartsick.' Those few words revealed a soft spot in his great heart, unknown to the majority of men."

PROFESSOR PARKES refers in a few words to Doctor Gunn's philosophy of manipulation in the reduction of hip and shoulder dislocations:—"The profession at large have always been very greatly interested in the treatment of dislocations of the larger joints. Professor Gunn worked out with careful minuteness and to a successful termination the physical obstacles preventing easy return of joint-surfaces after their displacement, and the best procedures of manipulation to be adopted in securing the reduction.

"He spent many years in the careful dissection and preparation of joints, illustrating many varieties of dislocations, and absolutely demonstrating the hindrances presented to easy reduction and the best means of overcoming them. His extensive and abundant experience also furnished him with manifold instances of proving on the living body the truths elicited from his researches and demonstrations. Especially is this true with reference to dislocations of the hip-joint. He has proven beyond a doubt that he was *the first*, or among the first to teach the profession that it is much easier, as well as safer, to reduce dislocations of this joint by position and manipulation, than by means of the old plan with blocks and pulleys, and main strength. This was very ably and certainly set forth in a paper read by Doctor Gunn before the American Surgical Association at Washington in 1884.

"One of the main principles advocated by him and expressed with great terseness, was that of placing the dislocated member in exactly the same position which it had at the time the head of the bone was forced through the capsular ligament. When in this position, with tissues all relaxed by anæsthesia, the bone could easily be caused to retain its cover and, too, without the application of great force.   As a matter of fact, no surgeon ever had greater success in the treatment of these injuries, when based upon the truths advocated by him and applicable to them.   Not only was this true particularly in the treatment of recent dislocations, but also after the abnormal adhesions present in them were thoroughly and completely broken up.

"Doctor Gunn never assumed to be able to master all the difficulties belonging to the cases presented with so much diversity for consideration at his college clinics, but always freely admitted his liability to err, not infrequently expressing to the student in a somewhat quaint and forcible manner: 'If your fore sight was as good as your hind sight you would not make so many mistakes by a —— sight.'"

CHAPTER THIRTIETH.

DOCTOR GUNN never seemed in better health than in February, 1887, when he visited California. San Francisco and many other places were enjoyed, but none more than Santa Barbara. The W——s from St. Louis had been for months at "The Arlington" (a pleasant hotel where we found some Chicago friends). Mr. W—— pressed upon the doctor the use of his saddle-horse, which courtesy enabled him to scour the country, explore out-of-the-way places, and obtain magnificent, extended views of the sparkling blue waters of the Pacific. Six weeks of almost unalloyed happiness in this congenial climate unfitted us for our uncongenial Spring. As we actually arrived in a blizzard, this inhospitable reception made the doctor reiterate, that if he were twenty years younger, California should be his home.

A month later he had symptoms that suggested to him rheumatism of the heart. He looked forward to warm weather for relief,—warm weather came but not relief. His professional work was continued, his attendance upon his clinics was unfailing. One evening in the latter part of July, a physician came to have Doctor Gunn accompany him to the interior of the state to operate. When he said that he was too ill to go, we realized as we had never done before, the gravity of his condition. We proposed a sea-voyage; to this he replied, "I am not ambitious to be eaten by sharks!"

His attention had been called to the mineral baths at St. Clair. Being the most available point, the next day saw us *en route* for these springs. A few days after his arrival, he had a short discouraging illness; then he seemed better, or at least his pain was gone; this alone was sufficient to make him cheerful. He never tired of the river scenery, and the surroundings were agreeable. Some old friends and several new acquaintances made a pleasant social element.

Among those in whom we became interested, and who seemed equally interested in us, and who were endeared to me on account of their regard for my husband, were Mr. and Mrs. G——, young married people, and Mrs. S——, who had early passed through a shadow of trouble. Mrs. G——, once speaking to me of the doctor, said, " Though I have not seen so many mile-stones, it has been my good fortune to go about the world somewhat, and meet a great many people, but never until I met Dr. Gunn have I seen a man that so fully realizes my ideal, especially of what one would wish for in a father.   How proud his children must be of him, how they must love and honor and venerate him!"

One afternoon several of us were strolling along near the river, when this always bright and agreeable woman, with something like child-like pertinacity, insisted that the doctor should entertain them by telling about his courtship.   At her repeated requests, that he should "*tell it all*," he replied:—"If I should, you would find it very tiresome, though some of it *was very funny*."   Then with a lurking smile of humor, "Pardon me for the simile: My wife in those days resembled the Irishman's flea; she was sure of me, but I was never sure of her—*until I got her!*"

Comparatively, these were bright and happy days, most of them, and I mention this single incident to show the doctor's light-heartedness, in contrast to the weeks of depression that had gone before.

The G——s left a few days in advance of us.   A merry party with exuberant spirits went down to the landing to see them off.   Amidst waving adieus as the steamer receded from the wharf, the doctor's young friend threw him a poppy!—a parting gift; he caught it, waved a gallant farewell and they were gone.   Who could foresee the hour that brought me this letter from her?—

"CINCINNATI, *November* 13*th*, *1887*.

"My heart goes out in deep sympathy for you, while a spirit of sadness comes over me as I write, to beg the privilege of laying at your feet our humble offering of respect for your husband, Doctor Gunn, whom we had the honor to meet, and whom we have since so thoroughly appreciated. • Miss K——, whom I have lately seen, also holds his memory sacred, and like every one who ever met and knew him, blesses the opportunity afforded of having known a man so courteous and so distinguished.

" I shall never forget the walk along the river-bank, when he touched upon the romance of his life with humor that did not hide the pathos in his heart. More than ever that day, I recognized his dignified and noble bearing, blended with every impulse of a genial and kind-hearted man. To me he looked like a great general or leader born to command, and yet so tender in all his home relations, and so observant of social amenities. How well I remember throwing the poppy from the deck of the steamer! Was it prophetic? I can shut my eyes and see the glorious man he looked standing there, head uncovered, hat aloft, waving me that good-bye.

"He was one who drew appreciative hearts to him; it was impossible to be in his presence without feeling the magnetism of his good influence. How much such a life does for humanity! It would be in such an atmosphere that we should love to live, and we hope to blend our lives as beautifully as you did your own."

I return to one of the few remaining days, when we drove with Judge and Mrs. H——. The drive was long and pleasant. Alighting at the "Oakland," the doctor expressed his thanks for the enjoyment they had given him, adding, "I have had a capital time. I feel perfectly well and it won't do to *fool away* any more time here. I must get back to work."

Sunday evening, which was the following evening, he did not feel so well; Monday he did not leave his room, but Tuesday morning re-appeared at the breakfast table. Dr. T. W. M—— had been watching the doctor. Some hours later Mrs. H—— asked when we were going. I replied "On Thursday." "Well," she responded, "that will be time enough." "For what?" I said in surprise. Hesitating a moment, she answered, "Dr. M—— fears your husband is going to be ill, and thinks he ought to be at home." Was it possible we had deceived ourselves? No, it could not be quite possible, but the chilling purport of her words haunted me, and my heart sank to its lowest depths!

Thursday we left St. Clair, remained twenty-four hours in Detroit with some life-long friends of my husband—a visit which brings the saddest of pleasant memories. Friday night we were at home; we had just escaped. Sunday morning the doctor was seriously ill. It is painful to revert briefly to this illness,—to a night when his physicians thought he would never see the morning. Their unwearied efforts restored him to life. Afterwards he had a short convalescence, but when he again found himself prostrated with days and nights of suffering, he said, " It would have been better if the doctors had let me *die that night.*"

" JUNE,"—the doctor's saddle-horse, was a Kentucky thoroughbred; beautiful as the month for which she was named, and as intelligent, almost, as she was beautiful. Black, her coat, like the sheen of satin, glistened in the sun-light. Her small head, small acute ears, eyes ever vigilant, broad, flat shoulders, light sinewy legs, and other points, denoted her patrician blood. She was a little over fifteen and a half hands high. At first the doctor hesitated about taking her, but was assured that a thoroughbred of her size could carry him with ease, and that in a year or two she would grow heavier. In carrying him she bore over one-quarter of her own weight.

She could single-foot rapidly, though the doctor seldom speeded her. To her bridle was attached a coquettish nose-strap of fringed leather, just touching her nostrils. By a motion of his hand, he had taught her to place herself at his side. He mounted easily and when in the saddle was mobile and magnificent, while she with her light hoofs just spurning the ground, moved proudly and gracefully along.

Dismounting at his door, the doctor threw her bridle-rein over the saddle to indicate that he was through with her services. She would then take a small circle on the avenue, proudly turn the corner and walk majestically to the stable at the end of the street, where a groom was usually ready to receive her. If not, after standing a moment, she would turn, take a broad circuit and come again upon the platform. This time, if she received no attention and was kept waiting, she would neigh, or with her hoof paw on the closed door.

She responded immediately to the doctor's raised hand, whether several rods away on the lawn, where sometimes she was permitted, or in her stall, from which backing carefully, she turned and crossed the stable floor, wheeling quickly in order to place herself at the doctor's side, while he always caressed her approvingly.

Guests staying in the house seldom failed to witness this entertainment, when two or more of the family were sure to add themselves to the small audience of delighted guests. Once she was allowed to hurry over one of the bridges just as the bell had rung. Ever after when hearing the ring she would quicken her pace and skim over before the bridge could be opened, greatly to the amusement of those in charge.

During the doctor's supposed convalescence, he desired a new span of carriage horses. As this involved sending some of the others into the country, he decided that "June" should be one of them, saying, "Perhaps in the Spring when she comes back, her old master will be able to ride her." The morning she went (I saw her pass), I shall never forget the feelings that came over me, but turning as cheerfully as I could, I said, "Doctor, June has just gone! and you never saw her." "No," he replied, "I avoided looking out for fear I *should* see her."

The sensations awakened by the sight of a favorite brute bereft of a loving master, are none the less painful because the heart is full of a greater grief. June seemed, and now seems, a part of him; and in those old, familiar places where I have seen him riding so royally, the superb vision is photographed on the scene.

During the two weeks of the doctor's apparent improvement, he drove several times, but each day instead of the distance being increased, it was lessened. When again prostrated, foreseeing his doom, and fearing a lingering illness, he said: "God grant the struggle may not last long!"

A few days—and the light of a more glorious world, perhaps, dawned upon him, but to me the days were darker than the darkest midnight hour. From out that darkness, his intonation of a name falls upon my ear and leaves me—in the desolation of despair!

CHAPTER THIRTY-SECOND.

THIS and the succeeding chapters contain a part only of the many loving letters and tributes which flowed in upon me after Doctor Gunn's death. I regret that I cannot put them all in print, as well as the generous testimonials received from the hospitals and medical societies with which he was connected.

PROFESSOR CORYDON L. FORD.

"ANN ARBOR, *November 7th, 1887.*

.   .   .   "I was astonished and pained at the message received on Friday evening, for I had always anticipated that Dr. Gunn, with his strong physique and vigorous intellect, would long survive my own feeble organization, to bless and serve the invalid, for which he was so fitted by nature and attainments. . .

"Until I received the telegram I had supposed that the doctor enjoyed the same vigorous health as when we last met. I sorrow for his death as that of a brother beloved. For more than forty years of professional life, many of which were side by side, we labored in our sphere to relieve human suffering and to teach others to do so. Thousands will regret his early removal as prematurely closing a career of unusual success in his chosen field of labor, by which the world loses a faithful servant, and the medical profession an inspiring example, whose influence will, happily, be perpetuated in numberless survivors.   .   .   .

"There is also the added comfort of a companion whose death thousands join in lamenting, for your sake, for their sake, and for the sake of humanity. . . A true man has fallen, but his influence does not end; the thousands who have profited by his invaluable instruction and the contagion of his enthusiasm will carry it on and cause it to be felt for many a year to come."   .   .   .   .   .

REV. GEORGE FRANCIS NELSON.

"GRACE HOUSE, NEW YORK,
"*November 16th, 1887.*

"How can I tell you, my dear friend, of the profound sympathy which the unhappy news from your household has stirred in my heart. The memory of old-time pleasant hours under your roof is so fresh and dear to me still, even after this long lapse of years, that your bereavement touches me with a shock as if I had

but yesterday come from your fireside, to hear to-day of
the shadow that has quenched its brightness.　．　．

"What a rare personality was Doctor Gunn's!　He
was one of the few men I have ever known whose very
presence was an inspiration.　With most of our friends,
perhaps, the graces of character which endear us to
them, are gems that brighten only in the light of our
intimate knowledge; they do not have the setting
always that seems best fitted to make them plain to
every eye.　But now and then we meet men whose form
and bearing at once suggest even to the most casual
observer, the strong and gracious character within.
Such a man was the friend for whom I beg the privilege of mingling my mourning with your own.

"How well I remember the room where we sometimes sat together at table!　There was a window of
richly tinted glass overlooking the waters of Lake
Michigan, and giving to lake and sky, to stately ship,
or patched and lowly sail a coloring of strange, exquisite beauty.　And what a symbol that radiant window
was of the gifted physician to whom it belonged!　How
it suggests to my thought that charity of his vision
which transfigured all that it viewed, and made the
crippled beggar equal to any prince, for the ministrations of its mercy.

"There is another thing I love to recall.　It is Doctor Gunn at his telescope. What enthusiasm was his when he brought out the lens that made the starry skies come closer with their pure looks! What new interest he awakened in the group of his evening guests on the summer veranda! And was it not a sign of a life that uplifted all it touched? He was never a dreamer. The force that he turned to the star-lit vaulting of the night was the force that bent in toil over day-time tasks.

"I shall not soon forget the ring of his voice nor the manly light of his face, and I am comforted not a little that I felt the pressure of his hand the last time I was in Chicago. What a heritage memory gives us sometimes! Some light of sweetness fades out of that vision which opens in the present and hopefully comforts in the future, but memory has garnered up something of its richness in the years that are gone, and now sets its kindly influence like star-gleams breaking the night of sorrow. Surely such a memory wakes and works now in your grief.

"I cherish most of all the memory of his strong and stainless spirit. I knew something of what he was out in the busy world where his skill and energy made so bright a mark, but it was my privilege to know him better still at his own fireside, and it was there under his kindly roof, where from time to time I had the good fortune to be one of his guests, that I learned to esteem him with a hearty thoroughness which made every moment of his friendship a precious one.

"But his eyes, perhaps, thirsted for the light of other worlds than our own. He was glad to awaken such a thirst in his friends. And to all who knew him this was but a sign of a heart that may have learned amid all its hopes and toils to look away from earth for its sweetest peace.

"Beloved physician and Christian friend, may God keep alive in us the memory of thy wisdom, and comfort us for thy loss!"

DR. CLAUDIUS H. MASTIN.

"MOBILE, ALABAMA,

"*November 14th, 1887.*

"I was greatly shocked when I heard of the affliction which had fallen upon your family. Doctor Gunn and myself were very warm personal friends, and while our acquaintance had been of short duration, it soon ripened into a genuine friendship which I had learned to value. Although known professionally to each other for many years, our personal acquaintance dates back only to the summer of 1883.

"We met first in Philadelphia at the house of our common and lamented friend, Professor Samuel D.

Gross. We were both in attendance upon the annual session of the American Surgical Association. Dr. Gross was President, whilst the Vice-Presidency was vacant by the death of Dr. James R. Wood, of New York. It so happened that I was on the nominating committee, and through my influence Doctor Gunn was chosen for that office. After the death of Dr. Gross, the Presidency of the association was filled first by Dr. Moore of New York, then by Dr. Briggs of Tennessee. When I again came into position, I nominated your husband for the Presidency, and of course his election was assured.

.   .   .   .   .   "We were in the habit of frequently corresponding with each other, and at this time I have a large number of his letters on file as valuable documents. It is probable you may find many of mine among his papers. Since the first day we met in Philadelphia, in 1883, there has been an uninterrupted friendship between us. My first interview with him so impressed me that I was irresistibly drawn to him by his manly, chivalric bearing, his graceful manner, and his distinguished personal appearance.

"In all my intercourse with your husband, I never found him aught else than a polished gentleman and scholar. He had all the attributes of a noble man.

From close observation, I always form a very just estimate of men, and am not often mistaken in my diagnosis. From the first time I ever met him, I thought
him to be just what time has proved to be true; and I
fancy that old heraldic insignia, with its ribbon bearing
the motto of some old knight of yore, "*Aut pax aut
bellum*," is justly and honorably worn by a worthy son
of an honored line.   .   .   .   .   .

"His paper before the association that year, impressed me that he was no ordinary man intellectually.
There we shall miss his wise counsel, his genial society,
and his distinguished *personnel*. I cultivated an
acquaintance of which I have given you an outline,
—one which was full of pleasure for me. I can hardly
add to the many flattering testimonials already written
on the life and character of your husband. It would
afford me the greatest pleasure to say something more
in the way of an eulogy upon his life and to add my
grain of sand in rearing a monument to his memory.
In his death his friends have sustained a terrible blow,
the American Surgical Association has lost one of its
most valued fellows, and the profession of America
one of its brightest jewels.

"I will not longer intrude upon your sorrow, nor
attempt to offer you the valueless balm of consolation,
for it would be cold charity for me to speak to you of

his worth.   His memory lives in the hearts of his professional friends, and it will be long before the void he has left, can be filled."

MRS. KATE H. LYMAN.

WASHINGTON, D. C., *December 1st, 1888.*

"The remembrance of the valued friendship with which your kind husband honored me has prompted this expression of sympathy and appreciation, which is, however, utterly inadequate to express the esteem and reverence due to a man of his genius, scientific acquirements, and high professional learning.

"A memoir, it seems to me, my friend, is a sad retrospect of the dear lives which have made life happy, which taken in connection with our own, made nature lovelier, friends dearer and living one bright dream of happiness; not the sad recollection of those days which shut out the loved ones from our view, throwing over earth a pall and filling us with woe and despair—days when our only sense was our misery and the poignant knowledge of our loss.

"Let us leave this retrospect and go back to the happier days—the days when we were all together in your happy home.

"My first recollections of Dr. Gunn are so closely

allied with those of his wife and children, that for me they are the sacred memory of a life not lived in vain.

"At the time of the great fire in 1871, those days of gloom were met by him with courage for himself and the utterly wrecked college of which he was a distinguished member, and with sympathy and encouragement for the suffering and unfortunate. That is to me a peculiarly memorable time, and recalling his earnest solicitude and interest is 'A sorrow's crown of sorrow' in 'remembering happier days.'

"He was markedly conspicuous in public places by his distinguished bearing; and as President of the American Surgical Association in Washington in 1885 will long be remembered.

"His enjoyment of the social entertainments was most gratifying to his friends here. The occasion of his meeting the great philanthropist of this city, W. W. Corcoran (since gone to his rest), was an occasion not soon to be forgotten. It was a noticeable group, the aged host, receiving that body of distinguished men, prominent among whom was Doctor Gunn with his handsome face and commanding figure. As he bowed low with the courtesy and veneration due to the recognized benefactor of this city, and as each spoke words of greeting expressive of the respect due to the other, all present paused for an instant. It was their last meeting, and its impressiveness seems now to have been prophetic of the change since come to both.

"But I could go on forever dreaming of this great nature. In the words of his successor in Rush College, 'How his place can be filled it is impossible to tell.' But hearts do not break, and lives do not cease, and the world moves on carelessly as though a hero had not fallen by the way. Who can tell but that his great mind has passed on to more complete perfection, has solved the problem which must come to all some time, and that he looks with pitying eye upon our poor endeavors and disappointments, he having realized the full fruition of all hope? Who can tell? May we not hope that these days of tears, and prayers, and aspirations, are the fuller accomplishment of a Divine purpose for the happy reunion with the loved ones gone before?

"That you may have encouragement for the purposes of your life, and strength to accomplish all before you, and that friends may seem dearer for the sweet sympathy extended, and life become at least peaceful and hopeful, is my dearest wish."

DR. ROSWELL PARK.

"BUFFALO, NEW YORK, *November 5th, 1887.*

.   .   .   "I should do myself scant justice did I fail to at least express my sympathy for you . . as well as to tell you of my own personal loss. The doctor had indeed been a true friend to me, and I revered him and had learned to regard him almost as one might a parent. How much I owed him I could better tell if you knew how favored I have been here where his friendly influence placed me."   .   .   .

"BUFFALO, NEW YORK, *January, 1888.*

.   .   .   "I send herewith a little tribute of respect to Doctor Gunn's memory which I hope will at least not displease you:—

"'It is almost needless to say that there was much in the character and ability of Professor Gunn which young men should try to imitate. In regard to those relations between doctor and patient, not only the most cordial but the most sacred, he was punctilious to a degree. Never could a word be elicited from him that could disturb these relations or breed distrust.

"'In the many delicate positions in which a consultant often finds himself, no one was more considerate, more honorable than he. In his habit of saying nothing unkind of or to young men he showed himself his juniors' kindest friend. It never was my lot to call in any one who was more considerate in all these respects than he; yet never for an instant sacrificing the interests of the patient. In all that was courtly and noble, I have never seen his superior.

" 'Of his abilities as a teacher and operator, others who have seen him and known him longer than I, can speak more fittingly, I have been so fortunate, however, as to see him time and again hold the attention of large audiences absolutely riveted upon himself and his work; and to those who really know what clinical lecturing is, this means the possession of didactic and oratorical powers of the highest order. His commanding figure, his beautiful command of his subject, his grace of diction, his intrepidity of operating—all these conspired to make his clinics memorable, as well as to inspire in his auditors that enthusiastic reverence with which every one of his former students remember him.

" 'Whether, then, one remembers him as teacher, operator, friend or citizen, Doctor Gunn must ever remain in one's memory as one of the commanding characters of the century—one that may find, as it ought, many imitators, but few if any rivals.'

"I also enclose what was an editorial notice of his death, that I put in the journal of which I am editor, 'The Medical Press of Western New York' of December, 1887:—   .   .   .   .

" 'In many respects like his even more widely known colleague (Langenbeck) was the late Professor Moses Gunn, of Chicago, who died early in November.

" 'A graduate of the college of Geneva, which college, by the way, was moved to Buffalo and made the Buffalo Medical College, a friend and class-mate of the late Dr. Rochester, he determined to hew his own path in the great West, and in 1846 settled in Ann Arbor. He took with him two trunks, one of which contained his personal effects; the other held the cadaver of a colored man, which he intended to dissect in the presence of his new professional associates. He soon gathered about him a class, and this became the nucleus of the medical school which was attached to the University of Michigan. In Ann Arbor as in Detroit Dr. Gunn established a reputation which brought him an extensive practice.

" 'When Dr. Brainard died of cholera, after the war, during the terrible epidemic which visited Chicago, Doctor Gunn was invited to occupy his chair in Rush

23

Medical College, which he has since filled to the eminent satisfaction and pride of all concerned.

" 'A man of jovial nature, earnest and most painstaking in his work, honorable to the extreme degree, an abominator of quackery in any form, a clear and admirable teacher, an intrepid operator—he endeared himself alike to the public and to the students whose idol he was.

" 'It will be difficult to find his successor either in the esteem of the Western profession or his capability of imparting instruction. He had been honored with the highest evidences of respect by his brother surgeons, having recently been President of the American Surgical Association.' "

DR. HENRY M. LYMAN.

"CHICAGO, *August 9th, 1888.*

.   .   .   .   "I was one of the firm friends and warm admirers of your husband, yet it was so little of friendly intercourse with him that I could ever enjoy, that my recollections are almost entirely confined to our reunions at the meetings of the Faculty or Trustees of the College, and its public anniversaries.

"I greatly admired his noble presence, his active energy, his clear comprehension of every subject brought before him, and his prompt decision when judgment was required. He always produced upon me the impression of a great, broad-gauged soul that could never descend to anything low or mean. He was an eagle always soaring in the upper air. It was a good thing for students and for the younger members of the profession to have such an example living before them —hence one of the sources of the regret which I feel over his loss.

"I wish I could add more from a larger acquaintance with my much honored friend, but the course of our lives lay so far apart that I really possess too little, in the matter of reminiscences such as you would naturally desire. Count me always as having been one of his most loyal friends."

A FEW words from Professor Hyde's address to the class on the morning after Doctor Gunn's death : —"A great man has gone from us. When we use the term great, we all know it has a purely relative meaning. . . . A man who is esteemed great after a life of intimate relationship with thousands of his fellow beings in many important, and even sacred trusts, we may regard as great in some worthy sense of the word.

"It has been my personal lot to know some of the great men of the world. . . . I have known a few men in private life who, though then but little esteemed, secured for themselves afterward a place which the world thought high. Now with this possibly narrow experience of greatness in others, I set it down in calm judgment that he who has gone, should have his name spread upon the roll of the truly great.

"This is not the place nor have I the right to occupy your time in pronouncing that eulogy upon his greatness, which will be uttered more worthily by other lips in another place.   Others will speak and write of what he was, what he did for his profession, what dextrous skill he had, what scientific attainments he possessed. Others will relate his history, from the days of his life in school to those of his professorship; will follow his footsteps over the western prairies in the piping times of peace, as well as over the battle-worn fields of Virginia in the army of McClellan during the struggles of war; and even over the lands beyond the sea whither he travelled for recreation and observation.

"I dwell on none of these points.   This is the hour for the tears of friendship, for the broken accents of the voice that mourns.   I loved him and he is gone!— that is my story of sorrow to-day.   You loved him too, I doubt not; but perhaps none of you like myself had this love strengthened by a thousand acts of unselfish kindness or tested by an unfailing regard, enduring for years and expressed always with the least demonstration and the greatest constancy.

"When I say this of myself, I say it of every member of the Faculty of the College.   We loved him, we all held him in the same tender regard.   Our sense of personal bereavement is our chief sorrow.   Words fail me in this moment of grief to tell all that is in our hearts relating to his personal association with us, his loyal attachments, his lofty ideal of honor, his unswerving faithfulness to duty, his steadfast trust in his friends, and his long self-denying labor. We are heart-broken in this sorrow, 'For God maketh our hearts soft, and the Almighty troubleth us.'"

DR. CHARLES T. PARKES, who succeeded Doctor Gunn in the chair of surgery at Rush Medical College, made the following remarks at the first commencement exercises of the college after the doctor's death:—

"To me has been awarded the privilege of making a few remarks on some of the characteristics of my immediate predecessor in the department of surgery in this institution, the late Professor Moses Gunn, A.M., M.D., LL.D. I esteem this favor a great privilege; still it is to me in part a task, because I fully appreciate my inability to do proper justice to the chosen theme.

"May we not hope, however, that upon this occasion a few plain words, quietly spoken, by one who loved him much, and reverenced him, if possible, more than he loved him, will tell the story as well as if it were enhanced by all the charms of oratory.

"Twenty years of the closest intimacy between two men, an intimacy almost daily in frequency, without a single manifestation of diversity of purpose, without any unpleasant words spoken, without even the indulgence in an ungenerous thought one toward the other, ought, when either of them is called upon to pay the last debt to Nature, to make the testimony of the survivor trustworthy. At the same time, and quite as surely, it fills his heart full of sadness to review the long period of happy and honorable association, so untimely ended, and to remember the loss we feel in the absence of the departed one—so sadly and solemnly suggested by this empty chair, bearing the emblems of mourning.

"One year ago, on the occasion of the holding of the commencement exercises of this institution, the President very happily felicitated himself, and congratulated his colleagues, on the fact that so many years had passed away without showing any break in the chain which bound us together as a corps of teachers. Alas! how short the period in the midst of which one of the firmest links has been torn asunder by the strong and resistless hand of Death! Professor Gunn, our beloved brother, has gone away from his labors and trials and worries, and who will catch up the thread now that is fallen from his fingers?

"The man who would inscribe his name high on the walls of the temple erected in commemoration of the deeds of great surgeons, alongside of the scroll bearing the name of Moses Gunn—upon the reading of which all men will gladly pay the obeisance of honor and respect—must be a perfect master of the construction and functions of the component parts of the human body; of the changes induced in them by the onslaughts of disease; of the defects cast upon them as a legacy by progenitors; of the vital capacity remaining in them throughout all vicissitudes of existence. He must be, at the same time, wise in human nature, wise in the laws of general science, wise in social amenities.

"Professor Gunn came among us more than twenty years ago, possessed of all these acquirements, and more. During his stay in our midst we have been the beneficiaries in the results of his tireless labors; the recipients of his many acts of graceful and kindly favor; the companions, among whom were enjoyed his fleeting moments of ease and recreation. With us there still remain man's triumphs and man's burdens—to him has come God's peace and God's rest.

"If it is given for me to choose the most noticeable of the many remarkable characteristics belonging to this great surgeon, it would be embraced in the expression: "Devotion to Duty." With him an ever-present and an every-day devotion, which the storms of winter and the heats of summer availed not to diminish nor dampen. A devotion as fresh and untiring as the ardor of youth's enthusiasm; a devotion as full of zeal as that which animated the hearts of the fire worshipers of old—the flame of their altar fires never went out. A devotion to duty, which we, his colleagues, will do well to imitate. Certainly a devotion which the students cannot do better than to cultivate; and if they do but cultivate it earnestly and continuously, there will surely come to them, as to him, the fullest measure of success and honor.

"It has always seemed to me that there is one period in the life of those unfortunate individuals afflicted with diseases demanding the surgeon's attention, which is more replete than any other with anxiety of mind and distress of spirit; often, it constitutes a perfect agony of suffering. It lies in the interval between the time when any present trouble is diagnosed, its nature determined, and the hour appointed when a surgical operation is to be done for its relief or removal. It is an interval of time which the merciful surgeon should never allow himself to forget. For the patient, every moment of it is full of the worst forebodings, engendered by the dread of the knife and the fear of death.

"No patient ever shed one tear too many, or felt one pang of anguish more than was absolutely necessary, on account of any forgetfulness or lack of punctuality on the part of Professor Gunn. With an appointment made, he was as sure to be present at the appointed hour, as the sun is to cross the horizon at its fixed and stated time.　More than once he has gone on with the execution of a complicated operation requiring several assistants, with myself alone to help him, and the unavoidably detained aids would straggle in, to be chagrined at witnessing an operation nearly or quite completed.

"It is only by undeviating promptness and certainty in keeping engagements of whatever nature, when once made, that the professional man can be sure that his day's work is well done; can gain or maintain stability of reputation; can keep his friends, confound his enemies, or hope to be rewarded with prosperity.

"Most men, in any vocation, come sooner or later to enjoy some one portion of their work more than all the rest.　The treasure of Professor Gunn's heart, professionally, was his free surgical clinic; the work he most loved was done here, and the doing of it gave him the most happiness.　No possible combination of circumstances, except absolute physical disability or absence from the city, seemed powerful enough to keep him out of the well known arena at the appointed hour of his coming.　Who can *ever* estimate the good done by this man, in this one department of labor; and all of it done for charity's sake?　His best efforts, his accumulated knowledge, his manhood's energies, his bodily strength, given away for years, as freely and bountifully as the air we breathe is given us.

"In this estimation of good done, there must be counted not alone the hearts he comforted, the pain assuaged, the deformities relieved, the diseases cured, by his skill and genius and courage; but it must be remembered as well, that the thousands of young men who have listened to the words of wisdom as they fell from his lips so eloquently and full of practical worth, have garnered up the jewels of his ripe experience and in their turn are spreading the same blessings among the homes of almost every hamlet, village, town and city in this broad land.

"Probably no person now living has witnessed as much of the professional work of Professor Gunn, as myself. The list, if made, would embrace almost every known surgical procedure, from the simplest act the surgeon ever does, to the most complicated undertaking he ever presumes to think of doing. On none of these occasions did he fail to be fully prepared, and instantly ready to meet any and all the exigencies or indications of the case in hand. This readiness could not possibly have been the result of any haphazard processes of thought; on the contrary, it was the outgrowth of the most painstaking and deliberate consideration of all the circumstances present in or surrounding the disease to be eradicated, or the injury to be repaired. Before going to any operation, it evidently was his rule quietly to sit down, and carefully, step by step, go over every one of the procedures indicated, and to set aside as carefully, in its proper place, every instrument or appliance necessary for their execution.

"Further, not only were the plain requirements of each case provided for, but as well, the possible accidents likely to occur under any care, were considered, and their harm, in case they happened, was reduced to the minimum, by their occurrence being promptly met with the proper remedy always at hand.

"In this characteristic of his, rests one of the main elements of his great success as a surgeon. I say to you that no man living or dead, no matter how great the halo of glory or recollections that may arise at the mention of the name, ever had more or better success attend his efforts to relieve the ailments of suffering humanity, than followed as the direct sequence of the work of this truly eminent surgeon.

"One word in token of the honesty and modesty of the man, and my story is ended. I do not refer to his honesty in common things. Every line of his countenance, every motion of his magnificent form bespoke him an honest man. I allude to his honesty in giving professional opinions. No patient's understanding was

ever befogged by any trickery of words, or disingenu-
ousness of expression, or misrepresentation of facts.
Professor Gunn's opinions were always given in plain
words, easily understood, although perhaps sometimes
bluntly spoken. No doubt could remain in any patient's
mind as to his opinions when once expressed. They
were always expressed modestly as well, entirely free
from ostentation, egotism or self-assertion.

"There comes to me an instance of this trait of
character which occurred during the second year of my
pupilage as a student of medicine in this college, and
the first of his connection with it as a teacher. I happened to be present at a consultation between several
surgeons--among the number was Dr. Gunn—held to
consider the nature of a tumor. The examination was
carefully made, the growth was large, and to me, a
novice, seemed sufficiently characteristic. When it
came time for Professor Gunn to give his opinion, he
said, 'Gentlemen, I have practiced surgery long enough
to learn that it is a wise thing in a doubtful case to be
modest in expressing an opinion. I do not know what
this tumor is and think it had better be let alone.' In
my short experience it has been my good fortune to see
diseases considered, and operations for their relief done
by many prominent surgeons in many places; but I
have never met one who excelled, and very few who

equaled Professor Gunn in exactitude of diagnosis or skill in execution.

"His self-reliance was wonderful in its perfection, at times startling, at the ease and steadiness with which it enabled him to approach safely close to the vital parts of the living body. To him a hair's breadth was oceans of room, and yet never any display of recklessness. All this is readily understood, and proper appreciation awarded, when his wonderful attention to details and unerring knowledge are remembered.

"No man was ever more just to his fellow practitioners. I have stimulated my memory many times, since assuming this duty, in order to bring to my mind any instances, on his part, of adverse criticisms of colaborers. I do not recall any. His time was too precious to expend, his mind too fair to indulge in the fruitless results of personal animosities, spites or wrangles.

"Perhaps some one may say:—'You have sounded his praises, now let us hear of his faults.'

"I never hear any one speak of the faults of Professor Gunn without my eyelids closing involuntarily, and there comes up before me a vision of the heavens on the brightest of nights. There are the fixed stars; their light is never dimmed; they are unchangeable and everlasting. How pleasant it is to carry the eye from one to another, trying to estimate their difference in beauty as they seem to vie with each other in glory! Suddenly there flashes across the view a flaming meteor, momentarily obscuring all else, as it passes quickly on into outer darkness. Who will say that the beauty of the scene has been marred by the intruder; nay, it has been increased.

"So with our friend; his virtues and excellences are as the fixed stars; they become brighter and fuller the longer and oftener they are examined; they are impressed upon our hearts indelibly. His faults, if he had any, have gone like a flash into oblivion."

CHAPTER THIRTY-FOURTH.

REV. DR. CLINTON LOCKE.

"THERE are certain relations between a pastor and a parishioner, certain confidences between a rector and one who has been intimately associated with him, which often enables the one to say things about the other, which might not come with so good a grace from any other man.

"Such were the relations between Dr. Moses Gunn and the writer of these lines. They had long been united together as rector and warden, and for many years as a valued member of the medical staff of the hospital of which the writer is president, and above all they were dear personal friends and accustomed to meet each other in the most free and friendly intercourse. This may color the writer's sentences and influence his judgment, but the memoir of which this forms a part is the tribute of loving and friendly hearts and is meant to speak warmly and partially. It is not some cold compilation of an uninterested historian writing about some one dead a century or two ago.

"I well remember in the year 1867, Dr. J. Adams Allen saying to me:—'I have found a new parishioner for you and I can thoroughly indorse him as a good churchman and a noble fellow. He is my old friend Moses Gunn.' Soon after, Dr. Allen brought him to see me, and I was struck, as every one was, with his splendid physique. Tall, stately, well-proportioned, every feature of the face and every movement of the body expressing energy and force, he was in every sense of the word, a noble looking man; and seemed to grow more so as he grew older.

"He met me with that frank cordiality which put us both at our ease, for he said in a moment:—'I was at church last Sunday; I like the little church, I like you and I liked the sermon, and I know I shall be happy there.' No rector could resist that, and that first interview was the beginning of a long and lasting friendship.

"Let me speak of him first as a churchman. He had gone through as much mental and spiritual conflict as men of his profession are apt to do if they are at all thoughtful men. That materialism which saps the faith of so many of his fellow doctors had spread all its specious glamour before him. He had weighed its arguments and found them wanting. He said to me once:—'I often doubt terribly, but I say to myself,

24

I looked this thing all over once, I went through the arguments and I decided that the immense balance of testimony was in favor of Christianity, and I cannot take time to go all over it again.'

"He was not even willing to admit the claims of systems of evolution which Christian men think perfectly reconcilable with the faith of the scriptures. He said they could not be scientifically proved to his satisfaction, and that he was impatient of mere theories. He told me once that he thought sermons on the difficulties between science and revelation very unnecessary, for there was no real difficulty, their spheres did not touch. I did not agree with him in this, though I find many devout doctors think as he did.

"I remember once when the sermon had been on the 'Powerlessness of infidelity to move the great mass of the people,' he stopped after church to say that the sermon had done him much good, and that he would make use of some of the arguments in his talks to students. Many times he has said to me 'I wish I had more faith.' There are but few of us who cannot re-echo his sentiments and share his yearning.

"He was a member of the Protestant Episcopal church from sincere and honest conviction. He was what we call now an old-fashioned high churchman, holding firmly to the doctrines of Apostolic Order and

Sacramental Grace, and any violation of any kind of vow or obligation was to him unbearable. His Prayer-Book to him was next thing to his Bible and he held with the utmost firmness to its regulations. He was not given to 'new things' as he called them, and any change in the ceremonial had to recommend itself very plainly to his judgment before he would thoroughly accept it.

"When the parish resolved to adopt the vested choir and to give up the very excellent quartette, to whose fine rendering of the music he was much attached, he was quite disturbed; but he grew to like the music, and said to me before he died:—'It makes the service much more devotional than the old way, I must confess it.'

"In church he was always thoroughly devout and one of the most attentive listeners a preacher ever had; not only attentive but appreciative; and never forgot to bestow that word of commendation which is ever so grateful for a rector to have, when he knows it is not the outcome of hollow, insincere flattery.

"During the best years of his life his connection with a large hospital, which required Sunday morning duties, often obliged him to be absent from his place in church. Once while he was so ill, when he heard I had been told it was impossible to see him, he said:—'I do not think it would hurt me to see my pastor; at least I feel that I ought to see him.'

"Let me speak of him as a parishioner. He took for many years an active part in the management of the parish, being a vestryman, and after that for some years one of the wardens. These offices were to him not mere places of honor, but duties which he conscientiously discharged and to which he gave his closest attention.

"He gave always a proportion that he thought just, and no argument could make him give more, or sanction any measure which he did not think could honestly be carried out. Not only did he do faithfully his duty as an officer of the parish, but he aided in the development of the social side. After the fire, it was necessary to give that feature more prominence than is now done, and it was always a pleasant thing to me to see a surgeon so eminent and whose time was so closely occupied, devoting himself to the pleasure of others in whom he had no interest, except that they were fellow parishioners.

"I often asked his advice about parish matters, and always with profit. He was perhaps a little conservative for one as pushing as I then was, but I have reason to remember him many times, when I recognize that his course was wise and his suggestions those which it was best to follow. I was sorry when he felt that his duties on Sunday precluded any longer retaining the wardenship.

"As a friend Doctor Gunn was always constant and true. His friendship was not one of words but of deeds. Never can the writer forget when he went to consult the doctor about his son's commencing the study of medicine, how affectionately he was met, how the doctor immediately placed at his disposal all his influence, and prepared to take the young man under his own care, and to look after him as if he were his own, and he did so nearly to his dying day, so that next to his own family there were none that felt his loss more deeply than the rector and his wife, for they recognized what their son had lost in a friend and counselor, and how impossible it would be to supply the place of him who had gone.

"Doctor Gunn's manners were very courteous, and well might be called elegant. He conversed well in general society, was fond of it, and wherever he went, and no matter how great the assemblage, was always a conspicuous figure. In his consulting room and by the operating table, there was a quietness and a decided manner, which, while very necessary there, would be out of place in the drawing-room; but he well knew how to make the distinction between the two places.

" In St. Luke's Hospital, with which he was long connected, and where the writer (being president) often saw him, he was thoroughly beloved by both nurses and patients. He was never at a loss, never gave dubious directions, never asked for impossibilities. Common-sense characterized all his actions, mingled with a tenderness for his poor suffering charges which always called forth my admiration. I often consulted him about the affairs of the hospital, and always with profit. He had its interests at heart and rejoiced over every mark of its prosperity. I feel sure that the same would be said of him in the other large hospitals with which he was connected and to which he rendered the most important services.

" It is not my place to speak of him as a professor in Rush Medical College, or as a surgeon of the very first rank. Those are phases of his life which are best described by his brother doctors, who can much better understand their merits than one who merely views them from an unlearned standpoint. He was a man of extensive reading, outside of his profession, and was ever occupying himself with some favorite hobby—not a useless one. Once it was German, in which he became a proficient; later it was French, which he read with the greatest assiduity; then again it was astronomy to which he gave himself with enthusiasm, and in which for a long time he took the greatest delight. Horsemanship was natural to him and like the Centaurs of old, horse and man seemed one!

"It is seldom that one so distinguished passes a life so long, with so few enemies. He never provoked opposition, although most decided in opinions and tenacious of his own judgment.

"He died amid universal regret; who that ever saw it can forget that crowded church, filled with the distinguished as well as others, showing how truly they all felt the loss the cause of humanity had sustained?

"It was a most impressive funeral; and not the least of it was the burial just as the shades of night were darkening. One could scarcely distinguish faces. The few lanterns that were held up to enable the priest to read the words of committal, and to aid those charged with the last sad duties threw a wierd and solemn light on the scene. Here was left his body, but his soul, we trust, was already in that Paradise of the Blessed where God's servants rest from their labors.

"Let me end this sketch with the words which I pronounced over his grand form, draped for burial, as it lay in his open coffin before the altar in the hour of his funeral:—

"We sometimes feel when we are summoned to pay the last tribute of respect to the dead that the passing away of the personage we are burying is of no importance anyway.   The world was no better for him; a negative quantity; his death, as Scripture says, 'a keel passing through water which leaves no trace behind.'   But we feel differently from that to-day.   The man around whose coffin we are gathered will be widely missed.   It does make a difference to the community whether he lived or died; he does leave a place which will not readily be filled.   A marked man in many ways: Marked in his personal appearance; in every assembly he stood distinguished for his glorious presence, and we all know how much that impresses itself on every one.   Marked for his energy and eagerness; although no longer young, no young man was ever fuller of fire and dash, and swiftness of execution. Marked for his dexterity; with unerring precision the knife in his hand found its place, and did its work. Marked for his accurate knowledge of the human body, and the cleverness and finish with which he ever imparted that knowledge to the thousands who these many years have come under his instruction.   Marked for his courtesy and kindness, treating the poorest patient as though she were a duke's daughter.   Marked for that steady purpose, that unflinching devotion to his art, that brilliant perception of each case, which raised him to the highest rank of his profession.

" But let me in this place, leaving his professional career to those far abler than I to picture it, speak of him in other lights. He was marked for untarnished honor and unswerving integrity. He carried almost to a passion his strict discharge of obligation, and carefulness in business accounts. He was marked for an intense sympathy with the struggles and lives of the young men whom he led. He was marked for a simple, unostentatious, religious life. He had very little patience with modern materialism—very little patience with the infidelity some of his profession see fit to put forth. He believed in the gospel of Jesus Christ— long ago cast in his lot with it, and lived in the profession and practice of it until his death. He regretted often that professional duties kept him so much from the services of the sanctuary. He was for some years senior warden of his church, and for many years one of its most honored members. I mourn him as a dear friend as well as a valued parishioner. He lived a long, busy, useful, model life. He has entered now into his Christian rest. May he sleep in peace, and may perpetual light shine upon him."

A FEW LAST WORDS.

ANNIVERSARIES are always pleasurable or sad.
A time comes in our lives when they are all sad.
The anticipations and realities of Christmas had unusual
charms for Doctor Gunn. This remembrance of their
father's happiness must forever be enshrined in the
hearts of his children.

Christmas morning of 1888 was bright and sunny,
but no darker day could dawn for me. A light fall of
fleecy snow covered the spot to which we had made our
sad pilgrimage. On the pure drapery we laid immor-
telles and holly. How strange and unnatural it seemed
and how futile any attempt to penetrate that veil which
hides from us the future! Waves of sorrow surged
through my mind as we retraced our journey; and as
we reached our home, the direful reality came upon me,
that the *soul* of Christmas was forever gone.

On one of the last days the doctor said, "Do you
know we have lived together nearly forty years? In a
few more months, it will be forty years." He kept
account of all such anniversaries, but this account was

left for me to keep with the blackest thread of anguish that could be woven into the woof of an anniversary.

In a tender letter of sympathy from Mrs. Custer, are a few words in reference to herself, which I hope she will pardon me for quoting:—

"In this last hour I have finished the proof of my book about my beloved husband. For eighteen months it has wrapped me round like a cloak I could not unloose day or night. In living over again the days that are forever gone, I have suffered anguish; but the comfort it gives me to pay tribute to one I love, has given me strength!" . . . . .

"There is nothing that can give you courage but a full life. Work has been my salvation. May our Heavenly Father open a way to you to forget yourself! . . . . .

Her words have been re-echoed in my heart. To dwell with loving care on one, who was to me the type of true manliness, has been the solace of my companionless hours.

Those who had known him long and intimately could not know all his inner life. He thanked God for mere existence.   He never outlived the romance of his love, and perhaps it is not too much to add, that over a period of almost forty years, in letters to his wife, were passages worth living—and dying for.

And now that the sad pleasure of my work is done, I feel the dread pall of my loneliness settling down around me; I see no light, nor the out-stretched hand that guides me on my way—I grope and stumble in my path, and take the journey step by step—alone!

www.ingramcontent.com/pod-product-compliance
Lightning Source LLC
Chambersburg PA
CBHW030220130726
47898CB00014B/1464